the
dice was
loaded
from
the start

Also by David Annand
Peterdown

the dice was loaded from the start

DAVID ANNAND

corsair

CORSAIR

First published in Great Britain in 2026 by Corsair

1 3 5 7 9 10 8 6 4 2

Copyright © David Annand, 2026

The moral right of the author has been asserted.

All characters and events in this publication, other than those clearly in the public domain, are fictitious and any resemblance to real persons, living or dead, is purely coincidental.

'Now we are Six' from "Now we are Six" by A.A. Milne
Copyright © Pooh Properties Trust 1927
Reproduced with permissions from Curtis Brown Group Ltd
on behalf of The Pooh Properties Trust.

Adapted lyrics on p. 204 from 'Romeo and Juliet' by Dire Straits,
written by Mark Knopfler

All rights reserved.
No part of this publication may be reproduced, stored in a
retrieval system, or transmitted, in any form, or by any means, without
the prior permission in writing of the publisher, nor be otherwise circulated
in any form of binding or cover other than that in which it is published
and without a similar condition including this condition
being imposed on the subsequent purchaser.

A CIP catalogue record for this book is available from the British Library.

ISBN 978-1-4721-5587-0

Typeset in Caslon by M Rules
Printed and bound in Great Britain by Clays Ltd

Papers used by Corsair are from well-managed forests
and other responsible sources.

Corsair
An imprint of
Little, Brown Book Group
Carmelite House
50 Victoria Embankment
London EC4Y 0DZ

The authorised representative
in the EEA is
Hachette Ireland
8 Castlecourt Centre
Dublin 15, D15 XTP3, Ireland
(email: info@hbgi.ie)

An Hachette UK Company
www.hachette.co.uk

www.littlebrown.co.uk

For Naomi

*'And I dreamed your dream for you
and now your dream is real'*

MARK KNOPFLER, from 'Romeo
and Juliet' by the Dire Straits

Wednesday 16 May

Pemberton Place was a short street, only twenty-one houses, and it was closed at one end, giving it a kind of self-contained, almost island-like quality, which made it easy to stand out if you were new, or if you were different. And the Andersons were both, having moved there only nine weeks earlier, and being, along with their two children, pretty much the only residents of the street who weren't past retirement age.

Max stood on the front step of number fourteen, waiting for someone to answer the door. He and his wife, Karolina, had received a handful of social invitations since moving in but this was the first that either of them had been able to accept. Wine and nibbles and a film projected on to the west-facing wall of Tabitha Gayle's open-plan kitchen.

'Max,' she said censoriously, looking down at him from three steps up. 'We've been waiting for you.'

Tabitha was five foot ten and wore her hair short. For much of her life she had been the head of voice at the British Academy of Music and Dramatic Art. Even now, some years into her seventies, her posture telegraphed its dynamic balance and everything she ever said was delivered, you sensed, to those right at the very back of the upper circle.

'Sorry I'm late,' he said. 'The little one took ages to get down.'

'Come in,' she said, sweeping open the door. 'We've saved you a place.'

Like all the other houses on the street, Tabitha's was an early

Victorian villa with a wide, high-ceilinged hallway, decorative tiles on the floor, picture rails and cornices.

'We're all through here,' she said, leading him into the kitchen.

The lights had been turned off but there was enough light for Max to fully take in the chaos of the room. Tables had been pushed against walls. Plant pots had been placed upon surfaces. A cat's scratching pole was balanced on a sideboard.

The dining chairs were lined up in rows. At the back of the room, a film projector sat on the top shelf of a pine dresser of the sort that Max was told, but struggled to believe, had once been fashionable in the 1980s.

There were a dozen or so chairs, all but one occupied by residents of the street. No one there was entirely new to him. His two children, aged five and three, and both possessed of an abundance of golden curls, had, upon moving in, become instant local celebrities, and he had talked to pretty much everyone present, even if only briefly, as they fussed over the kids in the street.

Tabitha stood at the front and addressed the room as Max sat down, near the back, on the last available chair.

'For those of you who don't know, tonight's piece is a short film called *Canvey*. It stars a young woman called Natalie Clark, who was my favourite student in my last year at BAMDA. She was a rough little thing when she came to us. Clearly talented. Great energy.' Here, she smiled knowingly, indulgently. 'Too much piss and vinegar, though. Too much attitude. We taught her discipline. Explained to her that acting isn't something you can just *do*. That it's a skill that needs to be learned. A craft. Three years later she walked out an actor. And I'm very proud of her.'

The man sitting next to Max chuckled quietly to himself. Gordon Barraclough, who lived at number twelve. A semi-retired architect in a jacket, chinos and Chelsea boots. Max had talked to him a couple of times. He was a man who semaphored his appetites unapologetically. The smell of his cologne. The way he occupied space. All of it was somehow libidinal and openly acquisitive. Karolina called him 'Red Flag', but Max liked him; his laughter was infectious and puckish, and even when he was boasting he seemed to be alive to his own ridiculousness.

'When Tabitha was in charge, the Academy was more brutal than the parachute regiment,' he whispered to Max. 'She used to break them like horses. Remake them from the ground up.'

Max grinned.

'Where might I get one of those?' he whispered back, pointing to Gordon's glass of red wine.

Gordon reached over to the table to his left and grabbed Max a clean glass.

'We always gather like this when one of hers gets a part,' continued Gordon, using the music of the opening credits as cover. 'Because it happens so rarely.' He pulled a face. 'Admissions policy was always militantly about talent over looks. The hill they liked to die upon. They were, as she has told us all, many, many times, "in the business of creating actors, not movie stars". Admirable of course but fundamentally misguided.'

'As all the talented fat kids discover upon graduation,' said Max.

'Exactly,' said Gordon, chortling merrily while he poured Max a large glass of wine. 'As the fat kids discover upon graduation.'

The credits finished and both Max and Gordon settled in and turned their attention to the film being projected onto the wall.

Canvey. Max had seen it before. It had done well on the festival circuit, won prizes at Berlin and Venice. He watched for a couple of minutes, enjoying the intimacy of the handheld camera, how it brought you right in, captured the claustrophobia of the island and the people who lived there.

Eventually, though, his attention drifted. First, to the couple in the row in front of him. Fiona and Douglas. They lived a few doors down and across the road. Academics, he thought. Or had been. Max had never seen them apart and there was something about the way they were together that made it difficult to imagine them separately. It wasn't that they had morphed into a single entity, finishing each other's sentences, inadvertently colour-coding their outfits. In fact, they remained markedly distinct; he soft and understated, she prickly and purposeful, quick to laugh. Nonetheless there was, Max felt, a kind of co-dependence to them, the presence of the other clarifying perfectly their individual roles, like an all-conquering tennis doubles partnership who move in perfect choreography, know their strengths, never go for the same ball.

Max had talked to them half a dozen times in the street and was always amused by the militant practicality of their clothes: high-performance waterproof jackets, complex Velcro-heavy sandals, technical hats with neck flaps that came out at even the merest hint of sun.

He felt his phone buzz in his pocket. It was a WhatsApp message from Karolina, who was at her desk, in their spare bedroom, working on a project that required her to keep US West Coast hours Monday to Friday. She had been told that the project would last for a month, but six weeks on there was no sign of it ending and so, once he got their two young children to bed, Max was, of a weekday evening, at a loose end. Or at least at a sort of loose end. The deal – which had never been concretely articulated, but had emerged organically, its parameters established by precedent rather than diktat – was that he could go out, but only locally, so that he would always be on hand in case one of the children woke up. They never did, but that wasn't to say they never *would*, and in any case, neither Max nor Karolina were in any hurry to undermine an agreement that allowed both of them to experience a kind of gratifying magnanimity, that sense they had both conceded exactly the right amount; had been generous, but had also held the line.

Even though he was often exhausted by the time he had fed and bathed both children, read to them, and coaxed them to sleep, it felt wrong, given their circumstances, *not* to go out. Like it was an opportunity wasted. A chance at life. Out-there-in-the-world *adult* life. The sort that he had missed so fervently during his first four years of fatherhood.

And so out he went. To the local cinema. To the cafe round the corner where he would read and write. And now to a film club hosted by Tabitha Gayle, who was the closest thing he had to a local friend even though she was old enough to be his mother.

How are the Boomtown Rats?

Max replied with a rapid succession of WhatsApp messages, his phone angled so that in the dark no one could see what he was doing.

> They are out in force
> Lots of hearing aid static
> House is hilarious
> WAY too much furniture
> Wine is awful. Obvs

He watched the icon in the top corner of the screen as it moved, indicating that Karolina was writing.

> Ha!
> Gutted not to be there.
> Next meeting starts now
> Love you
> x

Max replied with a single kiss and put his phone back in his pocket.

The film was nearing its end. Natalie Clark was building up to her big moment, eyes red, snot trails wiped across her cheeks. Tabitha was right. Natalie was good. Totally lacking in vanity. Just the right side of showy. He smiled. A credit to her drama coaches.

He leaned down, picked up his glass from the floor and shifted his weight slightly in his chair so that he could see past the various heads to the front row, where Jonathan and Bryony Cox were sitting side-by-side, his arm resting along the back of her chair.

The Coxes lived in the house at the end of Pemberton Place,

number twenty-one, which stood apart from the others on the street. It was detached and architecturally distinct, surrounded by a garden big enough to contain two substantial outbuildings. Max hadn't really met either of them properly yet, and neither had Karolina, but the Coxes were self-evidently the royalty of the street and so they speculated hysterically about them, their relationship, the extent of their wealth.

Bryony had her hair up, as she always did. A kind of artfully sloppy bun held in place by a long tortoiseshell clip, loose strands falling over either ear. She was younger than the others. Max knew this because she was an artist, famous enough, at least in her world, for there to be biographies of her on the internet. She painted large canvases that sat, to his untrained eye, somewhere between the figurative and abstract. It was a body of work that had, according to one critic, 'contributed in a small but not insignificant way to the history of English painting'.

From where he was sitting, Max could just see her profile. Her features were delicate, her face finely lined. In her nose there was a tiny silver stud – almost too small to see until it caught the light and sparkled briefly. There was something about her that put Max in mind of a spirited Shakespearean beauty.

Max looked again at Jonathan. His shirtsleeves were rolled up to the elbow, exposing tanned forearms that tapered satisfyingly from elbow to wrist. They were the kind of forearms you could imagine covered with sea spray, winding a length of rope round the cleat of a boat. The kind Max might have had, he thought, had he been a wholly different person.

On-screen, the credits rolled. There was a lull and then Gordon let loose a bellow of approval. The applause that followed was loud and sustained. Max was the first to stand but quickly the others all followed and for a full minute the whole room stood clapping wildly. Tabitha stood at the front of the room, accepting the adulation as if the film had been hers alone.

Once the applause had finally subsided, Max was tasked with reordering the room. He folded garden chairs, put a rug back into place, carried a table from one side of the room to the other. At various points both Gordon and Douglas made noises about helping him, but neither of them actually did.

After about ten minutes, Max returned the scratching pole to what he guessed might be its rightful place and decided that he had done enough. By any metric there was still an overabundance of stuff pretty much everywhere you looked, but the room at least had a semblance of order.

Tabitha placed a hand on his arm.

'Thank you,' she said earnestly.

Max nodded humbly.

'It is a great performance,' he said. 'You should be very proud.'

Tabitha squeezed his arm, smiled. There was something watery and maternal about the way she was looking at him.

'I think we need to get you another drink,' she said eventually.

'That would be lovely,' he said, as he let her lead him towards the table where she left him in front of a large serving dish of bite-size supermarket samosas and half a dozen open bottles of wine.

The guests were arranged around the room in clusters of two or three: some on stools at a breakfast bar, others sitting round a large dining table, a few standing in the kitchen. Max stood at the edge of conversations, made the odd joke, smiled appreciatively at anecdotes.

After a while, Gordon appeared at his shoulder. They were the two men who had come to the party without their partners, and it made them, Max realised with a slight sense of panic, a sort of double act.

'Can I top you up?'

'Always,' said Max in a classic register of his, which was a kind of jocular ironic detachment. 'You never need to ask. The answer is always yes.'

'Good man,' said Gordon, having chosen, clearly, to interpret this through the prism of his own bonhomie. 'My position exactly.'

'I mean, it doesn't really do anything to fill the void,' said Max in a voice that was flattened out, but with a hint of a smile, 'but at least it's something, right?'

Gordon looked at him appraisingly, momentarily confused at how seriously to take all this. Not very, he eventually decided.

'So you're in number fifteen,' he said.

'Yes,' said Max, although it wasn't, he noted, actually a question.

'Funny old woman lived there. Mabel. She must have been knocking on a hundred when she died. Had been in the house since the fifties. She was bloody miserable most of the time but I liked having her here. There aren't many of them left. The real old guard.'

Gordon popped an olive in his mouth.

'I don't even know if her sons are still alive. I know they were living in Australia. Whoever inherited it, they cashed out. Sold it to a developer. We were worried that they would stick it on Airbnb. Bloody relief when you moved in.'

Fiona overheard this and turned to them and said: 'It really is so nice to have a new young family on the street. Your children are such beauties. The curls on that little boy.'

Max felt a ripple go round the room, like a shift in a shoal of fish. They stopped their conversations, turned themselves to him.

'Having you here reminds us all of when we did it,' added Tabitha. 'My eldest was just a baby when we moved here.'

'My god, Tabitha. Was that thirty-five years ago?'

'Nearly. We bought the house in '85.'

'The pioneers of Pemberton Place,' shouted Gordon merrily, 'civilising the north London Badlands.'

'Oh, nonsense, Gordon, we weren't civilising anything.'

'Don't listen to her, Max. My mother wouldn't visit us for the first five years we lived here.'

Douglas, who had been talking separately to Jonathan, leaned in to the conversation and, with his eyes widened for comic effect, said:

'When we applied for our mortgage the first bank we talked to said they didn't do loans on houses north of Sedgemoor Road.'

Gordon laughed fulsomely at this, one hand on his chest.

'I remember a lovely spring morning sometime in the mid

eighties,' said Gordon, still chortling, 'when I had to come to Douglas's rescue after he almost cut off one of his own fingers trying to get rid of the cast-iron security grille on his front door.'

'The previous owner had put it on,' said Douglas to Max. 'In those days it wasn't an entirely irrational thing to have but it did make you feel a little like you were a battery hen.'

'Old Johnny-come-lately wasn't here then, back when we had cages on the doors,' said Gordon with a smirk on his face. 'He didn't move onto the street until the nineties.'

'1989,' said Jonathan.

Gordon waved his hand.

'The West was won by then.'

Jonathan turned to look at Max.

'It really wasn't,' he said dryly.

There was a lull in the conversation and as quickly as the attention had turned to them, it turned away again. Tabitha and Fiona were discussing some upcoming social occasion. Douglas was talking to Gordon, the two of them laughing over an old joke.

'We haven't met yet,' he said to Jonathan. 'I'm Max.'

'Jonathan Cox,' he said. His handshake was strong: sandpapery and slow-moving. Like an old but very impressive ship. Max felt momentarily unsure whether to try to match it or acquiesce, uncertain which was more manly, more noble. In the end he did a bit of both, intensifying his grip once the moment had passed, which extended the handshake a beat too long and made it oddly, embarrassingly, intimate.

'Welcome to the Pemberton Place film festival,' said Jonathan with an arched eyebrow.

'I've been to Cannes a couple of times,' said Max, recovering his composure. 'Not actually all that different to this.'

Jonathan smiled.

'Me too. Similar levels of ego.'

His hair was grey, but thick, and just long enough to have a sort of sweep to it. Max noticed the white buttons on his blue linen shirt. There was a kind of implacable solidity to him. The way he fully occupied all three dimensions, possessed the sort of depth that Max had always felt he lacked.

'What did you think?' he said. 'Of the film?'

'I thought it was good, actually,' said Jonathan. 'Nicely shot. Not exactly original though. Bit of a Truffaut wannabe.'

Max raised his gaze, his attention caught.

'The bit where she steals the milk isn't even really an homage,' he said incredulously. 'It's basically a shot for shot recreation.'

'Precisely,' said Jonathan. 'It's a total rip-off.'

'Normally, I'm on board with whatever borrowings a director wants to make. But that,' said Max, pointing at the wall onto which the film had been projected, 'that was just too on the nose. You can't just copy something like that. You've got to do something with it.'

Jonathan smiled.

'*400 Blows*,' he said. 'That's an old film for you to like.'

Max shrugged.

'I mean, it's an old film for *you* to like, isn't it? Came out in 1959. You must have just have been a kid.'

'It didn't come out in '59. It was later than that. I remember going to see it.'

'I'm pretty sure it was '59.'

'Truffaut is sixties and seventies.'

'Yeah, but it was his first film so ...'

Jonathan looked at him sceptically and then pulled out his phone and googled it. The look on his face was one of genuine surprise. At being wrong, Max felt. But also at having been challenged in the first place.

'Good for you,' he said eventually. 'I stand corrected. 1959. I was nine years old. So I suppose I didn't see it on its first run.'

'I prefer *Shoot the Piano Player* anyway,' said Max.

Jonathan smiled at this, then he paused for a second, as he took Max's measure, his eyes ever so slightly narrowed. But the grin that followed was warm and indulgent. Max felt the heady feeling that he prized above all others: that of the clever boy who has said the right thing.

'I did some work in film distribution when I was young,' said Jonathan. 'Seventies. Early eighties. Never any Truffaut. But I was involved in the financing of some interesting deals.'

'Really?'

'Quite of lot of Fassbinder. Some Bertoluccis.'

'*Really?*'

'It was different then. There was an audience. Not that anyone made any actual money from it.' He stroked his face idly, looked past Max for a second or two. 'But that wasn't why we did it.'

'You distributed Fassbinder,' said Max, slightly awestruck. 'Did you ever meet him?'

'Not really. We were at the same parties. Shook hands. But we never really spent any time together. Bertolucci however …'

But that was as far as Jonathan got before there was a loud yelp and someone shouted.

'HENRIK!'

A grey and black tabby was on the table, nose-deep in a bowl of shockingly pink taramasalata.

'It's not Henrik, it's Oscar,' said Bryony as they all crowded towards the table. 'The little rogue.'

'It's Samuel,' said Jonathan. 'You can tell by the markings on his back.'

'It's Bertolt,' said Tabitha, picking the cat up off the table with one hand and throwing it onto the floor. 'He's a greedy little bugger.'

'*Bertolt*,' said Max, now tipsy enough to be openly rolling his eyes. Gordon clocked this.

'You can laugh,' he said, 'but our Bertolt's no Marxist. Never known an animal so committed to personal accumulation.'

Max laughed at this and that was all they needed. He got the full show. *The irony of the Gayle family cats*. It was an ensemble piece. Everyone contributed. Anecdotes. Jokes. Long, lavishly detailed stories. Photographic evidence was produced, videos called up on phones. Henrik being frivolous. Samuel gregarious. Oscar ascetic. Bertolt a glutton.

Max got the distinct sense that a fair amount of creative

interpretation had been necessary for all four cats to display such obviously antithetical attributes to their namesakes. But he understood the significance of it to the group, the delight they took in the telling and retelling of the tale, and so he submitted graciously, laughing at all the right moments, even contributing a terrible but well-received joke about a litter tray and *Krapp's Last Tape*.

By this point most of the guests had left and those still there had retired to the living room. Tabitha and Douglas were in armchairs, Fiona and Gordon on one sofa, the Coxes on the other. Max had tried perching on the arm of one of the sofas but it made him awkwardly taller than everyone else and so he had settled on the floor, sitting on a cushion with his back against the wall.

'Gordon,' said Bryony. 'I had completely forgotten to ask. It was this weekend, wasn't it? How was the wedding?'

'Oh god,' he said. 'It was a nightmare. They didn't have rings. They both had tattoos done on their ring fingers, which they had covered up with, you know, make-up. Theatrical make-up. That kind of thing. And then when it came to the moment they dunked their hands in this font or whatever it was. The kind of thing you baptise a baby in. And off came the make-up.'

'The church let them do that?' said Fiona, looking appalled.

'Don't be ridiculous, it wasn't in a church. It was in a field. You should have seen it, Fiona. The groom's got a great big beard. He was wearing a straw hat and a bow-tie. He looked like one of the guys from *Three Men in a Boat* if he'd gone to seed and was sleeping rough.'

'Gordon's niece got married at the weekend,' explained Tabitha to Max. 'His sister's daughter.'

'She had all these bloody flowers in her hair and the bridesmaids were wearing tunics. The first dance was round a bloody maypole. They danced just the two of them for a bit and then their friends all joined in and wrapped them up in the ribbons. It was supposed to symbolise the binding of their relationship or something like that.'

Here, Gordon looked despairingly into the middle distance.

'It was like a greeting-card version of the *Wicker Man*.'

There was laughter, glasses were refilled.

'Well, I think it sounds charming,' said Bryony.

'Apparently, they spent six months planning it,' said Gordon, with a dismissive wave of the hand. 'God knows what it cost.'

'We got married in a pub,' said Fiona. 'Registry office and then a room above a pub. Thirty guests. The whole thing cost £12 and it was over by eight o'clock. It wasn't a form of self-expression. We did it to have sex.'

Bryony clapped her hands in delight.

'We did,' said Douglas with a chuckle. 'Fiona's father was not a man who welcomed the prospect of his daughter living in sin.'

'My wedding was absolutely ghastly,' said Gordon. 'Andrea's mother organised the whole thing and invited all her friends. My brother, my best man and I were the only vaguely modern people there. Everyone else there was bloody Edwardian.'

'And Andrea. She was young, too,' said Bryony.

'Yes, of course. And Andrea. She was young then. At least calendrically.'

'*Gordon*,' said Fiona, slapping him on the arm. 'Enough of that.'

'And then Julia's wedding was the total opposite,' said Gordon, warming to his theme. 'We had to pay for the whole bloody thing and weren't allowed a sniff at the guest list. Barely got an invite ourselves.'

'I'm assuming Julia is your daughter?' said Max to Gordon.

'She is,' said Bryony, answering for him. 'And she's very nice. The poor thing. Imagine how nervous she must have been about the father of the bride speech, having this insensitive lump as her dad.'

'My speech was a model of bloody restraint, I can tell you,' said Gordon. 'Anyway, thank god *they* didn't get tattoo rings. The dickhead left her after eighteen months.'

And on it went. This great show of their lives. Max sat on the floor, a glass of wine to his left, a bowl of crisps to his right, drinking it in.

It was nearly midnight when he felt his phone buzz in his pocket.

I'm going to bed x

Max slipped into the toilet to call her.

She answered on the second ring. Her voice was slow and sleepy, which always made her sound even more Swedish.

'You sound like you've had fun,' she said.

'It has been a very informative fact-finding mission.'

'But fun, no?'

'Yeah, it has been fun.'

'So, are you in the gang now?'

'I'm not sure about that. The only question anyone asked me was if I wanted my drink topped up.'

'But they were nice, no?'

'Oh, yeah. Totally. They're vain and entitled and utterly lacking in self-awareness. But they're kind of wonderful with it. I mean, they're boomers. What were we expecting?'

Thursday 17 May

It was seven o'clock and the sun was setting on Pemberton Place. The light on the buildings was orangey-pink, some of the windows squares of pure gold. The gentlest of breezes was shimmering through the blossom on the street's six cherry trees.

Max, who was walking home, his rucksack on his back, paused for a second, felt a smile rise to his lips.

This was where he lived.

Quite a contrast to their street in Kreuzberg with its tide-mark of anarchist graffiti and its annual May Day riot. His apartment had been the on third floor. Bike parts in the hallway. Always the smell of cooking fat.

He had lived in Berlin for nine years, all but one with Karolina. For most of those eight years, when she wasn't on maternity leave, Karolina had been working, as she had for almost her whole adult life, first in Stockholm and then in Berlin, at a long-established international NGO, putting together funding mechanisms for global wetland restoration projects.

But then, six months earlier, just before Christmas, the offer had come. From one of the charity's major donors, an American bank with offices all over the world. They had worked closely with her for years and now they wanted her to be part of a new team, help sculpt the bank's rebooted environmental strategy.

Karolina's immediate reaction had been to turn it down. She was an environmentalist, not a banker. And this, to her, was a distinction that was self-defining, existential even.

But her contact at the bank had been prepared for this and slowly she had worked on her. Sure, we'll be nearly doubling your salary, she had told her, but really you should be thinking about this as an opportunity to effect change from the inside. Control budgets. Direct funds where you think they would be best spent.

A month later, the bank made a second approach, offering a little more money and considerably more autonomy. And again she said no, but then, just a few days later, a project of hers collapsed. One that she had been working on for three years. An on-the-ground, woman-led drive to protect mangroves in Java.

And so when the third offer came, she relented. She had spent too many years watching money wasted, she told Max. Too many good projects had gone to the wall. This would be a chance to take hold of the reins, really get something done.

Then came the caveat: they wanted her to relocate to London. For a week or so, the two of them had prevaricated. They were happy in Berlin. The kids were settled. But then the bank told them about the rent allowance. The ridiculous rent allowance. The *offensive* rent allowance. And that had tipped the scales. Could we spend half and keep the rest, they had asked. No, they had been told, you have to spend it all.

And so on a blustery weekend at the end of February, Max and Karolina left the kids with her mum and flew to London, where they spent a couple of very surreal days viewing properties of the sort they had never previously imagined living in. A Georgian stable complex in Islington that had been converted into a four-bedroom bachelor pad with a hot tub and snooker room. A stuccoed maisonette in Notting Hill which they were told *sotto voce* was the preferred London home of an unnamed pop star. An enormous open-plan flat that occupied the whole top floor of a nineteenth-century waterfront warehouse near Tower Bridge.

But in the end they had settled on the house on Pemberton Place, in part for the neighbourhood: its proximity to the Heath, the charming oak-panelled pubs, the fabled bookshop, the Deco cinema. But mostly for the house, which was beautiful without being ostentatious. Number fifteen was, by any metric, ludicrously expensive, but it was also, perversely, a not unreasonable sort of place. Semi-detached, solidly Victorian; it was the kind of home in which you could acceptably imagine raising your family.

Max paused outside, one hand on the garden gate. The front garden magnolia tree was flowering, its pale pink petals pointing up at the sky. Did he miss Berlin? He paused. It was hard to say.

Back in 2009, for those lacking a Green Card and a way into New York, it was commonly accepted that Berlin was *the* place to live. Aesthetically, it had spoken to him. The angularity of the city. Its history-haunted modernity. The way it came at you. Unforgiving. Relentlessly urban. He had gone there to test himself against the whetstone of it.

Back then, in terms of work, it didn't make much difference where he lived. He was directing commercials and music videos, but never more than a handful a year, and they tended to be shot in Prague or Barcelona so it made no difference whether he flew in from London or Berlin. It was also cheap in Berlin, which suited him, because although the advertising gigs were paid at a spectacular day rate, there were a lot of false starts, weeks spent working on pitches that went nowhere, and, averaged out over the course of the year, his annual wage was nothing special.

More than anything, though, Berlin was fun. The close-quartered, smoke-filled bars. The summer afternoons swimming in the lakes. The days spent writing in cafes. The nights in Neukölln, bonfires burning by the canal. The art-world after-parties in warren-like nightclubs that had about them a trace of the cabarets of the 1930s.

For all this, though, he hadn't found it a wrench to leave. It wasn't so much that the Berlin moment was over. (Although he had been aware for a couple of years that while the overall number of Americans had stayed reasonably constant, they were, increasingly, the wrong sort of Americans, the right ones having all moved en masse, it seemed, to Lisbon.) More that *his* Berlin moment was over.

He looked up at the house. The stained-glass panel above the front door. The double bay window. The decorative brickwork.

As much as he had loved his high-ceilinged Kreuzberg apartment with its parquet floor and south-facing balcony, he had, deep-rooted in his soul, a yearning to live in a house with a kitchen door that opened onto a garden, and the bedrooms arranged, in the timeless fashion, on the floor above the living room. He was forty-two years old. He had two kids. It had been time, in truth, to come home.

Max slid his key into the lock and pushed open the front door. In front of him, a scooter lay on its side, its wheels scuffed, a unicorn sticker peeling from its underside. He counted three active tote bags, all of which, he knew for a fact, contained an open packet of rice cakes.

As he was hanging up his jacket, Karolina emerged from the kitchen, holding her laptop. She had her reading glasses on, through which she squinted at him down the hall.

'How was your day?'

'There comes a point in everyone's life when they realise they should have been a doctor,' he said. 'It is one of life's many cruel ironies that it comes just at the moment when you realise that you're too old to retrain.'

Karolina half-smiled. 'Right,' she said.

Max sighed.

'I did meaningless things for credulous people. *Plus ça change.*'

This was delivered in Max's deadpan, self-pitying tone, which aimed at being both worldly and blithe, while also communicating that he knew, obviously, that these were the problems of the absurdly entitled. But there was a crack, occasionally, in the delivery, that revealed a more authentic self-pity: one he himself could occasionally hear but could never really face.

The problem for Max, or at least one of the problems, was that it had all started so brightly. By the time he was twenty-six, he had made a feature film. Not quite all by himself, but almost. It premiered in June 2004 at the Edinburgh Film Festival where it was shortlisted for, but did not win, best debut.

This early success brought him to the attention of a couple of middleweight producers and for a few years, his name had been in the frame to direct other things. Bigger projects with proper budgets. Twice, he was attached to existing scripts, which he got paid to re-write and develop, but on both occasions the financing didn't materialise and they petered out into nothing.

Over time, he could feel the producers slowly lose interest, and so he resolved to go back to working on his own scripts while he made money directing music videos and the occasional television commercial.

Which is what he did for nearly ten years, first in London and then in Berlin. Over time, the budgets for music videos steadily shrank. And the number of television commercials he was invited to pitch for slowly dwindled before drying up completely when his commercial agency went spectacularly bust overnight. For a few years after that he had picked up piecemeal work here and there. He directed short films for tourist boards, edited promotional videos for Karolina's charity, helped video artists represented by a friend's gallery.

It was the kind of working life that might have been just about sustainable if you were twenty-six and single, but fell a long way short of what was needed for a father of two. Which was why he was, as of nine weeks earlier, working three days a week as the client content lead for Luxio Films, who made corporate videos for clients in the UK, Europe and the Middle East.

He did his best to fashion a smile.

'The only really important thing we have to teach the kids is that the only jobs worth doing are the ones in picture books: doctor, fireman, farmer.'

Karolina leaned in and kissed him, before she started up the stairs. She was smiling impishly.

'What?'

'I am trying to imagine you as a fireman.'

Max went to protest this and then decided against it.

'Or a farmer,' she said.

'I could have been a good doctor, though, couldn't I?'

Karolina made a face at this, which involved much widening of the eyes.

'Really? I think I would have been OK. Quite good. The bedside bit anyway. If not the science stuff.'

Karolina looked down at him.

'You would be good at the bedside bit.'

She was halfway up the stairs, he standing next to them, looking up at her.

'Butt.com soft,' he said, which was what he always said whenever they were arranged a bit like the balcony scene.

Karolina laughed. It was one of their long-standing jokes. Five years earlier for Valentine's Day, he had ordered sunflowers, dictated the dedication over the phone. 'But comma soft what light through yonder window breaks question mark,' he had said. 'It is the east comma and Karolina is the sun.'

The flowers arrived on the Sunday morning with the dedication handwritten by the florist. *Butt.com soft. What like light through yonder window broken . . .*

'It is the east,' he said in a not-joking voice, 'and Karolina is the sun.'

She smiled.

Max shut one eye, looked down the corridor at the kitchen.

'How's it been?'

Karolina laughed ruefully.

'It was an afternoon of false flags,' she said. 'And friendly fire.'

'Moscow or Pyongyang?'

'Both.'

'Oh god. I'm going to get it, aren't I?'

Karolina looked at her watch.

'Three minutes until the meeting starts,' she said.

She kissed him over the banister then disappeared, once again, into the spare bedroom. Max took a long deep breath in through his nose.

'Darlings,' he shouted as he walked into the kitchen. 'How has your day been? I have missed you both so much!'

'Arthur sneezed into my yoghurt.'

'I'm sure he didn't.'

'Yes, I did,' shouted Arthur gleefully.

'Well, I'm sure he didn't mean to,' said Max with as much jollity as he could muster.

'I did mean it,' shouted Arthur. 'I really did.'

At which point Alma picked up Arthur's yoghurt and sneezed into it and the evening went rapidly downhill from there.

Wednesday 23 May

Jonathan's work dinner had been brought forward at the last minute and there was nothing he could do about it. Which was a pain because it had been in the diary for weeks and the thing about six-handed canasta was that it wasn't, obviously, a game that you could play with five. Max was, they were keen to stress, the *first* person they had thought of, being free as often as he was and being so young and so good at picking things up quickly. And, of course, such lovely company.

'It's so kind of you to help us out at the last minute,' said Tabitha.

They were sitting round Fiona and Douglas's dining room table underneath a Moroccan lamp which cast a warm yellow light over everything it touched. On the table were three Moorish bowls filled with different kinds of olives.

'Well, let's see,' he said, looking at his improbably large hand, which contained, disconcertingly, two jokers. 'I hadn't even heard of canasta until this afternoon. I watched a YouTube tutorial on my phone while the kids were in the bath but I'm not sure that I've really grasped the nuances of the game.'

'Don't worry,' said Gordon. 'You're playing with Bryony; she's had years of carrying her partner.'

Max looked at Bryony, a scarf in her hair. A long cashmere cardigan and a black rollneck. She was wearing glasses to read the cards, over which she looked at him.

'Don't listen to him, Max. Jonathan and I are the Torvill and Dean of Pemberton Place canasta.'

'I'll deal,' said Gordon. 'What's the ante? Two hundred quid?'

'Oh, Gordon, honestly.'

'You don't want to spice it up a bit?'

'What are you talking about?' said Tabitha. She turned to Max. 'Ignore him. I don't know what he's talking about. We never gamble.'

'Max looks like he fancies a bit of a flutter.'

Max made a little deflationary gesture.

'I'm not much of a betting man,' he said. 'Too uptight and controlling.'

Gordon's nostrils flared. Max could imagine him at the baccarat table at Aspinall's. He had the quality of a man who had made and lost many fortunes. And he had a contemptuous streak to him, an intolerance of weakness. Max understood that it was something he triggered in men like Gordon, which brought it maddeningly to their attention and therefore wasn't without its own kind of power.

'You don't want to live a little?' he asked grumpily.

'Leave him alone, Gordon,' said Douglas, studiously not looking at Fiona, as he did when he was about to say something that might be just the wrong side of the line. 'I can't imagine he's got a penny to spare with all the rent he's paying on that house.'

Fiona groaned.

'Honestly,' said Tabitha. 'Max, please ignore them both.'

But it had been named. And that made it unignorable. They seemed to realise this simultaneously and blushed collectively, their breath held for a second. He was, after all, a guest.

Max laughed. 'Did you think *we* were paying the rent?' he said. 'My god, no. Karolina got this new job and they wanted her to move here. They pay the rent. I mean, we could never ...'

'Oh,' said Tabitha.

'We did wonder,' said Fiona. 'What it was that you did to be able to afford it.'

'She worked for a charity for nearly twenty years. Wetlands preservation. Not sexy but so important. An American bank financed some of her projects and so they knew her work. They headhunted her. But she's not a banker. She restores mangroves.'

'Ah,' said Douglas.

'I mean, when it comes down to it. She doesn't do it herself, obviously. But that's basically what she does. She finds money to protect peatlands.'

Shoulders dropped. Smiles spread across faces.

'I *knew* it would be something like that,' said Bryony.

The tension had dissipated completely. They were new to the street, Max and Karolina, but they represented continuity. Right-mindedness. The Pemberton Place way of doing things.

For ten minutes they talked wetlands. Max outlining some of the projects she had helped make happen. Preservation schemes in Scotland and Sri Lanka. Targeted micro grants for coastal communities in Indonesia.

'What a wonderful thing to be doing,' said Fiona to a murmur of assent.

Max smiled. No one had responded so enthusiastically when he had told them about his work, but at least no one had asked him how he felt about Karolina being the breadwinner. If they had done, he would have been gracious and self-deprecating, he hoped, however complex his true feelings about the matter might be.

'When are we going to get to meet her properly?' asked Tabitha.

'Soon,' said Max. 'She's very keen to meet you all, too.'

Drinks were refreshed and then, finally, hands were dealt. Max got a good one and, much to everyone's delight, made a canasta on only his second turn.

Bryony blew him a kiss from across the table.

'Beginner's luck,' he said with a smile.

The last of the evening sun had gone and the room, lit now only by the Moroccan lamp, felt even more like a Bedouin tent. In one corner, there was a divan bed covered with a Persian carpet. In another, a basket full of Peruvian straw hats with leather trims.

Across from him, Bryony laid three jacks on the table in front of her.

'Nice,' he said.

'No communicating between partners,' said Gordon.

Max pulled a face for the table, mimed zipping his lips shut. He placed his hand face down on the table in front of him, let his eyes wander round the room.

One wall was taken up entirely by a bookshelf. The paperback spines were faded and cracked; the colours of the earth: beige, ochre, tan. Lots of Iris Murdoch and Ellis Peters. Bernard Malamud. *Shōgun*, obviously. On top of the books were *objets trouvés*. A carved horn. A nautilus shell. A couple of vintage cameras. A necklace made of seeds.

Next to the bookshelf, on the wall, there was a poster. From the 1960s, he thought. Or thereabouts. A block-print illustration. A style now imitated to the point of cliche. But this one was an original, clearly, its white bits having yellowed over time. An advert for El Al's route to Istanbul.

Douglas followed Max's gaze.

'We flew that route the year that came out.'

'It's a lovely poster.'

'Istanbul,' said Fiona. 'It was another world in the 1960s.'

'I bet,' said Max.

'The Grand Bazaar. What a place. The things you could buy there. It was an eye-opening experience.'

Gordon picked a card and threw a three of spades on the discard pile.

'Beirut was the same,' he said. 'The souk was wild. Colleague of mine acquired himself a human skull while we were there.'

'A real one?'

'I wasn't with him when he got it. But it was definitely the real thing. He told me his children used to play a game where they took the teeth out and had to put them back in the right holes like it was a jigsaw puzzle.'

Fiona hooted in delight. 'You're not supposed to talk about things like that any more.'

'*For good reason,*' said Bryony.

She looked plaintively at Max in an attempt to disassociate herself from the conversation.

'When were you in Beirut?' said Max.

'1972,' said Gordon. 'Three years before it all went wrong. Worldliest place you could possibly imagine. Food of the gods. Wine like honey. Most beautiful women you've ever seen.'

He sighed, smiled at some memory.

'I was there working for James Stirling. A ridiculous pipe dream project. Was never going to come to anything. Totally unrealisable. Perfect for me, though. I got paid to lark about for six months.'

The tabletop bore the scars of four decades of family life. Red-wine rings and faded felt-tip pen. Scratches so numerous that at points they seemed to suggest a kind of cuneiform, intelligible only to the near-at-hand.

Max drew a card and placed a five of clubs on the discard pile.

'I would love to have been to Beirut before the war,' he said.

'What a place,' said Gordon. 'So glamorous. Brilliant buildings going up everywhere you looked. We used to get in the car and drive up to Niemeyer's fairground up in Tripoli. A massive site, thousands of men working on it. Such a shame it never got finished. The days it was being built, it was like watching the future arrive in real time.'

Gordon chuckled to himself and then precipitously a sadness came over him and for a moment he looked uncharacteristically vulnerable.

'Once you've lived there you can't help but be marked by what's happened to the city since,' he said, not looking directly at anyone. 'So much of it was beyond their control. And when these things start they're terribly difficult to stop.'

'Incredible to think how much the Middle East has changed over the course of our lives,' said Douglas, as he placed three aces on the table in front of him.

'Beirut was the centre of it all,' said Gordon, gathering himself up again. 'Very open-minded. Very relaxed. Very international. The lead architect on the job I was on was from Berne. Charming man.

He told me that the average Swiss man drinks two bottles of wine a day. Or at least back then they did. He had a grappa every day with his eleven o'clock coffee. And then a bottle of white with lunch.'

'Thank god that building never got built,' said Tabitha. 'Who would have dared go in the parts of it that were designed in the afternoon.'

Max looked at Tabitha's gin and tonic. Her first, and still two-thirds full. She drank in fierce moderation and, although she did her best to hide it, her displeasure at the wider group's indulgence was permanently parked in the middle of the room, ostensibly obscured, but evident to all in outline, like a car under tarpaulin.

'It would have been fine,' said Gordon with a dismissive wave of the hand. 'He was a wonderful architect. Fantastic draughtsman. Terrible narcolepsy, though. My main jobs while I was there were to tally up his expenses and wake him up when he fell asleep at the wheel.'

For an hour, they played cards and told stories. Max mostly listened. Morocco. Tehran. Rome. Rio. The tales of travellers from an antique land. He was an endlessly willing audience for all this and they knew it.

'If you could go back to one place as it was back then,' he asked eventually, 'where would it be?'

Fiona didn't hesitate.

'Barcelona.'

'Oh, yes,' said Douglas. 'Absolutely.'

'We were travelling around Spain and got stuck there.'

'We couldn't leave. It was so dark and moody. There were parts of the old town that felt *actually* medieval.'

'People sold animals in the street. On the Rambla.'

'There were squares you had to run through,' said Douglas as he gathered up the cards. 'At night. We would run across them. Although most of the thieves were terribly small.'

'They were like characters from a Genet play, the thieves. It wasn't hard to outrun them. The police, however . . .'

She paused, pulled her fingers through her hair.

'It was a year after Franco had died but his lot were still in charge. Vile men. The Guardia Civil. They would come at you with batons. Men, women; didn't matter. But still the people came out and sang. In the streets. Songs in Catalan. We marched with them.'

Her eyes rimmed with tears.

'It was something to behold. A kind of awakening.'

'I bet,' said Max.

Fiona shook her head briskly as if to flick clear the sentimentality like other people did with rain.

'We went back a couple of years ago,' she said. 'It's just Disneyland now. Open-topped buses. Packs of people trudging round. This endless bovine trudging.'

Max smiled to himself.

'The masses ruin everything eventually, don't they?'

'Excuse me,' said Fiona. 'That is not what I meant . . .'

But she never got a chance to say what it was that she *had* meant because she was interrupted by a voice.

'You've finished.'

Everyone looked up. Jonathan was standing in the doorway.

'The front door was on the latch.'

'Did we not tell you, darling?' said Bryony. 'So sorry. Max stepped in.'

'I rushed back.'

'We won,' continued Bryony with a kind of willed gaiety. 'He has a remarkable talent for being dealt jokers.'

'I mean, fucking hell, Bryony. They had just ordered some extremely good quality cognac.'

'Sorry, darling.'

'I called three times.'

'My phone is in my bag.'

'I don't think we've got any cognac,' said Douglas mischievously. 'I think I could do you a Baileys, although it would probably have to be without ice.'

Gordon laughed.

'Nothing like a warm Baileys when you've just missed out on the vintage Courvoisier.'

Jonathan scowled at Gordon – possibly, Max imagined, because it was lower risk than scowling at his wife.

'Please have my seat,' he said.

'I can sit here,' said Jonathan, taking a stool from against the wall and pulling it alongside the table.

'Wine?' said Fiona.

'Abso-bloody-lutely.'

'Coming right up,' she said, standing up to get him a glass.

'How was the meeting?' asked Douglas.

'Fine,' said Jonathan irritably, before he caught himself and more courteously added: 'Productive actually. We made quite a lot of progress. A prospective new client was over from Sweden and he was sharp and informed and has the right instincts, I think.'

Fiona placed a glass in front of Jonathan and filled it generously.

'Lucky you,' said Gordon. 'I was in the office today. We're hiring for a new project that we've just won.'

As far as Max understood it, the *we* here might more accurately have been a *they*. Gordon's role at the practice, which still bore his name, was that of an emeritus director. And his appearances at the office were welcome so long as they were infrequent and uninvolved. At least in Tabitha's telling of it.

'This guy turns up. For his interview. Project lead. Important stuff. A big job. Four-million-pound build. And he turns up on a skateboard. The man is forty-eight years old! He has grey hairs in his beard. He might have been a *grandfather* in my father's time. And he turns up on a bloody skateboard.'

'In baggy jeans and a baseball cap?' asked Fiona impishly.

'Of course!'

'Gordon stopped wearing jeans in 1987,' said Bryony to Max. 'And the fashion world breathed a sigh of relief.'

'And then do you know what Jules said?' continued Gordon, blithely ignoring her. 'He said to this guy – this forty-eight-year-old man who has turned up to Barraclough Green Architects on a skateboard – he says to him: "Ordinarily this is the point when I ask interviewees if they'd like a cup of tea or coffee but perhaps you'd prefer a glass of orange squash?"'

The table roared.

'Are you a skateboarder, Max?' asked Jonathan pointedly.

Max demurred. For much of his life, he would very much have liked to have been a skater, one of those boys with long hair and plaid shirts, living in Seattle maybe, or San Diego. He had had a couple of classmates at school who had approximated that life, hanging out at the half-pipe on the local rec, summers spent surfing in Cornwall. He had envied them, those kids who find that almost spiritual thing in the feeling of movement. But it hadn't been him.

'No,' he said. 'I'm more of an A to B, two-wheels kind of guy.'

He paused.

'Just without your penchant for Lycra.'

Jonathan's bike had a carbon-fibre frame and retailed at £2,500, which Max knew because he had googled it.

Gordon guffawed and slapped the table.

'He needs to wear shorts that tight to keep his haemorrhoids in,' he shouted.

Jonathan said nothing to this, but, using his eyebrows and a very subtle movement of his head, communicated to the table a kind of wry acceptance.

'It's also kind of hard to fix a child seat to a skateboard,' said Max. 'Let alone two.'

'I saw you the other day,' said Fiona. 'One on the front. One on the back. So cute!'

'I was taking them to the aquarium,' said Max. 'Have you been? It's quite good but it's phenomenally expensive.'

'Oh god, isn't it? I took Dorothea's kids there once. It cost me an absolute fortune.'

'It wasn't until we got there that I realised that five-year-olds pay full adult price. So we're in the queue and I say to my five-year-old, "Tell them you're four." She looks at me like I'm Kim Philby and I've just asked her to betray her country. The horror on her face. You wouldn't believe it. So I say to her, "Come on, it's not like you carry ID. They basically have to take my word for it." And she's standing there, completely mortified, like everything she's ever known about me has turned out to be false. And obviously at that point I'm starting to have my doubts, too, but an adult ticket is eighteen quid so I say to her, "I'll get you a milkshake." And she looks at me and she says incredulously, "You were going to get me a milkshake anyway." Which was true, and had been much discussed. By this point, we're getting close to the front of the queue and I have to start whispering. And I say to her, "All right, don't say anything. I'm not asking you to lie. Just stay quiet, OK? Let me do the talking." And then we get to the front of the queue and I am just about to order the tickets when she shouts, at the top of her voice, "I'm five!"'

The story had gone where it was obviously going and the responses that greeted the punchline were mostly gentle laughter laced with recognition. Apart from Bryony's, which came out as a screech, so hard and so high that it silenced the room.

'What?' she said. 'I thought it was funny.'

'Yes,' said Jonathan. 'But was it *that* funny?'

There was a moment. A beat. Jonathan looked at Max. Max looked at Jonathan. There was something going on, Max knew, but he couldn't really tell what it was. Was he being auditioned? Or was he being warned off?

'I'm going to refill this,' he said, picking up the water jug.

'How refreshing,' said Fiona, throwing a look at Gordon. 'A man who recognises that he doesn't have a divine right to be waited on hand and foot.'

The open-fronted units gave the kitchen the feel of a chaotically curated anthropological museum. On display were clip-lid jars filled with pulses, dried fruits and unidentifiable grains. Bottles of oil with saturated labels. Spices from long-shuttered supermarket chains. There were ceramic tagine pots in a variety of colours. Bamboo dumpling steamers. Rusting pasta makers and heaped paella pans.

'How many tagines can one family eat at any given time?' asked

Max under his breath as he walked back into the room with the refilled water jug. But no one was listening. There had been movement at the table. Seats had been switched and there were two distinct conversations going on at either end of the table, with Bryony in the middle, not quite in either.

He sat down next to her, topped up her water glass.

'I have been told you're a director,' she said.

'That's right.'

'Let me guess.'

She sat back in her chair, sized him up.

'Documentaries,' she said. 'I'm thinking high-minded stuff. A life of Shostakovich for BBC Four, that sort of thing.'

Max shook his head.

'Commercials?' she asked with a sceptical eyebrow raised.

'I made a feature film,' he said.

'*Really?* Which one?'

'It's called *Flamingoland*.'

Bryony turned her head to the side, her right eye half-shut.

'Wait a second,' she said. '*Flamingoland*. Have I seen that? Could I have seen it at a film festival?'

'Maybe.'

'I used to go to them, film festivals. I mean, I still do, just not as much.'

She was wearing a long set of beads, which she twisted round one finger. She smiled.

'Set in that funny fairgroundy place. With the animals. It was quite good, wasn't it?'

Max cocked his head to one side, didn't say anything.

'You directed *Flamingoland*?' she said. Her voice was warm and round, soft from the wine.

Max didn't know much about science, but surely there was a new charge to all this, like the ions in the air had been upended. He could feel Jonathan watching them from the other end of the table, but he didn't acknowledge him. Instead, he kept his eyes fixed on Bryony and smiled humbly.

'Wrote and directed,' said Max. 'And pretty much produced.'

'An *auteur*.'

'Godard was an auteur. I made a film.'

'But it *was* quite good, wasn't it? It was funny and charming and it didn't have a big budget but it still looked good. It had a style to it.'

Max didn't answer this but he didn't need to – his wide grin was communicating everything that needed to be known.

'But that was ages ago, though,' said Bryony. 'What have you done since then?'

'There have been other scripts,' he said. 'And some music videos. And a few commercials. And lots of corporate videos.'

Bryony winced in sympathy.

'I know people in the trade. It's horrendous. You get so close and there's money lined up and then an actor pulls out and the whole thing collapses like a house of cards, never to be picked up again.'

Max smiled at this gnomically. This had not happened to him for a very long time. None of his recent projects had got anywhere near having actors attached to them, much less the kind of actors who ever turned anything down.

'Are you working on something now?'

'Yeah,' he said. 'I mean, it's just at the script stage. Or rather, it's not even at the finished script stage. It's an almost-done first draft.'

Bryony put her hand on his forearm, gave him that smile.

'Still,' she said. 'You're writing.'

'I am.'

'How exciting,' she said. 'An auteur walks among us.'

Friday 1 June

From Monday to Friday, their life was like a precision-cut jigsaw, each piece meticulously chamfered so that it slotted exactly into place. Karolina worked five days a week but didn't start until noon on Tuesdays and Thursdays. Alma did five days a week at school, Arthur, two and a half days at nursery. Max worked three days at Luxio Films. Twice a week, Maja from Gothenburg – whom they had found via a website, and who was writing her doctoral thesis on the phenomenology of boredom – picked up the kids and talked to them in Swedish until he got home at 6 p.m.

All of which, once you'd slotted it all together, left Fridays from 9 a.m.–2.30 p.m. as his time to write. Which is what Max would have been doing if he hadn't been sitting up in bed, two pillows behind his back, watching *Flamingoland* for the first time in years.

He was three-quarters of the way through the film. The lead character, played by a young Eddie Thomas in his first role, had just been dumped by his girlfriend and he was walking through Flamingoland, the faded theme park where he worked. It was sunset and the park was shut, made odd by its emptiness. In the background, you could see the stilled swirling saucers, pale pink and powder blue, and beyond them, a rollercoaster.

Max felt a soupy wave of nostalgia. He had worked at the park himself for five summers straight: the two while he was at sixth-form college and then his three years as an undergraduate. It no longer existed, having gone into administration not long after he had made his film, but it had been a brilliantly weird place. Part theme park, part zoo, its various attractions were an engagingly disjointed expression of the owner, John Armstrong's passing fancies: a netted habitat for six re-housed ring-tailed lemurs, the east of England's first log flume, a Magna Carta-themed diorama, half a dozen fairground rides and, at the centre of it all, thirty-two black-beaked Andean flamingos.

Five summers working there – always taking on the lowliest of tasks and always available for an after-work pint – had endeared Max to Flamingoland's management team and so, when he returned a few years after his last shift to ask if he could shoot there, they had enthusiastically given him the run of the place once the last guest had left.

Max sipped at his cup of tea and watched as Eddie walked up the steps of a carousel and sat in Cinderella's carriage. He had been just nineteen then, Eddie, but he already had it: that thing that made you want to watch him, that combination of weirdness and vulnerability and everyman charm.

Max watched him light a cigarette. Watched the smoke curl out through the carriage door as he exhaled. It had been shot on digital but it looked like film. The heavy early evening orange light had helped no end. But the reason it looked so gorgeously grainy and atmospheric was down to his vintage lenses: his beloved vintage lenses. He had acquired them as teenager on a half-term trip to Norfolk. His parents had given him some holiday money to spend at a car boot sale and he had been drawn to that box of tactile and mysterious objects, the dulled aluminium casings both obviously old and still thrillingly modern. They had given the film its hazy shimmer and the freewheeling sunflares that occasionally, out of nowhere, filled the frame.

He watched Eddie get up and walk out of the park into the wheat-fields that surrounded it. The sun had set and they were into the golden hour, that deep dusky window of light that had been particularly warm and rich that day, and watching Eddie, almost in silhouette as he walked through the wheat, you could convince yourself that a couple of Hertfordshire fields were the epic plains of Terrence Malick's Midwest.

Max smiled. *Days of Heaven* had been a favourite of Ron's, the measuredly flamboyant owner of Cinema Paradiso, Stevenage's only independent video rental shop. Ron stocked multiple copies of *Home Alone* and the Indiana Jones movies, but he had also carried Jarman and Jarmusch, most of the New Wave, and Wim Wenders's entire back catalogue. And his signature three-for-two VHS offer meant that the Anderson family invariably left his shop with a couple of crowd-pleasing blockbusters and something else. Something unexpected. Something pulled off the shelf as an afterthought, taken simply to make up the numbers. Something that somebody liked the cover of: *Slacker* maybe, or *Drugstore Cowboy*. *Paris, Texas. Down by Law.*

For Max, these third-choice videos, which he had almost always watched alone, late in the evening, after his sisters had gone to bed, hadn't simply provided him with an education in filmmaking, they had concretised his world view, his sense of a culture that was divided into the mainstream – which was artificial and jejune, compromised and degrading – and the independent space outside it where precious feelings could be honestly expressed and the world could be grasped in a way that was sophisticated and complicated and true.

On-screen, Eddie started to move through the fields more quickly. He wasn't quite dancing but he wasn't walking normally either. And that's when it started. The opening bars of the song.

Max tapped out the bass line against the keypad of his laptop. It was still just right, the soundtrack. Modest Mouse, Built to Spill, The Corrections. All of them bands that hadn't been buried in layers of middlemen. Bands whom you could just write to, as an earnest fan, and, if you were honest and open-hearted, you might get a response from the lead singer. Max felt again the feeling that he had experienced at the time: a great swell of gratitude that all of them had written back to him and all of them had agreed to let him use their songs for a peppercorn fee.

And then it happened – as of course he knew it would – but still it was a kind of jolt. Eddie was standing in the field in the gloaming, waist deep in wheat, when a flamingo walked into shot. It was in silhouette, but it was still self-evidently a flamingo, with that unmistakable S formed by its neck and beak; those wrong-way-round knees.

Max had known that although the flamingos had their flight feathers clipped, they would, on occasion, leap the fence and explore the local area, before heading home to their steady supply of brined shrimp, but it wasn't something that he could have engineered. It had just happened.

He remembered the magic of that moment, the astonishing quiet on set. He had been standing there, behind the camera, his breathing stilled as the flamingo had straightened its neck, looked at Eddie. He hadn't broken character, Eddie. Not for an instant. He had just stood there, holding the flamingo's gaze for a few seconds, until it disappeared back through a hedge and was gone.

Max paused the film. He had seen enough. It had dated, as all things do, but it was still cool, still just right in its detachment.

He flipped his laptop shut and walked out of the bedroom. He wasn't an auteur, not any more. But he had made a film, once. And he could do it again.

Down in the kitchen, he flicked on the kettle and listened as it creaked into life. There was something strangely reassuring about the sound, the way it brought a sense of life into the house, which otherwise had been redecorated to fastidiously eradicate noise. The double-glazed windows shut tight. The carpets were double ply, the drawers soft close. The fridge barely murmured.

Max pulled the box of teabags from the cupboard. The silence was so absolute that he often found it hard to concentrate. Such a contrast to the apartment in Berlin, with its knocking pipes and overhead footsteps, its omnipresent hum of ambient noise: distant bass lines, playground shrieks, the stop and start of the traffic on Prinzenstrasse. He had become so accustomed to it that it was a kind of comfort, a confirmation that he was alive and in the world.

For all that the noise of the city had been a kind of inspiration to him, he hadn't, in truth, actually written that much while he was in Berlin. There had been a short film, early on, that he had scripted, and then shot on a shoestring. It had done the thing that short films do, which is to flare up briefly, before disappearing into the ether, barely to be seen again. And then there was a feature script, which he had given up on halfway through. And then another, about two Americans in Berlin, which he had persevered with way beyond its natural lifespan.

He put the teabag in a cup and poured in the boiling water. The reality was that living in Berlin had been the achievement. The long nights on the cobblestone Admiralbrücke, drinking wine and eating pizza from boxes. The chess games on open-windowed cafe terraces. The beautiful women on their high-handlebarred bikes. The night rambles. The clubs. The parties. The people. Berlin was the sharp end. The needlepoint. And pulling it off, that life, in that place, at that time, *that* was what he had done all those years.

He sat down at the kitchen table and spread his notes out in front of him. The opening scene was a murder, which made clear the identity of the murderer, but not the victim. The action then flashed back six months and the script got its forward momentum from the viewer trying to work who the main character would end up murdering. A cinematic whodunnin. No one had done it yet.

In his head it would be a ninety-minute film but if HBO wanted to turn it into a recurring series he would, he felt, be willing to compromise his ideals.

Two hours later, at one o'clock, he realised that a barefoot Karolina had walked into the kitchen without him noticing. She was looking over his shoulder at the printed pages in front of him, saw the shape of the document, the centre-aligned text, the Courier font, the inky mess of scribbles and addenda, underlinings, crossings out.

'Still going,' she said, dryly.

Max gathered the papers together, embarrassed that it was taking so long. Embarrassed that it was all so highwire, so fanciful.

'Is anyone ever going to get to read it?' she asked, as she pulled open the fridge door, scanned its contents.

'Yes. Definitely. Soon, but not yet.'

Karolina looked over at him, her hand still holding the fridge door, and raised an eyebrow.

'I promise, soon.'

'OK,' she said, returning her attention to the contents of the fridge. 'Tell me more about the card game. How did Zelda cope without F. Scott?'

'He came actually, later on. It was odd. He was kind of, I don't know, a bit weird about me being there I think.'

Karolina stood up, a block of cheese and two tomatoes in her hands.

'What do they think of us, living on their street?'

'Well, they're obsessed with you,' said Max.

'What?'

'That's what they say. Or at least that's what Tabitha and Bryony say. *We're obsessed with your wife*. They tell me pretty much every time I see them.'

'What does that mean?'

'They like your hair. And your coats. And the way you put together an outfit.'

Karolina was at the kitchen counter facing away from him as she sliced a loaf of bread, but through her hair he could see her smiling.

'I think they also like you because you don't run and they have a real aversion to anyone who runs. Running seems to be totally infra dig for all of them.'

'What was the house like?'

'Hilarious. Like being at a 1970s South American flea market. Hats and rugs everywhere. Obscure musical instruments. I'm sure there were like actual ransacked artefacts openly on display. There wasn't a monkey in a cage but it wouldn't have been out of place. Would get you cancelled in a heartbeat now . . .'

Max leaned back in his chair and crossed his legs.

'But, also, what a house. I mean, it's ramshackle and full of dead insects, but it's so expressive. It's so *them*. Everything feels redolent of something or some time ... I mean, she's not easy, but she's kind of amazing. And he's just lovely.'

'So are you like *in* with them?'

'I'm not sure. I think sort of. But also definitely not. I mean, I'm not in the inner circle, obviously.'

'Are you like the Lindsay Lohan character in *Mean Girls*?'

Max laughed.

'Actually, the women aren't the problem. It's the ...'

'Wait a sec,' said Karolina, her face a picture of impish joy, 'are you like Lindsay Lohan in *Mean Girls and* Lindsay Lohan in *Freaky Friday* all at once?'

Max took a second to compute this, unravel the references.

'Oh my god,' he said in mock horror, looking down at his body. 'Look at me.' He ran his hand through his moderately thick hair. 'I haven't literally become a seventy-year-old.'

Karolina raised an eyebrow as she walked past him, transporting her sandwich back up to her desk.

'Not yet,' she said. 'But we can all see the direction of travel ...'

Thursday 7 June

The drinks were last minute but it was one of those evenings when really it would have been a kind of a moral failure not to. The low light was full-bodied, generous to everything it touched. The air was soft; the wisteria at their heavy-scented best. Swifts wheeled above the gardens. Somebody, somewhere, was playing a cello by an open window.

For Max, it had been a long and particularly spirit-crushing day at work and so when the invitation had come he had readily accepted, knowing that Karolina would be tied up in meetings all evening. The kids, exhausted after their afternoon swimming lesson, had crashed out at 7 p.m., which meant that he was, for once, the first to arrive.

'Oh, those are lovely,' said Bryony, ushering him in.

He was carrying a bottle of rosé and a bunch of flowers.

'Karolina insisted I bring them,' he said, handing them to her. 'I told her you were all only interested in alcohol but she wouldn't listen.'

She tutted and led him down the hall to the kitchen.

'That poor woman. I don't know why she stays with you.'

The kitchen was barn-like. A sloped ceiling, the structural beams and wooden floor all painted white. The table was white. Everywhere you looked there were paintings: huge abstract canvases, ink sketches on paper, Russian icons in delicate frames.

'Wow,' said Max.

'I'm going to put these in water straight away. I was just about to go out and cut some mint.'

She pressed a pair of scissors into his hands and opened the back door.

'Be a darling?'

The garden was wild and copious. Max walked down a crooked path between two huge banks of flowers, each overflowing its borders. A long light-dappled table ran under a weathered pergola, thick with honeysuckle. In the far corner, he could see a love seat huddled under fruit trees. There were bird tables and peanut balls. Insects everywhere, abundant life.

A minute or so later, he was on his haunches, scissors in hand, about to cut what at the very least was a mint-like plant, when he heard Bryony approaching from behind him.

'This is a lovely garden,' he said, standing up. 'I mean, if it were mine I would obviously stick a sixteen-foot trampoline in the middle of it, but I suppose Jonathan's best bouncing years are behind him.'

Bryony gently took the scissors from him. She looked at him like an indulged son, one who has strayed from the path but is still the favourite.

'I sometimes think it's my first love,' she said. 'Gardening. I find it a very philosophical experience. You cleave close to life when your hands are in the dirt.'

She tucked her arm into Max's and guided him back to the patio.

'If you grow up in the countryside, it never leaves you, that connection with the soil. It's the pedestal on which the entire edifice rests.'

Max screwed one eye shut.

'I grew up in the suburbs,' he said. 'Tinned minds, tinned breath, all that.'

She smiled at him.

'A country boy would have known the difference between lemon verbena and mint.'

She bent down and took a cutting from a large terracotta pot, containing what Max now recognised was obviously mint.

'Put mint in the borders and it'll take your whole garden.'

Max smiled, tugging his forelock.

'It would have been perfectly nice with verbena,' she said. 'At least you weren't about to feed us all foxgloves.'

In the garden two doors along, a dog barked and a handful of sparrows hurried up into the air.

'Is that where you paint?' he said, pointing to the building at the end of the path.

'It is,' said Bryony, standing up with a clump of mint in her hand. 'Let me show you quickly. The light in there is amazing this evening. It's like being in a jar of honey.'

The studio was double height. The top of the north-facing wall and half the roof had been taken out and replaced with a Crittall-style glass box, which opened the whole place up to the sky.

In the middle of the room was an easel. On it was a half-finished painting. Around it were dozens of stretched canvases. Some had been started, some were still white. A large pile were leaning against the wall, backs facing out, the staples visible.

'I just took an order,' she said.

Her paintbox was like a little wooden suitcase, which sat on its own table, lid up. Inside were tubes of paint, curled up like snails. On the far wall were shelves, heaving with things. Palette knives in glass jars. Boxes of charcoals. A tray of pastels. Bottles of turps. A paint-flecked radio.

'It was a stable block originally. You can see the line there,' she pointed to an old weathered joist that ran in the brick, halfway up the wall. 'That's where the hay loft would have been. It had already been gutted when we bought the house. A mechanic used it as a storage unit. We put in the ceiling of course.'

On the easel was a canvas. To Max's eye it looked a lot like so many of her paintings, which were loud on the edges and quiet in the middle. This one was mostly green, but in many different tones. The paint was layered up, so thick on the periphery that it was still tacky.

'It's finished,' she said. 'Or at least, I have stopped. None of them are ever really finished.'

'It's beautiful,' said Max because etiquette demanded it, but also because it *was* beautiful. The contrast between the gauzy absence at its centre and the greens around it, which were murkily and moodily abstract, refusing to be reduced to leaves or grass.

'Is it?' she said, blithely. 'It's funny to me to think that these objects might be things that are considered beautiful or are coveted or have value.'

It had a practised quality to it, this line, but Max was happy to play along. There had been shows, he knew. Some commercial success. And then later in life, something of a rediscovery after two of her paintings were included in large museum show reappraising overlooked women artists.

'The recognition is neither here nor there,' she continued. 'For me, the process is everything.'

Max allowed himself a little smile at this but said nothing.

'The work is all about ellipsis,' she said. 'The absence of the thing in the middle.'

They stood for a few seconds looking at the canvas in that slightly reverent way which always feels like the thing to do in such situations.

'Do you know what I mean?'

'I think so,' said Max. 'There's no endpoint. They're not going anywhere.'

'Exactly,' said Bryony, turning reflexively to look at him. 'That's exactly it.' She smiled. 'That there is nothing at the centre is the point. I want the process to be foregrounded all the time.'

She took a step back from the canvas, which compelled Max to do the same, ensuring that he saw it from another perspective.

'Because the process is the transformative act. When I'm painting I am able to break through into a kind of spiritual place. Where you can intuit pure forms. Where you can connect with your sense of the divine.'

Max made a non-committal gesture. He hadn't found this necessary for his whodunnin script.

'Every time *I* try to break through to roam with the gods,' he said dryly, 'I find that they're never in.'

Bryony was animated now and barely heard him. The stud in her nose flashed in the light. She talked about the hours at the canvas, the feeling of a brush in your hand. The state of crystalline thinking that it engendered, the feeling of being both utterly present and beyond thought. Max mostly nodded along, somewhat delighted and somewhat engaged, but also keen to get back to his glass of wine.

'It's a kind of slow, methodical pacing that has a kind of transcendence to it. The pacing. Not the product,' she said as they walked back through the garden. 'I achieve a kind of coherence when I'm doing it. A sense of order.'

The sun was dipping behind a tree, throwing shadows across the lawn.

'When I'm writing a script it's like I have a huge blank canvas behind me, everywhere I go. Like the cloth that would become the Bayeux Tapestry before it had been started.'

'Yes,' she said, tucking her arm into his again. She was a head shorter than him and leaned into him slightly as they walked.

'And everything that I see or read or hear has the potential to add to it. A line of dialogue. The way someone walks. A joke. All these things contribute. A few stitches here. A whole scene there. Everything has the potential to feed into it. Everything has the potential to be transformed.'

'Everything has the potential to be transformed,' she said. 'That's the way artists see the world.'

Back in the kitchen, Max sat at the breakfast bar, elated, despite himself. It wasn't simply the generosity of the parallel, the sense of legitimacy that her imprimatur conferred on what he'd done, but how it opened up the future, made writing feel urgent again, viable.

Bryony upended a brown paper bag, tipping a dozen figs onto the counter. They were yellowy-green and veiny, like tiny varicose pears.

'Everyone assumes that the black ones are the best but the Italians know that the Lattarula is queen of the figs,' she said, as she picked one up and squeezed it ever so gently. 'You need to hold them in your hand, get a feel for the thickness of the skin, get a sense of whether it is thinning. If it's thinning then it's ready.'

She put the fig back in the bag, picked out another. Felt it. Smiled. Cut it in half. The flesh inside was pale orange, dense with juice.

'I lived in Umbria for a while in my youth,' she said, unapologetically picking up a piece of fig with her fingers and passing it to Max. 'We picked these off the trees on our way down to the river and ate them with the juice running down our chins.'

Max ate the fig, watching her, as she cut the ends off two packets of feta and drained the water into the sink.

'I was twenty then. Auburn hair and long arms. The local boys called out to me in the night.'

The counter was cluttered, the recipe book dark with stains. She broke the blocks of cheese with her hands, tossed craggy hunks into a bowl.

'What took you to Umbria?' he asked.

'Art school,' she said. 'A year-long exchange. It was in an old palace. We slept three girls to a bed. Parts of the building had no electricity or running water. We used a chamber pot and read by candlelight.'

Max sat at the bar, chopping the mint and listening to her as she told him about it, the hard technical lessons, hours and hours spent mastering chiaroscuro, line, perspective. There was a new kind of compact between them now, an intimacy. The conversation was unhurried, digressive. Her wooden bracelets rattled as she moved.

'The 1970s,' she said. 'A million years ago.'

But also not, thought Max. It didn't take much to imagine her – that twenty-year-old – with her long arms. So much of her was present still. The ease. That casualness of beautiful women, the abundance of their gestures.

The doorbell rang.

'I'll get it,' said Max.

'No, you cut the baguette,' she said, passing it to him as she walked round the kitchen island. 'At an angle. I don't want tiny little slices. I want them longer than that.'

When she returned a minute later, Tabitha was with her, wearing a black cape fixed with a brooch.

'Max,' she said, in a voice that managed somehow to be both warm and stern.

'Hello, Tabitha.'

She walked behind him and as she passed, she paused and pinched the neck of his jumper, rubbed the wool between her fingers to get a feel for its weight. They had a habit, the pair of them, of touching him in a way that would be unthinkable for him to reciprocate.

'Your wife dresses you well.'

Max looked down at his outfit. As well as the jumper, he was wearing his new pleated wool trousers, yellow socks and a pair of faded brown leather brogue boots given to him many years earlier by a stylist at the end of a commercial shoot.

'She had literally nothing to do with anything I'm wearing.'

'Nonsense,' said Tabitha.

'We've seen her outfits,' said Bryony. 'She has an eye.'

'It's the woman who sets the tone,' said Tabitha.

Max was spreading whipped feta onto the slices of baguette. He groaned despairingly.

'Maybe in the 1950s,' he said.

Tabitha raised her head to its full height and looked down her nose at him.

'How old are you?'

'Forty-two.'

'Forty-two is a good age for a man,' said Bryony.

'Yes,' said Tabitha. 'Forty-two is good these days. Women peak earlier of course, but forty-two is still good for a man.'

Max did one of his eyes-wide half-snorts.

'You can say that when you're our age,' said Bryony. 'When you know things.'

Tabitha nodded.

'How old is Karolina?' she asked.

'Thirty-eight,' said Max, laughing in disbelief. 'Shall I put her out to pasture?'

'That's a good gap,' she said.

Bryony nodded.

'Five years is better, but four is good.'

'According to whom?'

'Natural law,' said Tabitha. 'I married a man younger than me. It was a mistake.'

'Right,' said Max. He waited for a beat or two, thought about pursuing this further, but then decided against it.

'I'm assuming the mint goes on these?' he said.

Over the next half an hour, the house filled. Gordon sauntered in looking like he had already had a gin and tonic or two. Fiona was next, without Douglas, who was in bed with a fever. Finally, Jonathan returned from work and walked into the kitchen reading a letter that he'd clearly just opened. He stopped in the doorway and looked over his glasses at the scene in front of him, seemingly deciding how he felt about it, before he tossed the letter on the sideboard, smiled broadly, and poured himself a glass of wine.

Bottles were pulled from the fridge. French cheese unwrapped from stiff white paper. These impromptu drinks. The nonchalance of them. A bottle of white in an earthenware pot. Arms reaching across the table. Italian figs. Bone-handled cutlery. The easy choreography of it all.

Max was at the head of the table. The conversation was like a river. Always the same and always different. What could he do but allow himself to be swept along?

Three hours later it was 10.30 p.m. and everyone had gone home except Max, who had his sleeves rolled to the elbows and was tipsily washing up all the things that couldn't fit in the dishwasher.

'You really don't have to do that,' said Bryony.

'I know,' said Max merrily. 'It would be a pretty hopeless way of saying thank you if it was something I had to do.'

She folded a tea towel over the back of a chair.

'You're a charming boy,' she said. 'And it was a charming evening. But I am dog-tired and I am going to bed.'

Jonathan was sitting at the table, a half-drunk bottle of red wine at his elbow. As she passed him, she laid a hand on his shoulder.

'Don't stay up too late.'

She closed the door behind herself just as Max was placing the final roasting dish onto the drying rack.

'You're well trained,' said Jonathan.

Max dried his hands on the tea towel.

'I only did it to make you and Gordon look bad,' he said. 'Five minutes of work. So easy and so worth it.'

Jonathan laughed and pushed a chair away from the table with his foot.

'Sit down,' he said. 'Help me finish this.'

Max sat down and accepted the proffered glass. For a few seconds they sat in companiable silence.

'God, it's nice just to be able to drink a glass of wine,' said Jonathan eventually. 'My son-in-law . . .' He paused and looked over his shoulder to check that Bryony was definitely out of the room. 'He can't just drink a glass of wine. "It's small batch, Jonathan," he has to tell me. Like that's somehow moral.'

Max smiled as he took his glass by the stem and swirled it so the wine hung pleasingly on its sides.

'His name is Toby,' he said. 'He likes kitesurfing. He wears bracelets.'

The candle on the table burned itself out and a thin column of smoke fizzled into the air. Jonathan brought his index finger and thumb to his mouth, wetted them on the tips and then pinched the wick.

'Two glasses in and he can't stop banging on about his men's group. I have absolutely no idea what makes him think that I would have any interest in ayahuasca.'

Max laughed through his nose, put his hand over his mouth.

'My future grandchildren will have half his genes.'

Jonathan pulled a lump of dripped wax from the side of the candlestick.

'Do you play chess?'

'Depends what you mean by that,' said Max, leaning back in his chair. 'I'm not at the openings and defences kind of level, but I know what goes where.'

'Fancy a game?'

'Sure.'

Jonathan switched on a standing lamp and a warm orange light filled the living room, which was abundant but ordered. A piano stood to one side, its lacquer gleaming. On the walls were paintings in heavy gilt frames, charcoal sketches, a line drawing in pen and ink. Art books lay on the coffee table, their spines aligned. Brocaded lamps sat on circular side tables. Walnuts were piled in a bowl, a brass nutcracker lying beside them. A bamboo palm cast spiky shadows on the wall. The gold-tasselled throw cushions were, somehow, obviously French.

The chess set was already out, the board sitting on a low table between two chairs, the pieces arranged in perfect formation.

'This is a beautiful set.'

'Nineteenth century,' said Jonathan. 'The craftsmanship on the knights is exceptional.'

He picked one up, ran his finger along its back.

'Bryony bought it in some antiques shop in the middle of nowhere. She had the board made for me. My fiftieth birthday.'

He pointed down at the different woods used in its construction.

'Ash and beech for the squares. Walnut frame. And this thin line around the squares is zebrawood.'

Jonathan sat in the reading chair, an angled lamp peering over his shoulder. Max sat in the one opposite.

'I learned to play at primary school,' said Jonathan as he picked up a pawn from either side, mixed them together below the table and then stuck out two fists, inviting Max to pick one.

'Mr Jenkins taught us. He was a nasty piece of work but he was good at chess.'

Max picked a fist and Jonathan opened it to reveal a black pawn.

'He liked to use his belt, Mr Jenkins. Sometimes a ruler. He could do you a proper welt with a ruler, could Jenkins. Right across the palm. There was something kind of beautiful about it. The way it ran right across your hand, the lines so straight.'

He spun the board through 180 degrees so the white pieces were on his side.

'Passing the eleven plus was a rebuke to that old bastard. I left him there at that crappy bloody primary school and I never looked back.'

He took his queen's pawn and moved it forward two spaces.

'You went to grammar school?' said Max.

'St Cuthbert's College, 1961 to 1968. They shut it down the year I left.'

Max brought his queen's pawn up two in reply.

'Missed the farewell party. I had already hitched halfway to northern Germany by that point.'

He brought out his king's knight.

'I thought I was Laurie Lee. Patrick Leigh Fermor.'

'Irongate Wharf to Constantinople,' said Max approvingly.

'That's right,' said Jonathan. He smiled and Max smiled and for a second they both glowed with that feeling of exuberant hope that surges through you when you meet someone new, whose Venn diagram of interests and experiences overlaps largely but not wholly with your own, leaving space for stories to be told and discoveries to be made.

'Although they didn't hitch, they walked,' said Max, still smiling, as he brought forward a pawn one space in preparation for a kingside castle.

'I didn't have time to walk, did I? Had to be at college in the September. I wanted to do the whole Iron Curtain. The Baltic to Trieste.'

'You hitchhiked the whole way?'

'Hitched, hiked, rode the rails,' said Jonathan as he moved his other knight. 'With my old pal Ben Muirden. Hardly a shilling between us. We slept in barns, fields, siding cars, a dredging barge on the Danube.'

'I hitched all around New Zealand,' said Max. 'I was nineteen...'

For twenty minutes they played chess and rhapsodised the romance of the open road. They talked about lifts from nuns and lifts from soldiers, about feelings of pure freedom and absolute possibility. They refilled their glasses and lamented the death of hitchhiking and the end of adventure.

'You couldn't do it now,' said Jonathan.

'You couldn't,' said Max. 'I don't know why, but you just couldn't.'

With the board open and the balance of play about even, Jonathan picked up his bishop between his second and third fingers. He held it up by his head, upside down, like one might do a cigarette. He paused, pensively, looking down at the board.

'Nothing ventured,' he said

And then, with a practised flourish, he used the bishop to take Max's knight.

Max looked down at the board and then looked again. He calculated the permutations and then he passed up the opportunity to take Jonathan's bishop and chose instead to move his kingside rook.

'Check,' he said.

Jonathan looked down at the board. There was no cover available. He had no choice but to move his king one square to the left. But doing so opened him up to a fork.

'Fuck,' he said. 'You're going to take my queen.'

Max looked up at him, unable to supress his gloating smile.

''Fraid so,' he said.

Thursday 14 June

It was a stretch, really, to call it a park. It was a plot on which you felt there might once have been a couple of houses. Perhaps they had been bombed in the war. Or just demolished back in the days when the street was rundown and crumbling. Either way, it was now a patch of grass with a few trees, a small playground and single tennis court surrounded by a high wire fence.

Everyone called it the Square locally, despite it being neither square, nor at the centre of things. Max had only been living on Pemberton Place for two months, but already he had identified the Square as a place where he experienced entropy in real time, a place where he pushed swings and stood at the bottom of the slides, incapable of any kind of useful thought, until he was a little closer to death.

He sat on the playground bench, half-watching Arthur whoosh down the slide, arrive at the bottom and run round to do it all again.

Was forty-two a good age for a man?

In the days since the drinks at Bryony and Jonathan's, the weather had turned. He pulled his jacket across his chest. *Forty-two*. Wasn't it a kind of desperate age? Halfway, or thereabouts. The point at which things could still be righted, but only just. An age freighted with a kind of scrambling urgency.

Arthur came down the slide, only this time on his front.

'Nice one,' said Max.

Arthur grinned.

A cold breeze blew across the square. Maybe forty-two *was* a good age for a man if you'd had children, like they had, in your twenties. Max felt the onset of a familiar anxiety. It had seemed like such a smart move, having children late. Like they'd cheated the system and got away with it. Lived these epic youths and still managed to have a family. It was only lately that he'd started to see whole the enormity of the wasted days, the stasis. The years and years of drift. They looked so thin now, those pre-fatherhood days. He had waited too long and he could never catch up.

Arthur slid down the slide and saw a pigeon perched on the roundabout.

'Go away, pigeon!' he shouted and ran at it.

The pigeon flew away. Thrown by the bird's sudden flapping, Arthur tripped, face-forward with no attempt made to break his fall.

Max rushed over and hauled him up. He seemed shaken but unharmed. Together, they looked down at his body. Nothing but a muddied knee.

'New trousers.'

Max looked despairingly at the buggy but he knew what he knew: he had come out without any.

'Sure thing, let's go home and get some.'

'No, stay here.'

'I don't have any trousers here.'

'New trousers,' said Arthur with a snarl.

'If you want new trousers, we'll have to go home.'

'I want new trousers here.'

'Well, we can't do it here. We can either stay here in those trousers, or we can go home and get some new ones.'

To his right, Max could see Tabitha walking into the Square with her granddaughter, Grace.

'New trousers here,' said Arthur with a stamp of his foot.

'I can't do that.'

And on it went. Like this. Only louder. And then much louder. And then before Max had a chance to react, Arthur was deep into one of his signature screaming fits which were high and hard and raging. Max endured this for a minute or two, talking softly with open arms, while trying his best not to catch the eye of any of the other adults present, most, but not all, of whom had the good grace not to stand and stare at him.

After a while, the screaming slowly subsided but all that did was clear space for Arthur to return to the conversation about his trousers, which predictably ran up against the same intractable dilemma that it had the first time.

'Change trousers here!'

'We don't have any other trousers here.'

On and on it went and then finally Max shouted.

Impotently.

Counterproductively.

Self-loathingly.

He shouted.

And off again went Arthur. Only this time, he was lying on his back and screaming up into the air.

Five minutes later, it was all over. Ancient history, at least from Arthur's perspective. He was back up on his feet and happily playing with someone else's abandoned ball. Max, for whom it was not all over, not by a long shot, was sitting dejectedly on a bench.

Tabitha came and sat next to him.

'I am patient and patient and patient and patient and then I lose my patience and I shout.'

'Everyone knows what it's like.'

'Every time I lose my temper, I feel it like a kind of corrosive spill. Like a battery leaking. This awful corrosive thing gets inside me and it just spreads everywhere.'

'We have all been there.'

Max leaned back into the bench.

'In your youth you have no sense of how much of your life is going to look like this.'

Tabitha leaned against his arm in comradely affection.

'It only feels like that for the short time you're in it. That brief period when they are young. And then before you know it you're nostalgic for it.'

'Really?' said Max. 'For this funny little square? Where it is always two degrees too cold. It's like it has its own malign little microclimate. Is it always like this, even in August?'

Tabitha smiled, said nothing.

'I'm only here because I couldn't face going to St Peter's.'

'The church?'

'There's a stay and play. It's not in the actual church – it's in one of the side rooms and they have toys and books out and there's a pot of tea. And sometimes someone has made a cake and it's ... it's *nice*.'

Arthur picked up the ball and threw it up the slide, watched it roll down in delight.

'But the thing about St Peter's is that I am almost always the only guy there. Like, the only dad there.'

Arthur threw the ball up the slide again and squealed in delight as it rolled down. He looked at Max, who gave him a thumbs up.

'Half the mums there look at you doe-eyed like you're some kind of saint. The other half look at you with this undisguised contempt, like *my husband would rather die than have his balls cut off like this*.'

On the bench opposite them a woman was changing a baby boy. She held him by the ankles in one hand and pulled him up like a trussed bird so she could wipe his bum.

'The other week, there were three or four guys there doing some work on the building. A gutter had leaked or something and so they were at one end of the room, taking down this section of the ceiling so they could get in and do whatever it was they had to do. They all had power tools and I was at the other end of the room, singing about five little speckled frogs.'

Tabitha laughed.

'Sat on their speckled log?'

'That's the one. One of the guys looked over and caught my eye just as I was pretending to jump into a pool where it was nice and cool.'

Tabitha took his hand and squeezed it.

'It's a different kind of masculinity,' she said.

'You can say that again.'

'The thought of my father doing that,' she said. 'Or even this.'

'At 10 a.m. on a Thursday morning?'

'At any time of week.' She nodded at Arthur. 'This will make such a difference to them. Such a present father.'

'Really? There's no sign of that yet. They're animals.'

Tabitha turned to look at him.

'Is he Vlad or Kim?'

Max turned his head sharply to look at her. He had had no idea she knew that was what they called the children. He felt his cheeks reddening. It was like being caught out by your mum. How could she know? Karolina couldn't have told them. Had someone heard it over a garden fence?

'You know it's a joke, right?' he said, his head scrambled. 'Karolina wrote her graduate thesis on the paradox of rationality in game theory.'

'Ah,' said Tabitha.

'It's just a riff on that.' He paused, sighed. 'And, I mean, our kids *are* dicks a lot of the time.'

Tabitha laughed and shook her head.

'Alma is Vlad,' he said. 'She's capable of wild and crazy shit but there's always a calculation to it. 4D chess, *Art of War* kind of stuff.'

Max looked up at his son, who was sitting on a climbing frame shaped like a tractor, smiling beatifically.

'He's Kim. The real headcase. He doesn't have any ballistic missiles but if he did I can guarantee you that he would be randomly lobbing them into the Sea of Japan just to keep everyone guessing.'

Tabitha laughed her high-throated laugh.

'And it's a pretty effective strategy because he knows we're always going to be the grown-ups in the room. Or at least Karolina is. She's like the UN. She believes in diplomacy and democracy and everyone having a voice. And that means you've got to keep talking to the North Koreans however crazy they are.'

Tabitha got up and walked to Grace, who needed some help getting into a swing. Max followed.

'My problem,' he said, as they walked, 'is that I like to think I'm the UN as well, but really I'm the US. My foreign policy is at least half the problem. I like to think that I believe in a rules-based system but really I'm just another belligerent duking it out in the trenches.'

Max stood in front of the swing so he and Tabitha were either side of it and he could push Grace back towards her grandmother.

'But you just get what you inherit, right?' he said. 'Your generation are the Britain and France of the whole thing. You drew all the lines in the wrong places.'

Tabitha laughed at this.

'As soon as you're old enough,' he said to Grace in a coochy-coo kind of voice. 'I'm going to explain to you why everything is ultimately Granny's fault.'

'Don't listen to him, Grace,' said Tabitha. 'Whatever he says, you're much safer with me.'

She nodded her head to encourage Max to turn around and when he did so he saw that Arthur had somehow liberated himself from the playground and was slowly waddling away from them towards the climbing tree on the far side of the Square.

'Oh god, back in a minute.'

'No hurry,' said Tabitha.

By the time Max caught up with Arthur he had already hauled himself onto one of the tree's broad lower branches, where he stood staring at a girl about his age, who was standing on another of the branches next to a man whom Max took to be her father.

For what could only have been a few seconds but felt much longer, the two children stood on their respective branches, staring unsettlingly at each other.

'This is Arthur,' said Max eventually, because somebody really needed to say something.

'And this is Rosa,' said the man. He was wearing Japanese jeans rolled up a little to reveal paisley patterned socks. 'And I'm Dom.'

'Max.'

For a couple of minutes they chatted the usual parent chat: nurseries, daycare, the lunatic cost of it all.

And then, 'Swings,' said Arthur.

And, 'Yes,' said Rosa.

And so, together, the four walked back towards the swings. Tabitha was still there, pushing Grace on the baby swing.

'Tabitha, this is Dom,' said Max.

'Lovely to meet you, Dom,' she said as she pulled Grace out of her swing. 'These are all yours.'

'Oh, we didn't mean to drive you away. Ours seem to have lost interest.'

He pointed to Arthur and Rosa, who had run over to the roundabout.

'Not at all. We were leaving anyway,' she said, as she strapped her granddaughter into the buggy. 'Grace is ready for her nap. And I need a lie down too, what with Max accusing me of imperialist parenting.'

'*Imperialist parenting*,' said Max with a groan. 'I can't believe you got there before me, Tabitha. There is a book in that. Seriously, there is a whole *career* in that.'

'He thinks he had it bad,' she said to Dom. 'But he knows nothing. My generation were raised by Visigoths and Vandals.'

Tabitha smiled her cunning little smile and departed with what looked a bit like a curtsey.

'She's a character,' said Dom.

'The street is full of them.'

'You live on Pemberton Place?'

'Yeah. But we've only been here for a couple of months.'

'Nice.'

'Where are you?'

'We're on Chalgrove Close, two streets over.'

Rosa appeared in front of them.

'Surfing,' she said to her father.

Dom duly picked her up and stood her in the middle of the seesaw, where she planted both her feet in a practised way and stuck out her arms like she was catching a wave.

'Surfer Rosa,' said Max in the dry voice he reserved for puns that were obvious but also needed to be made.

Dom looked at him, broke into a broad smile.

'I'm more of a *Doolittle* man,' he said, 'but "Gigantic" is probably my favourite song of all time.'

'Brixton Academy 1991,' said Max. 'Front of the mosh pit.'

Dom did an exaggerated jaw-drop of a face.

'I was there.'

'No!'

'Yes!'

'It was the worst performance of "Debaser" I have ever heard...'

'But also the best,' said Max.

'Exactly!' said Dom, beaming. 'But also the best.'

For fifteen minutes, they pushed swings and talked Pixies. And then the gigs in London they had been to in the 1990s, Max coming down from Hertfordshire, Dom up from Kent. My Bloody Valentine. Smashing Pumpkins. Nights at the 100 Club and the Astoria. Indie discos that they had both loved, two quid on the door. But they couldn't find another event that they'd both been at.

Eventually, after much remonstrating from both children, they picked their respective kids out of the swings, and accepted that it was time to go home.

'Come to ours for dinner,' said Max. 'Next Saturday.'

'We will.'

'We'll listen to Pixies all night.'

'And Dinosaur Jr!'

'My wife will absolutely hate it!'

'So will my mine!'

Wednesday 20 June

They arrived, all eight of them at once, in a convoy at nine thirty in the morning. A van and three cars. Only the van could fit on the drive at number five and so they had to park the cars wherever they could find spaces, which meant that the unpacking process dominated the street for the three hours or so that it them took to ferry their things into the house.

And what a lot of things they had. Rucksacks straining at the seams. Cardboard boxes sealed with tape. Plastic bags spilling forth their contents. Piles of books that appeared to have been transported loose in the footwells of the cars and had to be carried down the street in teetering stacks. Futons rigged onto roof racks. Gingham check laundry bags so full they had to be dragged along the pavement. Two yuccas and a rubber plant which even from across the road you could tell had fungal leaf disease. A sofa that everyone agreed would need to be thoroughly fumigated before you ever caught them sitting on it. And, intriguingly, a full-size four-panel interior door, which someone speculated was probably being used as an improvised tabletop, a theory which spread quickly along the street and was established as indisputable fact not long after lunch.

Max had been at work and missed the whole thing but had, he felt, been brought comprehensively up to date, having already heard three different accounts of the spectacle by the time Gordon arrived for the early evening barbeque in the Coxes' garden.

'Did you see them?' he shouted as he kicked shut the garden gate.

He was carrying a bowl of his homemade coleslaw covered in silver foil. 'It took the whole morning. What a performance!'

'There are *eight* of them,' said Fiona in a tone of voice that suggested no further commentary was needed. She was walking idly around the lawn, wearing a floral dress and shoes that looked to Max like some kind of cross between sandals and hiking boots.

'It is four bedrooms,' said Douglas, even handedly. He was sitting at the patio table cutting hot-dog buns and half-reading a quartered newspaper, which sat next to the plate, crossword face up. 'Or even five, I suppose, if you make the dining room another one.'

The blue sky was scattered with white clouds. A light breeze shifting the leaves in the trees overhead. Sitting opposite Douglas at the patio table were a couple and another woman to whom Max had just been introduced and whose names he had already forgotten. Bryony was tossing a salad, Jonathan fixing drinks.

'I still don't know how they can afford it,' said Fiona. 'With the best will in the world, none of them exactly look like young professionals.'

'No skateboards?' asked Max.

'They're not going to be paying anything like market rate,' said Gordon, ignoring him. 'The house is in for planning. You can see it all on the council website. And it's not just the usual stuff. Ownership is listed as a limited company. But whoever owns it has got big plans. A big basement dig-out. Huge kitchen extension. An application like that is guaranteed to go back and forth. It'll take months. Could even be a year or two. They'll be rejected first time round. They'll appeal with slightly modified plans. There's a kind of dance you have to do to get a project like that through.'

'And I guess the owner is making some cash in the meantime,' said Douglas, as he dipped a tortilla chip into a bowl of hummus.

The barbeque coals were still burning, sending drifts of thin smoke across the garden. Max sat perched on a low wall, downwind from the fire, wondering if his own family's arrival had caused such a furore.

'I bet you even money the contract has a special break clause in it which means the owner can turf them out as soon as he gets planning,' said Gordon. 'You put a clause like that in the lease and you can't charge anything like market rate. They'll be getting it for a song.'

'Still,' said Fiona. '*Eight* of them.'

'How old are they?' asked Gordon as he levered the cork out of a bottle of wine. 'I just have no idea any more. They could be anything from fourteen to forty as far as I can tell.'

Everyone turned expectantly to Max.

'As I keep saying, I was at work. I haven't laid eyes on a single one of them.'

Bryony bit pensively on the end of a carrot baton.

'I'd say mid-twenties,' she said. 'A fair bit younger than any of our lot.'

'Are they really in their mid-twenties?' said someone. 'I had two children by the time I was in my mid-twenties. Did we look that young when were their age?'

'I was the first person to be young in my family,' said Douglas. 'Me and then my brother. No Macallan had ever done it before. They had been children, of course, but they were never young. They didn't know what to make of us and our jazz records.'

He shut his eyes and seemed to disappear somewhere.

'*A Night in Tunisia*,' he said. 'Art Blakey and the Jazz Messengers. We played it until the grooves were flat.'

The gate creaked open and in walked Tabitha, the corners of her mouth already half turned up in anticipation of mischief and delight.

'Did you see them?' she announced to the garden, all diaphragm and projection. '*What* a palaver.'

'Eight of them,' shouted Fiona from the far side of the lawn. '*Eight of them*.'

And off it went again. The unfathomable number of bikes in the front garden. How they could afford it. And, most pressingly, what *were* they doing with that goddam door.

Once it was over and things had settled again, Max found

himself talking to a couple who lived at number seven, Sandra and Robert, who had him pinned between them on a bench at the patio table, and who took advantage of his captivity by describing to him in astonishing detail the lives of their children. Throughout, Max made noises about refilling his drink or checking on the halloumi skewers, but his murmurings were either misunderstood or ignored, and he found himself trapped for twenty minutes, looking longingly across the lawn at Gordon, who was in a three-way conversation with the Coxes.

Jonathan was talking, the other two listening. Max strained to hear what he was saying, but couldn't. Jonathan always spoke softly, conspiratorially. Max smiled. The linen shirt. The vintage watch. The set of his shoulders. There was an absolute certainty to him, the way he held himself at a half-step remove, compelling you to go to him, occupy space on his terms.

Somebody said something and Bryony laughed, her head back, one hand on her throat. Max found himself desperately wanting to be there, in that huddle, in on the joke, energised by their charisma and the lavishness of their attention. But also, weirdly, quietly glad he wasn't. A ripple of trepidation ran through him at the thought of talking to them when they were together. He had established a kind of intimacy with both of them, but in each case the relationship felt private, still fragile and slightly illicit, and he couldn't imagine maintaining it in the presence of the other.

'And then there's Charlotte, our youngest,' said Sandra. 'She lives in Melbourne, Australia.'

'Well, just outside Melbourne,' said Robert.

'Yes, just outside,' said Sandra. 'She's a speech therapist ...'

After ten minutes more of this, Max finally freed himself and walked over to a trellis table, ordinarily a place to display pots and seedlings, now home to a variety of bottles, including a Chablis in a ceramic chiller. He was topping up his glass when Tabitha appeared by his side and started pouring herself an elderflower cordial.

'How's the speech therapist?' she asked *sotto voce*.

Max turned to look at her; there was a half-smile on her lips.

'You could have come and rescued me,' he whispered incredulously. 'I just did a full half an hour. I didn't even have a drink for most of it.'

'Everyone must do their turn.'

Bryony appeared to his right.

'Is Charlotte still on for that promotion?' she asked innocently.

Max choked on his wine.

'You were in cahoots,' he said. 'This is too much. I am being tormented on all sides.'

'It's OK, they're moving. You'll be spared further torture.'

'Really?'

'They're cashing in. Off to the quiet life in the Peak District.'

'Still,' said Tabitha, 'poor Max.'

'I know,' said Bryony. 'It's been a bad day for him and his beautiful family. They were the bright young things on the street, the talk of the town, and already their thunder has been stolen.'

'Ha,' said Max. 'I think we'll all be perfectly comfortable with the glare of attention being focused elsewhere.'

Bryony placed her hand on his forearm.

'You may no longer be the young pup of the street but you will always be our favourite.'

Max sensed the imprint of her fingers through his shirtsleeve. There was a casualness to the way she touched people, but also a calculation. He noticed her touch linger for a beat longer than necessary and felt a complicated slew of emotions – but most of all a sense of arrival.

Bryony caught his eye, held his gaze, smiled.

'Let's get something to eat,' she said.

He followed Bryony and Tabitha over to the table. The food was arranged on large Mediterranean platters. A pile of squeaky sausages, stripily charred on the grill. A stack of burgers oozing fat. Chicken legs marinaded in honey and mustard. A plate of sliced tomatoes. Pickles in a jar.

To one side of the table, looking a little estranged from

everything else, there was a small bowl containing three slightly sad-looking pieces of blackened halloumi.

Max was about to fork one of them onto his plate when Gordon appeared by his side.

'Oh god, you're not a vegetarian, are you?'

Max turned slowly to look at him.

'I am.'

'Bloody hell. What a pain in the arse.'

'Funny that, because it really is just to annoy you.'

'I ate halloumi in a pub once. Like eating a salty wet pillow.'

Max smiled.

'It has suffered at the hands of more than one pub chef,' he said. 'But it's pretty good if it's done right.'

Gordon picked up a Lincolnshire sausage and bit off the end of it with a great big grin on his face. Max looked at him unmoved. Gordon took another bite, moaned appreciatively.

Max, who had planned to keep his counsel, decided he wouldn't actually after all.

'You know, in the future they will look back on all this with the same kind of disbelief as we do at slavery,' he said. 'The wantonness of it. The egregious cruelty. People of the future will see it as a moral failure at a societal level.'

Gordon wiped his mouth with the back of his hand.

'Don't be ridiculous. Humans have always eaten meat. It's the most natural thing in the world.'

'It'll be a generational stain,' said Max lightly as he used some tongs to pick up a couple of tomato slices. 'In the future we will barely be able to see beyond it. It'll be a prism through which everything is judged.'

'I have never heard such nonsense,' said Tabitha from the other side of the table.

'If it's going to be a generational stain,' said Fiona, 'it'll be a stain on every generation back to Genesis.'

Max did his respectfully disagree shoulders, which was a kind of slow-motion shrug.

'I'm not talking about hunting with spears,' he said, as he spread some Dijon mustard on to the base of his brioche bun. 'I'm talking about the industrial phase. The last fifty years. We all know the reality of it. We turn away from it and choose not to think about the horror, but that doesn't mean it's not there.'

'There is plenty of good free-range meat,' said Bryony. 'If you shop at your local butcher.'

'Pastureland can be a very effective carbon sink,' said Douglas, as he ducked in and out to grab himself a couple of gherkins.

Max looked at the small table at the side of the grill. Alongside the dish that had held Bryony's own home-marinaded chicken thighs, were the empty packets of contributions brought by the guests. Supermarket burgers. Sausages from a high-street brand.

'People retain a fantasy of what farming is like from reading picture books as children,' he said as he placed two lettuce leaves and a pickle in his bun. 'And it's a total delusion. The reality is five thousand pigs in sheds with no windows and you know it and I know it.'

On the grill there were eight drumsticks, their skins charring, fat dripping from them and flaring with a sizzle as it hit the hot coals.

'A billion chickens a year,' said Max, delivering it all with his usual jollity. 'Just in the UK. A *billion* a year. And it's happened over your lifetime. The metastasizing of it.'

Gordon went to say something but then didn't. Max caught his eye and held it. He experienced a delicious lightness, a feeling of wholeness and rightness.

'*A billion chickens*,' he said. 'Think about the fossil record. People will look back on it in total bewilderment. At the egregiousness of it. They'll think of it as a kind of Caligulan excess.'

Finally, he picked up the blackened halloumi pieces and placed them in his bun.

'Anyway,' he said, 'hope you enjoy your food.'

Later, when the guests had all gone and the condiments had been returned to the fridge and the serving dishes washed up and Bryony had gone up to bed, Max hung the tea towel he'd been using on the oven handle and then paused, just for a second, creating a window for Jonathan to invite him to stay for a Scotch.

Once they both had an inch of whisky in their glasses, they thought briefly about playing chess, but decided, in the end, to listen to music in Jonathan's ground-floor home office with its two Barcelona chairs and walnut-trim record player.

While Jonathan pulled a John Coltrane record from its sleeve, Max stood in front of the shelves of LPs, hundreds of them, packed in tight, many of the spines faded or cracked so that the collection took on a kind of massed papery indistinguishability.

As the first notes of Coltrane's saxophone sounded through the room, *The White Album* caught his eye, its spine that bit thicker than those around it, though it was no longer really white. Instinctively, he reached out to touch it and as his eyes adjusted to the low light he noticed that it was surrounded by many of the band's other records. *Let it Be. Abbey Road. Revolver.* He pulled *Sgt. Pepper's* from the shelf with what he hoped was due reverence and it came out with the back of the record facing up; a great expanse of red with all the lyrics printed on the back.

'I was seventeen when that came out.'

Jonathan was sitting on his chair, his glass in his hand. He shook his head, almost imperceptibly, as if his sense of wonderment remained undimmed.

'I can't tell you what it was like to hear those songs for the first time. It was like a coded message had been sent out to an underground army. The old order had ended. They didn't know it yet, but we did.'

Max turned over the record. The Peter Blake cover had faded a little but they still popped, the four of them in their dayglo satin marching suits, a burst of colour against the black-and-white cut-outs behind them.

'I don't know if I would have gone to art school without *Sgt. Pepper's.*'

Max scanned the faces in the crowd. A few were familiar. The obvious ones. Marx. Marilyn. Elvis. Marlene Dietrich. But most of them weren't. Suddenly, and with a sharp sense of sadness, he saw that it wasn't his, this. And of all the things that were, nothing was as good.

'You went to art school?' he said as he put the record back on the shelf.

'Hornsey in '68. Right into the thick of the action.'

Max sat down next to him, a confused look on his face.

'In Hornsey?'

'We occupied the art school for six weeks in 1968.'

'Oh really?' said Max, perking up. 'Like an *under the pavement the beach* kind of thing?'

'It didn't start like that. It was unexciting stuff to begin with. The accommodation wasn't good enough. We needed a proper common room. There was something to do with the funding of the student union that seemed incredibly important at the time, but I now can't remember a thing about. But we were in there for weeks. Eating there. Sleeping there. And we talked and talked and talked and slowly it became something else. It wasn't about the common room any more, it was about how to live . . . how to organise society. Buckminster Fuller came and talked to us. So did Joan Littlewood. R. D. Laing. It was an amazing time.'

Opposite them was a rosewood mid-century desk with an Anglepoise lamp and a desktop computer. Bookshelves. A wall of framed posters. Some films. Some gallery group shows. The room smelled of whisky and old books. There was jazz playing on the stereo. Max felt momentarily overawed at how deeply earned it all seemed.

'I learned more in those six weeks than in the rest of my time there, which I mostly spent being told I had no talent as an artist. Couldn't paint. Couldn't draw. Barely could have got by as a bricklayer, let alone a sculptor.'

Jonathan laughed at himself.

'Not that any of it was anything I needed to be told. I knew it myself. But I knew it didn't really matter because I had a nose. And they all knew it. None of the posh kids had a nose like me.'

He nodded up at one of the posters on the wall. An old and faded thing, dated 1972.

'The show that started it all. Three months after graduation. I put it on with a guy called Sebastian Scott. Two grammar school boys on the make. We had forms of knowledge that most people in the art world didn't have at the time.'

The door to Jonathan's office was closed to stop the music from disturbing Bryony and it gave the room a cloistered feel, turning it, at least in Max's mind, into a sort of secret space where you could plot and plan, and truths could be spoken freely.

'Some corners might have been cut,' said Jonathan, smiling. 'A few figures were possibly inflated. But we pulled it off, the two of us. Made ourselves a bit of cash. Twenty-two years old. Funny, being twenty-two didn't feel that young then.'

Jonathan ran his finger pensively round the top of his glass.

'I suppose my dad had fought his way from Normandy to Paris by the time he was twenty-two, so putting on an art show was really neither here nor there ... Certainly wasn't going to impress him. Not that anything ever did.'

This line was delivered in a tone of voice that was more dismissive than it was melancholy, which meant that Max felt able to ask:

'Did he land on D-Day?'

'No. He landed a couple of weeks later, once the bodies had all been cleared up. He was a "D-Day dodger" as they used to call them. Dogged him for the rest of his life. I've often thought he would have rather died on the beach if it meant he could have been there on day one.'

'Did he talk about it much?'

'Not really. They just didn't, his generation. He had this look, though. You stepped out of line and you saw it. It was like he had opened this door, behind which there was a deep well of darkness. That look was him opening it a crack with the promise that he could open it further.'

Jonathan splashed another inch of Scotch into his glass.

'It kept us in line, that look.'

Max sat back in his chair.

'My granddad was in the 35th Light Artillery Regiment,' he said. 'He fought on Java until he was captured. Then did four years in a Japanese prisoner of war camp.'

'*Four years*,' said Jonathan. 'Jesus.'

'I'm pretty sure he spent his twenty-second birthday doing a twelve-hour shift in a Japanese quarry.' He screwed up an eye, smiled a little sadly. 'I spent mine dressed as Brian May at a Queen-themed karaoke bar in Tooting.'

Jonathan laughed.

'I wasn't even Freddie.'

Jonathan laughed again. 'Do ever you think about it? How you would have fared?'

'In Queen?'

Jonathan looked at him sideways.

'On that battlefield,' he said dryly and deliberately.

Max held his glass in his hand, felt the weight of it. How would he have fared? Disastrously, obviously.

'To be honest with you, I've never really thought about it that much,' he said. 'Modern warfare looks so systematised and technical. To operate any of those weapons you need years of training and all the jobs look so . . .'

'I don't mean being in a professional army,' said Jonathan. 'That's different. I'm talking about mass mobilisation. A conscription war. Poets and plumbers fighting next to each other on the front line. The romance of it. It was all we thought about as boys.'

He looked up at the ceiling, seemed to go somewhere else.

'It was the worst thing that ever happened to my dad, but it was the best thing as well. He spent the rest of his life in England as far as I can remember. I think he might have been to Spain once on holiday. Other than that I don't think he ever left the country. Worked as a sheet-metal worker. Lived half his life in a dreary little prefab on the outskirts of Portsmouth. But he'd liberated Paris. And he always had that in his back pocket. That trump card.'

Coltrane's sax was solemn, the piano keys insistent. Max could picture that prefab on the outskirts of town, its low roof, the rough concrete of its walls. It sounded like the start of a story.

'You're from Portsmouth?'

Jonathan smiled.

'For my sins,' he said.

For half an hour, they listened to records and talked Portsmouth and its public library and the eleven plus and the look on his dad's face when he told him he was going to art school. After they had refreshed their glasses, the conversation turned to the London gallery scene in the seventies and buying trips to Paris and partying with Baldessari.

'So you ran art galleries and then moved into film?' asked Max eventually, trying to sound as nonchalant as he could.

'It wasn't as neat as that. They were all mixed together for years. I helped put together a fashion brand for a bit. The film financing waxed and waned.'

'And now?' said Max with an involuntary simper.

Jonathan smiled gnomically.

'I put large amounts of other people's money into things that I think are going to do something.'

'Interesting,' said Max, for want of anything better to say.

'Yes,' said Jonathan. 'Yes, it is.'

Wednesday 27 June

The tyre was flat. Of that there was no doubt. The rubber at the bottom was creased and jowly, the rim of the wheel sitting worryingly close to the ground.

The woman trying to pump it up was one of the recent arrivals on the street. 'The millennials', as they had come to be known, even though no one had taken the trouble to establish whether or not they actually were millennials. It had been a week or so since they had moved in and Max had passed plenty of them on the street and smiles had been exchanged, but he was yet to actually introduce himself to any of them.

She was crouched down on her haunches and looked up as he approached.

'I feel that I have failed the sisterhood here,' she said, 'but I just cannot do this.'

The pump in her hand was the modern kind with two fittings, one for each kind of valve.

'It's not my bike. I borrowed it from my friend. And there are two holes on the thing and if I put that one on it feels far too loose but if I put that one on I feel like I'm going to break it. I tried putting it on the other tyre to see if I could make it work on that one but when I did finally get it on, all the air came out when I wanted it to go in.'

She looked up at him and crossed her eyes goofily.

'I can have a look if you'd like?' said Max.

She stood up. She was wearing a sleeveless denim all-in-one and glasses with a see-through frame. Her arms were dotted with tattoos that seemed to be positioned randomly – one here, one there – with scant consideration as to the overall composition. They were all line drawings in blue ink: a sticking plaster, the Nirvana smiley face, four dots in a diamond formation, Charlie Brown looking glum.

'That would be kind of you,' she said. 'I am already massively late.'

Max put his bag on the pavement and crouched down.

'This modern system is not at all intuitive. You have to screw this gold thing down on the valve before you put the pump on it, and this thing,' he said, pointing to the clip on the pump, 'needs to start down and then go up once it's on, which has always felt the wrong way round to me.'

Max clipped the pump into place and started pumping. In seconds, the tyre was fully inflated.

The woman yelped happily and stretched out her hand to shake his.

'I'm Zoe,' she said.

'Max.'

'Well, Max, if this was a nineteenth-century novel, we'd be half way to being married, wouldn't we? What with you gallantly re-shoeing my horse and everything.'

This, obviously, was not intended seriously, but it was delivered in a serious tone of voice and with full-beam eye contact, a combination which blindsided Max and made laughing feel weirdly inappropriate.

'Hmmm...' he said eventually, once he had composed himself. 'Only issues with that are me being already married. And the re-shoeing being a bit of a let-down.'

He pointed down to the tyre, which had already started to deflate.

'I don't think you're going to be riding off into the sunset anytime soon. Sorry.'

'Oh.'

'Do you have a puncture repair kit?'

She looked at him askance.

'Silly question,' said Max, smiling. 'I have one but I think it might be in Berlin.'

She pounced on this like a cat.

'Because who doesn't keep their practical bits and bobs in Berlin?'

Max smiled. 'I lived there until recently.'

'Of course you did.'

It was delivered, this line, with a smile, which made it hard to know exactly how to respond to it, which was confusing for Max because he was normally the one doing this sort of thing to other people.

'Sorry,' she said in response to his hesitation. 'Berlin sounds like a terribly exciting place to have lived.'

She was standing neatly, one hand in the other, head leaning slightly to one side. Max could feel himself being bested.

'I don't know,' he said. 'I moved from Hackney to the east end of a European capital city where the locals hated us for driving up the rent.' He shrugged. 'It was basically just Dalston with compound nouns.'

She smiled politely, as you might in the presence of an unmarried uncle.

'You've used that line before.'

Max laughed. There was a directness to her that was bracing.

'By the time you get to my age,' he said, 'everyone is just rehashing their back catalogue.'

She smiled again, this time more authentically.

'So,' she said, 'if you're just back from Berlin I'm guessing you haven't lived on Pemberton Place for long?'

'Not really. A few months. We're renting. My wife got a new job. She had been working for an NGO. And then they moved us here. And they pay our rent. Our ridiculous rent.'

Zoe cocked her head, bemused.

'An NGO pays the rent on *that* house?'

'Ah,' he said. 'No. She worked at an NGO for, I don't know, nearly twenty years. She's working for an American bank now.'

'Oh,' said Zoe.

'She's not a banker.'

'No.'

'Her work is sustainability stuff. She knows a lot about wetlands conservation. Mangrove preservation. That kind of thing. She puts together the financing of it.'

'For an American bank?'

'It's . . .' Max could see from the look on her face that nothing he said was going to make any difference. 'Yes,' he said.

Zoe didn't say or do anything but still, somehow, she radiated a quality of amused contempt. Like she had met him, or at least men like him, a thousand times before and never once had he, nor any of the others like him, said or done anything unexpected or interesting.

Max looked back again at the bike, eager to change the subject.

'I could probably get the tyre off with a spoon but I don't think you should do the inner tube with anything other than a proper patch,' he said.

'I have Sellotape.'

'I don't think Sellotape is going to do the job, I'm afraid.'

'Have I had the misfortune of being rescued by a bike maintenance purist?'

Max put up his hands, guilty as charged.

'There's an aesthetic satisfaction to it. Submerging the tube in water. Watching for the bubbles to find the hole. The way the tyre comes off.'

Max found himself wanting to impress her more than he should.

'It has a kind of wholeness to it. Something like Yeats's click of the well-made box.'

Zoe paused, looked at him sideways.

'*Yeats's click of the well-made box*,' she said. 'A gentleman *and* a scholar.'

Her hair, which looked like it had been recently cut, should, he felt, have been left an inch longer or cut an inch shorter. Nonetheless, she had a quality.

'What is it that you do?' she asked.

'I do film stuff.'

'Oh, really? *Film stuff.* That's enlightening...' Zoe stopped as a thought occurred to her. 'Wait a sec, you don't know anything about editing, do you?'

'I know my way round an edit suite.'

'Can you do it on a laptop?'

'Yeah, I can edit on a laptop.'

'Oh really? Could you, I mean, would you... *Might* you be able to help me with something?'

Max hesitated. There were all kinds of reasons to deflect. Not least the good favour of Karolina, whom he could imagine taking issue with the overall tenor of the conversation as it had gone so far. In her shoes, he would have done too.

'I just need a few pointers,' said Zoe.

Max clenched his fist, breathed out steadily through his nose. The sensible thing, obviously, would be to say no, but an attractive young woman was asking him, like directly actually *asking* him, to talk lengthily on something about which he knew a lot.

'Sure,' he said. 'I could give you a few pointers.

'Oh, you're such a lifesaver. That's so great. What's your Insta?'

Max took a deep breath.

'@maximum_overdrive76,' he said.

Zoe cocked her head, made an alarmed-looking kind of face.

'It's a Stephen King film from the eighties. Machines turn against their makers.'

'And you're called Max.'

'And I'm called Max.'

'Hence maximum_overdrive76.'

Max nodded. He was looking at her and she was looking at him with a kind of unsettling directness. It wasn't flirting, the thing that was going on, he didn't think, but it was adjacent to it.

'What does the Morse code say?' he asked, pointing at her right hand where a series of dots and dashes formed a kind of tattoo bracelet around her wrist.

'*Carpe diem.*'

'That's something I can get on board with.'

Zoe slung her tote bag over her shoulder.

'My flatmates talk about you,' she said as she prepared to go. 'The only not-old man on the street.'

'Do they?' said Max, feeling momentarily flattered and then horribly anxious.

'They call you *Cishet*,' she said.

'Cishet,' he said, complicatedly relieved. 'Makes me sound like a Sumerian king, doesn't it? *O glory to Cishet. King and conqueror. Knower of mysteries. Lord of his people.*'

He smiled.

'That's not what your flatmates mean though, is it?'

'No,' she said.

She readied her bike.

'But you could maybe be their heteronormative king?'

'Why not,' he said with a chuckle. 'I mean, if the position's vacant. Does the role come with ceremonial robes?'

Zoe smiled.

'Yeah, it does,' she said as she started to wheel the bike down the road. 'A navy blue overshirt.'

Max laughed.

'How convenient,' he called to her departing back. 'Cos, I've already got plenty of those, haven't I?'

'Yes,' she said, without turning back, 'you do.'

Saturday 30 June

'I've done a playlist for tonight and I have to warn you it has a lot of My Bloody Valentine on it.'

Max was in the kitchen at number fifteen, making a white sauce. Karolina was next to him, chopping a carrot into toddler-sized batons.

'Oh god, can't you just play Miles Davis like everyone else.'

'I've been messaging Dom about it. Even he thinks I've gone overboard on the Dinosaur Jr. Don't worry, though, he tells me that Maude will hate it just as much as you will.'

Karolina put down her knife so she could stir the macaroni boiling away in a large stainless-steel pan.

'They're called Maude and Dom?'

'Yeah, Maude is his wife. I'd forgotten her name until he messaged me this afternoon.'

Karolina held her wooden spoon in the air like an auctioneer with a paddle. 'Please don't say we're having Dom Carrington and Maude Stockwell round for dinner and you didn't tell me.'

Max's attention had drifted. The kids were in the living room watching the one TV show of theirs that he found quite charming – about a mouse who quietly dreamed of one day being a squirrel – and he could hear it through the double doors.

'I don't know,' he said, absent-mindedly. 'We might be. I don't know their surnames.'

Karolina pulled out her phone and typed quickly, before turning the screen to Max. The image she had conjured was a photo of Dom with a Leica hung around his neck.

'Yeah, that's him,' he said.

'Oh, *Max!*'

'Well, I didn't know, did I? Who is he?'

'Maude Stockwell and Dom Carrington. They're Kiln.'

'What's that?'

'They do interiors. And, I don't know, kind of everything. She does *Three Good Things*, which is massive on Instagram. He is the most amazing photographer.'

'Oh, OK. I didn't know that,' said Max, as he drained the pasta. 'But it doesn't matter, does it?'

'I can't believe they're coming here. The house is so *rental*.'

'I don't think they are planning on taking any pictures.'

'Oh Christ, Max. How long have I got?'

Max looked up the clock.

'They're going to be here in two hours.'

Karolina stood in the middle of the kitchen, desperately casting around for things she could improve.

'Can you hang the Jasper Johns?'

Max screwed shut an eye. The framed poster was six by four and had sat leaning up against the wall reprimandingly for the whole three months they had lived there.

'I think it needs special fixings,' he said, as he poured the white sauce over the pasta. 'I mean, have you ever tried to pick it up? It weighs a ton.'

Karolina groaned despairingly.

'What are you going to cook?'

'I was just going to do another round of this,' said Max, gesturing to the tray of milky white macaroni, onto which he was grating some mild cheddar cheese.

Karolina made a wretched noise and hit him with a towel.

'I'm doing the roast pumpkin,' he said, yelping. 'You know, with the salsa verde.'

'The one in the big tray that looks pretty?'

'I've bought all the ingredients.'

'Did you get cheese?'

'From the cheese shop. And crackers. Before you ask, yes, they're hexagonal.'

Half an hour later, the macaroni cheese was done. While it had been in the oven, Karolina had tidied the house with the manic energy of someone gathering their treasured belongings as the floodwaters rise outside the door. Max had made the salsa verde and oven-dried twenty-four baby plum tomatoes. And after one last episode and then another last episode, the mouse had finally been turned off, his dream deferred as always.

The four Andersons sat around the table, Max feeding Kim, Karolina feeding Vlad.

'So I finally met one of our newest neighbours yesterday,' said Max, as he blew gently on a forkful of macaroni.

'Oh yeah. Which one?'

'The brown-haired one. Lots of little tats on her arms.'

'Oh yeah. I've seen her.'

'She's quite a character.'

Karolina was holding a carrot stick, ready to pounce.

'What are they all about?' she said, darting the carrot into Alma's momentarily open mouth with lizard reflexes.

'Everyone thinks they've got a deal. Won't be there long. I guess they're students. Like postgraduates or something.'

'Oh cool.'

'Anyway, they need some help editing some film. I said I would show them the ropes. One of those offers that you make blithely and then find yourself beholden to.'

He reached his fingers into Arthur's mouth and pulled out the stringy remnants of a much-masticated green bean.

'I'm going to go round on Thursday after I've got the kids to bed.'

'Yeah, cool. Whatever. Just have your phone on.'

At 8.15 p.m. they arrived, Dom and Maude, bearing gifts. Raw chocolate. *Pétillant* wine. A small ceramic dish for Karolina.

'I've told the babysitter we're turning our phones off,' said Maude, as Max closed the door behind them.

She was tall and angular, just the right side of ungainly. Her dress was oversized and voluminous, the material so thick that it was almost quilted, like an over-blanket on a bed. On most women it would have looked ridiculous, Max felt, but on her it was strangely thrilling.

'We've given her a flare,' said Dom. 'And we told her that if she genuinely thinks someone's life is in danger she can send it up and we'll come, otherwise she just has to tough it out.'

'Our eldest was like, "Mum, do you have to go out?" And I was like, "They live round here and they are our age and they don't work in private finance. We are going whatever you say or do."'

Max laughed as he led them down the hall.

'Anyway,' said Maude with a sigh, 'all three of them are still awake so we'd better keep an eye out for the flare.'

She was striking, but carried herself with a slight crouch, as if to open herself up and stand tall would be too declarative, too aggrandising.

'In that case,' said Max, 'we should probably go fast out of the blocks. How about a negroni?'

'Amen to that.'

Max pushed open the door to the kitchen and ushered them in. The lights were low, the table set for four. Karolina had run a piece of fabric down the middle of it, arranged flowers from the garden in vases, decanted red wine into a jug. She had the oven door open and was checking on the clafoutis.

'Oh my god,' she said, looking up and clocking Maude for the first time. 'What a dress!'

'Be quiet,' said Maude. 'Look at yours!'

While they all properly introduced themselves to one another, Max pulled a bottle of Campari from the cupboard, watching Maude as she unwound her long scarf and tossed it over the back of a chair. Earlier that evening, while he was sitting in the dark, as was often necessary, at the end of Alma's bed, making occasionally reassuring noises as she fell asleep, he had googled Dom and

Maude. Their studio was multidisciplinary: a mix of photography, interiors and product design. All of this ran alongside Maude's parallel project *Three Good Things*, which had a website of its own and a huge following on social media.

The concept was simple. Every few days, she put together three complimentary objects and took a nice picture of them. Or someone did, probably Dom, as she was often in the photos, most of which were shot around their house with its abundant white spaces and singular pieces of furniture. Sometimes, the three good things were objects for the home, other times they were ingredients. Occasionally, they were the constituent parts of an outfit: a scarf, a jacket, a pair of earrings. Everything was tactile and textured, shot in reverent low light. There was a heavy emphasis on handcraft and material use. It seemed to aspire to a William Morris-y take on the world, craft as a kind of democratised version of high art. Although its version of democracy was one with a radically foreshortened suffrage, given the ferocious expense of everything featured. Max couldn't bring himself to describe it as a philosophy but he could imagine it being encapsulated by some abstract noun that was particular to the Japanese.

As he had scrolled through the images, humming every now and then as Alma stirred, Max had felt the pull of the life they presented. Patinaed copper pots and unglazed earthenware. Leatherbound books and layered fabrics. They weren't things that could save you, he knew that. But, he found himself wondering as he paused on an image of an Eames chair, were they solid enough to at least offer some ballast?

Once he had mixed the drinks, the four of them moved to the living room where they sat on sofas, Karolina and Maude on one, Dom and Max on the other.

Karolina and Maude just about endured the first three songs of the playlist but were in open revolt by the second verse of Pavement's 'Stereo'. In response, and despite their vocal protestations, Max insisted on playing a compilation of breathy jazz covers of the sort that you ordinarily only ever hear in Greek island tavernas.

For half an hour, they talked about where they would move, if they moved, which everyone they knew was always on the verge of doing. Somerset was lengthily discussed. House prices in Edinburgh. Berlin walk-ups. The kind of Lisbon loft apartments they could have got for a song if only they had moved ten years earlier.

Max recognised the restlessness. He felt it, too. He knew it would be forever out of reach, that mythical place that was both urban and spacious, edgily creative and blessed with good schools. A place of beautiful sunsets and people just like them. But to stop searching would be to give up, accept defeat.

'I mean, Frome is full of wonderful humans,' said Maude, as she picked the last olive from the bowl. 'Christ, I can think of two dozen off the top of my head. But the direct train only goes once a day and if you miss it, you're fucking stuck there.'

Max nodded his assent. No one present needed to be told the destination of this direct train. They all understood the push and pull of the capital. It had been the same in Berlin. The big cities were like open prisons: to live in one was to be always dreaming of escape, but years of habituation meant you were, for the most part, ignorant of and terrified by the world outside.

He cleared the empty glasses, listening to the other three discussing the merits of the Suffolk coastline. Had his parents ever had a conversation like this, even once? He couldn't imagine it. They had been born in Hertfordshire and had lived in Hertfordshire and would surely die in Hertfordshire, the mere thought of which sent a shudder through him. And yet, it had an enviable clarity, that kind of life. And it freed you from the tyranny of Rightmove.

He was in the kitchen, opening a bottle of white wine, when Karolina came in, looking for more crisps.

'When you say someone is a wonderful person,' he said quietly, kind of to her, kind of to himself, 'you're praising their personal qualities: their wit, their charm, their kindness, or whatever. When you say someone is a wonderful *human*, it sounds like you're praising their distinctly *human* qualities. Such great opposable thumbs. So upright and bipedal ...'

'You've got to stop staring at her forehead.'
'I'm not.'
'Yes, you are.'
Max frowned.
'I can't help it. Everything from her eyebrows down is normal, but her forehead is so ... *stretched*. It looks like a balloon that's been filled with clay, hard but also like it would be a little clammy to touch.'
'Don't ruin this for me. I like her.'
'I like her too. I like them both.'
'We need friends. *I* need friends.'

This was true. Karolina needed friends. Or at least London friends. She had dozens of them in Berlin. And Max liked them all individually. Collectively, though, he had started to find the thought of them oppressive. The sense he had that they were a kind of informal oversight committee, constantly monitoring him for transgressions and inadequacies.

'And *you* need friends.'

Max considered this as he pulled four wine glasses from the cupboard. He had friends. In Berlin, for sure. And in London. Although, when he actually thought about it, it was more accurate to say that he had friends who had once lived in London, but had now gone somewhere else. To Cornwall. Yorkshire. The Kent coast and Oxford. He was in touch with them all still, or at least most of them, even if he didn't see them that often. If contributing occasional jokes to the same WhatsApp groups counted as being in touch.

'I'll be good,' he said.

'You don't need to be *good*, whatever that means. Just stop staring at her forehead.'

They drank the bottle of white in the living room, laughing at the jazz covers each time a new one came on. For the most part, they talked work. Karolina told them about her job and how it had brought them to London.

'I'm not going to pretend that the hours don't sound awful,' said Maude, once she was done, 'but my god I wish I had a job. I can't tell you how much I miss the glorious sight of a monthly pay cheque.'

'*Really?* I'd love to have your freedom.'

'Is it freedom?' said Maude. 'I guess it's a kind of freedom. But honestly it's also just a relentless fucking hustle. We are just selling ourselves every day. I feel like I am constantly battling the algorithm. Trying to keep out there, being noticed, hoping that a job will come in.'

'You always seem so busy,' said Karolina.

'That's just us scrambling about to stay afloat.'

'I spent yesterday shooting the interior of the Singapore Airways lounge at Heathrow,' said Dom. 'My first decent money job in ages.' He ran his hand down the stubble on his throat.

'All the other stuff . . .' he said. 'The shoots for the niche travel magazines. The coffee-table modernism . . . I barely break even on most of those jobs.'

A smooth jazz version of 'Sweet Child O' Mine' came on the stereo.

'It was competitive back when I started,' said Dom, laughing at the terribleness of the song. 'But it's ridiculous now. Everyone's a bloody photographer these days.'

'Not like you, though,' said Karolina. 'Your pictures are beautiful.'

Dom smiled in appreciation at this, but in a way that also communicated an essential sadness.

'It was totally different when I started out assisting,' he said. 'The photographers I worked for were mostly monsters, but the care that got put into everything . . . there was a kind of sacredness to it. The images were obsessed over. Only the really great ones went out into the world. They were like the top eighth of this whole iceberg of work.'

He drank from his glass.

'Now there is just this endless churn of images. And still there are too many photographers.'

Max murmured his assent to this. There were too many everythings. Far too many. They had come of age in a time of complacency and entitlement. Everyone wanted it all and there was nothing like enough to go around.

'You start off with this long list of things you'll never do,' said Dom. 'Cars. Airlines. Fast food restaurants. Anything for the Saudis. And then you have a lean couple of months and you do something for someone. And you promise it will be just once. But once you've done it once it's suddenly normal and you find that you might as well carry on doing it.'

An air of sadness had settled over the room. A bossa nova cover of 'Boys Don't Cry' started and no one even managed a smile.

'Give it a few years and I'll be the in-house photographer at Lockheed Martin,' he said. 'Assuming AI hasn't already made me completely redundant.'

'Oh Christ,' said Maude, looking over at him. 'I didn't even know that was a possibility. Is that really a possibility?'

She smiled wryly, looked back at Karolina.

'Hopefully we'll get a few years of the Lockheed money before the machines take over.'

The white wine was finished. Together, they stood up. No one was unsteady on their feet, but they had drunk too much on empty stomachs and seemed to realise collectively that they needed a change of scene.

'Let's eat,' said Karolina.

They sat at the table, the couples opposite one another. Max put on some proper music and served the food. The pumpkin was charred at the edges, scattered with seeds. Bright green broad beans were topped with pink peppercorns. A plate of herby oven-roasted tomatoes sat on a bed of yoghurt.

'I just think your house looks amazing,' said Karolina, as she heaped some tomatoes onto Maude's plate, 'I mean, just from Instagram. You have such an eye. You've made it so beautiful.'

'It doesn't really look like that. I mean, apart from in the photos. Otherwise, it never looks like that.'

She reached for the wine and topped up her glass.

'I live with three actual children and one man-child,' she said. The delivery was both light-hearted and affectionate, and also, at the same time, neither. It was a line, Max sensed, that Dom had heard before. He didn't protest it, but he didn't smile either.

'Behind the camera there is always a slagheap of Lego bricks and L.O.L. dolls and bike parts that I have just piled up out of shot, which will be all over the floor again ten minutes later.'

Karolina laughed.

'I don't know how you manage with three. We're completely overwhelmed with two.'

'We had to have three to stay on brand,' said Dom, dryly.

Maude looked at Karolina.

'He's joking,' she said. 'They were all accidents.'

Maude held her pose at the end of this line. Max wasn't quite sure to what extent it was a performance, all of this. He clocked the hard glaze to her. However it was meant, she, surely, was her own intended audience. The one person whom she could guarantee would bear witness to her disappointment.

'When they said we could have it all, I hadn't realised that they meant *all* the stress of work and *all* the stress of motherhood.' She looked at Karolina.

'The fucking WhatsApps. It's practically a job in itself. Wading through the damn things while the men fuck off cycling in Dorset or to the Arsenal or wakeboarding or whatever.'

Maude spooned some salsa verde onto her pumpkin, communicating her disdain with a shake of the head. 'I don't even know what wakeboarding is.'

Max poured the wine, not daring to look at Dom. He understood his own culpability. They had promised much, men like them, but they had not delivered. They had had a chance to remake the world, achieve absolution for their sex, but it hadn't happened, not on their watch anyway.

Every time Karolina returned from a dinner with a friend, she would get into bed next to him and merrily precis the latest character assassination. This husband's absence. That one's retreat into himself. The emotional deafness. The selfishness. The two-day raves. The vinyl collections. The endless fucking cycling.

'The great thing about being a working mother,' continued Maude, 'is that it gives you the opportunity to fail at two things at once.'

She spiked a piece of pumpkin with her fork.

'This, by the way, is delicious,' she said, forcing a smile.

For twenty minutes or so, they ate and talked. Restaurants. Television. Films they were meaning to watch, books they were meaning to read.

Eventually, Max got up to refill the water jug. Only when he started running the tap did he realise that Dom had followed him into the kitchen.

'I don't know if you do, but I've brought some.'

For a second or two, Max stood helplessly in the middle of the room, trying to fathom what Dom might be talking about. And then he realised.

'Oh,' he said, wide-eyed. '*Right*.'

'I know we haven't finished all the food, but we started eating quite late and the babysitter is on the clock.'

'Right,' said Max again.

'I could go to the bathroom and line up a couple, leave one for you. Seems a bit unnecessary to go in together. It being your house and everything. And I do actually need a piss.'

Max blinked. Did he take drugs? He hadn't stopped, like you stopped smoking. He just hadn't for ages. Years. Hadn't even thought about it.

'I'm fine,' he said. 'Thanks.'

Dom disappeared upstairs and Max returned to the table with the full water jug. Maude had half-finished her plate, pushed it away.

'Karolina tells me you're a director. That sounds fun.'

'It is,' he said, as he sat down. 'On the rare occasions that I ever actually do it.'

'He's working on a script,' said Karolina.

Max swallowed. It was one thing talking about all this with Bryony and Tabitha. Quite another with people to whom he didn't seem young, still full of potential. He went to elaborate but instead found his thoughts drifting to *Match of the Day* and how poignant he had started to find it. Not because of anything that happened on the pitch, more the moments when the camera panned to the bench, and he saw the squad players sitting there, waiting for their turn, the hope and expectation on their faces.

For years, he hadn't been too troubled by the long periods of waiting that had characterised so much of his working life. He had always assumed, like the reserves on the bench, that things would play out as they were surely ordained to do, and, when the time was right, he would graduate to the starting eleven. Lately, though, he had come to realise that there are few things more ridiculous than still thinking of yourself as a promising tyro on the cusp of the first team, when it is obvious to everyone that you were in danger of being passed over completely, having never really got on the pitch.

The tealights on the table flickered. Max was aware that Maude and Karolina were sitting there, looking at him expectantly. He felt the grip of the alcohol, the way it took you and held you and stopped you from speaking. He went to talk but couldn't. And what, anyway, did he have to say other than that he felt, increasingly, like an unused substitute in his own life?

'It's a whodunnin,' said Karolina indifferently.

'Oh,' said Maude. 'That sounds interesting.'

'It's not a whodunnit, because you know who did the murder, just not who they killed . . .'

While she talked, Max cleared the plates. He was at the kitchen bin, scraping some food into it, when Karolina walked in, a serving bowl in either hand.

'I think they're taking cocaine,' she whispered violently.

'I know they are. He offered me some.'

'*What?* Why didn't you tell me?'

'Did you want some?'

'Of course not. The kids are upstairs.'

'I don't think he was planning on offering them any.'

'Jesus Christ, Max.'

He looked forlornly at the dessert.

'I don't think there is going to be much appetite for your clafoutis.'

Back at the table, Dom was opening a fourth bottle of wine. Maude had been upstairs and was now back down. The mood was hyperactive maudlin.

'I think about everything I have said and everything I have done and I am just constantly terrified of getting it wrong. Publicly. Two hundred and thirty-one thousand people. And I just need to offend one of them.'

Everyone was drunk now and the evening was starting to fray. Karolina was yawning, and kept looking exaggeratedly up at the clock.

'I just know that they are waiting for me to get it wrong, waiting to pounce. Imagine getting it wrong in front of all of them.'

Dom was up on his feet, reading the spines of the books on the shelves. He was moving along with the music, tapping out the bassline with his thumb. Max got the distinct impression he had heard this all before.

'What am I doing?' said Maude, gesticulating exaggeratedly. 'Posting all these fucking photos of the inside of my house? Sometimes, I lie there at night, thinking they're all looking at photos of this room, right now. Right now, they're all out there, looking at photos of my bed, this bed.'

She reached for the bottle and topped up her glass.

'I did a two-week experiment where I stopped using photos of me and just posted images of the stuff. Engagement fell by thirty-five per cent. *Thirty-five per cent!*'

Karolina looked like she was trying to summon a sympathetic gesture.

'I lose the followers, I lose the profile, I lose the work.'

The clafoutis sat sadly on the table.

'Sorry,' said Maude, suddenly aware, it seemed, of her total colonisation of the conversation. 'I love the idea of negronis but I always forget that they have gin in them.'

She smiled wanly, a faint dusting of cocaine visible on the rim of her right nostril.

'I have created a beast,' she said. 'And it feeds on me.'

Monday 2 July

Monday morning. The light outside was a cool grey, the moon still visible. Max opened his eyes, awoken by the sensation of a force, moderately but determinedly applying itself to his lower back. He turned sleepily to see Arthur lying on an inverted diagonal, his feet draped over Karolina's shoulders, his head now resting on Max's hip. Beyond Karolina, on the far side of the bed, he could see the antlers of Alma's stuffed reindeer, evidence that, at some point in the night, she too had padded down the hallway and got into bed with them, and was now nuzzling backwards into her mother's embrace.

Gently, he pulled Arthur's sweaty fringe away from his forehead. There was something tortoise-like about his torso, with its domed belly and defined lines. He watched his son's ribcage rise and fall, noticed again the slight flutter in his lashes as he breathed. He placed a hand on Arthur's chest and through it felt a connection to Karolina and then on to Alma. The four of them connected to each other like a chain-link fence. He shut his eyes. This drowsy bed. These limbs and stale breath. In a world where you were always just two steps from solitude, it was a kind of miracle, this.

'But it's a bank holiday!'

Two hours later, and Max had arrived at Tabitha's house with the children but without Karolina.

'Not in America, it isn't.'

They were standing in the hallway, Tabitha and Bryony, looking disappointed. Alma was insisting that Max crouch down and help her out of her shoes and, for reasons that were not entirely clear, her tights, while Arthur was rumbling down the hallway to god knows where to do god knows what.

'When are we going to get to meet her properly?'

'We're obsessed with her.'

'I know you are,' said Max who had successfully removed Alma's shoes and was now trying to peel off her tights, which seemed to have been vacuum-sucked to her legs.

'We feel like you're hiding her from us.'

'Why would I do that?' asked Max, a little grumpily. He was only just starting to feel himself again after Saturday's booze-soaked dinner with Dom and Maude.

'Because you're embarrassed.'

'I am not *embarrassed of my wife*,' he said, as he struggled on with the tights, Alma having turned unhelpfully onto her front.

'Not of *her*, of *us*.'

There was a noise that wasn't exactly a smash, but was definitely smash-like.

'Arthur,' he called plaintively down the hall.

'Oh, don't worry,' said Tabitha. 'I have seven grandchildren. There's nothing valuable left for him to break.'

Once everyone had disrobed to their satisfaction, they settled in the kitchen for a cup of tea. Or at least Tabitha and Bryony settled. Max mostly shadowed the children in a semi-crouch, eager to catch them before they electrocuted themselves or ate cat litter.

'Shall we get to it?' asked Tabitha, eventually.

'Yes,' said Max. 'Let's.'

He was there to help in the garden. Which he duly did, cutting back high-up creepers and pulling out deep-rooted poppies, while Tabitha and Bryony entertained the children. It wasn't a bad deal, Max reasoned, as he loaded cuttings into Tabitha's brown bin, and infinitely better than going to the South Tottenham soft-play centre, which had been the children's preferred plan.

After he had been going at it for about forty minutes, he was summoned back to the patio for tea and crumpets. Once the children had licked the honey off the top of the crumpets and disdained the rest, Tabitha laid a blanket on the lawn and the two of them sat on it, playing with a toy ship brought out from the house.

'You're a lovely family,' said Bryony.

The three adults were sitting in a row, facing the children, who were looking particularly winsome, the sunlight catching their hair.

'We see you in the street,' continued Tabitha. 'You carry yourselves lightly. You're easy, affectionate.'

'It's a show,' said Max, eating one of the licked crumpets. 'It's all *Sturm und Drang* at home.'

'You laugh a lot.'

'Gallows humour is the only way to get through the first years of parenthood.'

'Oh, come on, you make a very nice couple, you two.'

Max shrugged. It was true. They did. Everyone said so. Always had.

He took a sip of his tea. They had met at a party in someone's apartment, long past midnight. A guy was in the kitchen, grandstanding. She had rolled her eyes at just the right moment. And had then caught his. And in that very first look, they had recognised in each other something shared.

'We met at a good time in our lives,' he said.

Which was also true, he thought. At least up to a point. They had each brought with them remarkably little baggage. Both had had another pretty serious relationship, which had ended with just the right amount of heartache, and so neither was haunted by the sense of a life unlived. But they had both been, essentially, still young, hadn't got to that age when you start blindly swinging, desperate to grab on to whomever you can.

'How old were you?' asked Tabitha.

'I was thirty-four,' said Max. 'Karolina had turned thirty just a week or so before I met her.'

Max took another bite of the crumpet. Latterly, he had come to recognise that by your thirties you already are who you are. And so the two of them had looked to tessellate as best they could, rather than form themselves in the imprint of each other's contours, making and unmaking each other as they did so.

'Sounds like a very sensible age to me,' said Tabitha.

'Yeah,' said Max with one eye screwed shut. 'Although, I'm not sure if sensible is the thing you're really looking for in matters of the ...'

But that was as far as he got before he was interrupted by a voice drifting out from the house.

'Mu-um.'

'We're out here, darling.'

The woman who appeared out of the doorway was about ten years younger than him. Her hair pulled back in a ponytail. Hoop earrings. That front-foot energy of the London born and bred.

'This is Max. Who I was telling you about, who moved in down the road. Max, this is Imogen. My youngest.'

'Ah,' said Imogen. 'Max. We've heard all about you.'

She looked at him, cocked her head.

'Are you one of those con men who charms old ladies out of their houses?'

'*Imogen*,' said Tabitha.

'It's what Pete thinks,' she said to her mother. There was a flatness to her accent that had a practised quality to it.

'He was *joking*,' said Tabitha.

Imogen turned her attention back to Max. 'Peter's my brother and he thinks you are trying to trick our mum out of her pension.'

Max smiled.

'I don't think there is a single thing in the whole world that I could trick your mother out of,' he said.

Imogen smiled in recognition at the self-evident truth of this. She was standing on the patio, one hand on her hip, gesticulating vaguely towards the sandpit.

'You didn't hire these kids to make yourself seem more trustworthy?'

He looked over at Arthur, who was picking up handfuls of

raspberries and jamming them into his mouth and then wiping his hands on the front of his once-yellow T-shirt.

'Believe me,' he said. 'If you were putting together a team to pull off some scam and there was a choice in the matter, *no one* would choose to work with *these* two children.'

An hour later, he was at Bryony's. Seeing him working at Tabitha's had reminded her that there was a branch in her garden that had half-fallen and needed to be cut down. The children had happily stayed with Tabitha, watching television and eating sweets of the sort that were never allowed at home.

The tree with the problem branch was in a corner of the garden, next to an old brick wall. It was surrounded by tall-stemmed, purple-flowered plants and a bush that might have been a hydrangea, Max thought. He waded in, saw in hand.

'This is so kind of you. Really,' said Bryony, from behind him.

'Honestly, it's nothing. It'll only take five minutes.'

The branch had come down, but not wholly, and was connected still to the tree at shoulder height, the splintering wound exposing near-white innards. Max readied his saw.

'Don't tell Jonathan,' she said. 'About this.'

He looked over his shoulder at her. There was a flustered coyness to the look on her face, which he hadn't seen before.

'Men get so silly about these things.'

'Sure,' he said.

'I'm not saying he couldn't have done it. He absolutely *could* have done it, but it's silly to risk it. It's an awkward height. And his shoulder can be ... *problematic*.'

'Sure,' he said again. 'I won't say anything.'

Behind him, he could hear Bryony walking up to her studio and as he started to push and pull the saw, a new feeling ran through him, an unfamiliar combination of conquest and contrition, like a cuckoo abashed at having taken a nest.

Ten minutes later he was done. He had taken down the branch

and sawn it into three pieces so that they fitted, incognito, into the garden waste bin. A few quick turns with a spade was all that was needed to dig the small amount of sawdust into the earth. As he put the tools back into the garden shed he felt slightly embarrassed at the meticulousness with which he was covering his tracks, but overridingly a kind of electric thrill at the secrecy.

Across the garden, he could see her through her open studio door. Without washing his hands, he went and stood in the doorway, leaning into the frame with what the A-level student in him recognised as a kind of grubby Lawrentian impropriety.

She was standing in the middle of the space, her back to him, at an easel. Looking, rather than actively painting, an activity he felt he could legitimately interrupt, having just chopped up her branch.

'He told me you had a solo show in New York,' he said, from his place in the doorway.

Bryony turned to look at him.

'Is that what you talk about in your boys' den, drinking whisky into the night?'

Max smiled. 'Just small talk between moves while I'm schooling him at chess.'

Bryony walked over to the sink and turned on a tap, inviting him to wash his hands. 'March 1984,' she said. 'The Downtown gallery. Long defunct. It was on the corner of two streets, Prince and Elizabeth. Is that Little Italy? Or Nolita? I can't remember. They have all these neighbourhoods and silly names for them.'

Max ran his hands under the tap. He had first visited New York in the late nineties and had fallen hard, but had been conscious, even then, that he was late to the party.

'Nolita in 1984,' he said. 'That must have felt like the centre of the universe.'

A wave of scepticism rippled across Bryony's eyebrows.

'Well, it certainly *thought* it was,' she said, as she filled the kettle. 'And I suppose it had a kind of glamour, but it was a very hard place. There was a nakedness to the ambition on display there that was . . .' She smiled. 'It was what my daughter would describe these days as *cringe*.'

Max walked over to a shelf and took down a couple of hand-thrown mugs. He could still remember the first time he had walked up the subway steps, off a train from JFK, into the Manhattan maelstrom. The vertiginous rush of it, that first encounter with the urban sublime. And the instant confirmation that it was as thrilling in real life as it was on screen. It was inconceivable to him how anyone could fail to be entranced by it.

'Come on,' he said. 'It can't not have had a kind of charge to it. It *must* have done.'

'Yes, it had an *energy*,' she conceded, but without conviction. 'I was there for a week, doing the install. Jonathan could only come out just when the show started and so I was on my own a lot.'

She tossed a couple of teabags into a pot.

'And it was very dangerous. You could walk along the avenues fine, but the streets in downtown were very dark and forbidding. Some of them you had to run down. Don't catch anyone's eye, just run. It was very stressful.'

Max nodded along sympathetically but, really, this was exactly the stuff he was after. In his head, he conjured the shadowy streets of the East Village, the scene shot on 16mm, saturated and grainy. Lou Reed waiting for his man. Patti Smith and Mapplethorpe smoking on a stoop.

'Was the show a success?' he asked absent-mindedly.

'Oh god, I can't remember. I think it was fine. I'm sure at least some of the paintings must have sold. It was more than thirty years ago. Although I do recall that there was a fun party for the opening. I've got a photo of it in here somewhere.'

She walked to the dresser and opened a drawer, pulled out a folder full of keepsakes. Newspaper cuttings. Show notes. Flyers. Pages torn from magazines. Photos of her paintings hanging on gallery walls.

'All this stuff that you accumulate over a life,' she said. 'I mean, what are you supposed to do with it all? You can't throw it away but . . . Oh look, here it is.'

The image was black and white, painterly in its composition. Bryony was in the middle of the crowd, looking over her shoulder as if to catch the photographer's eye. She was in a shift dress, sylph-like, not yet thirty. Around her, the crowd seemed oblivious of the camera. They were all smoking, talking, looking at the work on the walls: a man in a camel cashmere coat, knotted tight at the waist; one woman in a tank top with a voluminous Afro; another in sheer fingerless gloves.

Bryony ran her finger along the crease in the photo where it had been folded.

'What a time,' she said, 'so fraught and so weird...'

Max looked at the image as she poured the tea.

'I sometimes think if I could be transported anywhere it would there, then,' he said.

'*Really?*' said Bryony. She looked abruptly at him. 'What, more than Paris in 1925, or Florence in ... I don't know ... 1500 or 1505 or whenever it was that Leonardo and Michelangelo were both living there?'

'They'd be amazing too, of course,' said Max, agitated by the feeling she had exposed the paucity of his imagination.

'Classical Athens,' she said, slightly contemptuously. 'Or pretty much anywhere in the 1780s.'

'Yeah, those too. I mean, there are obviously loads of historical moments that would be fascinating to return to.'

'A lot more interesting than bloody New York in 1984.'

Max poured the tea, feeling a little crushed and oddly compelled to defend his statement.

'It just seems like it was the last true bohemia,' he said quietly. 'You know, thrilling and free and modern, with all the good things that brings, but it wasn't self-conscious.'

Bryony scoffed. 'It was the most self-conscious place I've ever been.'

'That's not quite what I mean. Obviously, I wasn't there and I'm sure of course there were loads of self-conscious people, but the scene looked forward, not back. It wasn't a pastiche.'

Bryony looked at him kindly, clearly not exactly sure what he was talking about, but sympathetic nonetheless. She wrapped her hands around her mug of tea and moved the conversation on.

'While I was there I went to a lecture by Agnes Martin and got invited afterwards to drinks.'

'Agnes Martin,' said Max. 'I don't know her.'

'She was a minimalist. An abstract painter. Plagued by schizophrenia her whole life but what a body of work . . . Her mastery of colour was so total that it was almost spiritual. She was a titan. For me, for lots of us.'

Bryony's eyes moistened a little.

'Anyway, we were in a bar, in a big group. Lots of people. She was at the centre of it. Lots of big names. Art-world people. I was young then and not important.'

Bryony bit her lip.

'It's one of the great regrets of my life that I didn't summon the courage to talk to her, tell her how much her work had meant to me, what a lodestar she had been. How she had illuminated the sky for us.'

She felt instinctively for the hair on the back of her head, pushed her fingers into it – a reflex that Max hadn't seen before.

'I was intimidated.'

'I can't imagine you being intimidated by anyone.'

'She was seventy-two then and quite fragile, but still she burned.'

Bryony wasn't seventy-two, at least not yet. But still she burned, thought Max. She was a flame to which you could not help but be drawn.

Part of him longed to say it. To look at her and say it point blank. But to do so would have been to tip the conversation over the edge and watch it hurtle away from him, beyond his control. And anyway, it was unnecessary. She burned. And she knew it. And she knew that he knew it, too.

Thursday 5 July

The first thing to say about it was that the door was indeed being used as a tabletop. It was supported by the kinds of portable trestles that tradesmen use on site. Max felt the thrill of an anthropologist in the field. He had news to take back that would be eagerly feasted upon.

'Nice desk,' he said.

Zoe looked at it and dismissed it with a wave of her hand.

'We're not going to be here long,' she said. She was wearing a blue and white striped T-shirt, high-waisted jeans.

'No?'

'We're on a month-by-month deal. The landlord has put it in for planning. As soon as he gets it, we'll be out.'

The two reception rooms had been knocked together to create a large space, but still it was full. Two sofas, a futon, and two armchairs all in different styles. Old crates had been stacked to create a bookshelf of sorts. In two corners there were large boxes yet to be unpacked.

The beige carpet was tired, piebald in places. The arrangement of a previous configuration of furniture evident as sun-faded silhouettes.

'It must be unsettling,' he said. 'Not knowing how long you can be here.'

'Welcome to the lived reality of 2018,' she said, as she picked a jacket off the back of one of the two chairs at the desk and threw it onto a nearby sofa. 'The whole system is completely and totally fucked. This hardly feels any more unsettling than anything else.'

Max nodded sympathetically, but said nothing. The atmosphere in the room had soured a little. On his arrival she had been effusive, thanking him copiously for giving up his time, but already she seemed slightly resentful of his presence.

She sat down on one of the two chairs and opened a laptop.

'Are you OK to get started?'

'Sure,' said Max, as he sat down next to her. 'So everyone in the trade uses paid-for software but it's very expensive and takes a while to master, and the one you get free with your laptop is perfectly good and much more intuitive.'

He pointed to an icon, which she duly double-clicked, opening up the application.

'Right, where's the footage?'

'It's not ready yet,' said Zoe, slightly apologetically. 'I was hoping you could just run me through the basics.'

'Oh,' said Max, trying to mask his irritation. 'OK. Fine. We still need something to work on so I can show how to cut and splice and all that stuff. Any footage will do.'

Zoe tucked some hair behind her ear.

'Do you have any?'

Max paused. He had dozens of videos of his children on his phone, but the prospect of Karolina discovering that he had used one of them in this context filled him horror.

'Let's just shoot some now.'

He pulled out his phone and turned on the video camera.

'What did you do yesterday?' he asked her.

She looked at him, beyond the phone between them, piqued evidently at the presumptuousness, but then she refocused her gaze to the camera and, visibly softening, said, 'I watched your film.'

Max looked past the screen, straight at her, his chest tight.

'You did?'

She kept her focus on the phone, the merest hint of a smile on her face.

'Yeah,' she said. 'It's on YouTube.'

Max returned his focus to the phone screen, trying to maintain an equanimity of sorts.

'It wasn't what I expected it to be.'

'No?' said Max, outwardly placid, he hoped, while his heart hammered away in his chest.

'No.'

Max held the phone with two hands, breathing steadily in and out through his nose.

'It's so of its time,' she said. 'The awkwardness, the stilted dialogue. The total lack of anything resembling a plot. But it still shines through.'

He had his eyes fixed on his phone. Her face filled the screen.

'It?'

'Your love of cinema,' she said.

Max relaxed. The relief was like the breaking rains on a hot and humid day.

'It's obvious in every frame. As a viewer you can't help but fall for it.'

She leaned forward and took the phone from him. Surprised, he nevertheless let her take it, the camera still filming.

'We can edit this bit out,' she said with a smile, as she turned the phone round, pointed it at him.

'When did it start?' she asked. 'This great love affair?'

Max felt the dynamic shift on its axis, but was powerless to do anything about it. He hated being on camera. Always had. He took off his reading glasses. Not out of vanity, but to buy himself some time. Slowly, he folded the arms of his spectacles shut, slipped them into his breast pocket.

'You kind of always want to give a badass answer to this kind of question, don't you?' he said eventually. '*Paris, Texas*. Or *Chinatown*. Something singular. But really, for me, it was *Indiana Jones and the Temple of Doom*.'

He laughed quietly to himself.

'Widely recognised now as the most problematic of the first wave of Indiana Jones films . . .' He ran his hand pensively over his face. 'But it came out when I was eight and I was completely entranced by it. If it was released now I can't believe it would get the rating it got then – it's hilariously violent in places. I'm sure that was part of what got me. It felt so adult and exotic. That was that. I fell early and I fell hard.'

The last of the evening light cast long shadows across the desk.

'It's funny. Later, when I was in my teens and my twenties, films like that were what I *defined* myself in opposition to, that kind of big-studio corporate entertainment. The most mainstream of mainstream. But I look back on it now and ...'

He felt a sudden sadness that he had hitched his whole life to a caravan that was heading, if not off a cliff, then at least into the sunset.

'When I was a kid, movies were these incredible global events. When *ET* came out literally everyone watched it. I mean, *everyone* watched it. And *Home Alone*. And *Indiana Jones*. We went again and again. They were these kind of singular cultural events. They were the universal.'

He looked back at the camera and gave a defeated little shrug.

'And now they're not.'

Forty-five minutes later, once they had run through the basics of the software, uploaded the footage and cut it a couple of times, they decided that they were done for the day.

'Thai green curry for dinner tonight,' she said as they folded shut their laptops. 'I had nothing to do with its creation so it will probably be edible.'

There were four of them in the kitchen: one at the stove, the other three sat at a large dining table. A woman with a topknot had been telling some raucous story, underlining her points with dramatic waves of the arm, but she stopped abruptly upon their arrival and Max felt like a teacher walking into the classroom.

'This is Max,' said Zoe. 'He's been running me through the basics of editing so let's all be nice.'

'Hi,' he said, with a coy wave and what he hoped was a generous smile, remembering the nickname they had for him, and the great iceberg of disdain that it intimated.

A couple of murmured greetings followed.

'I could have taught you,' said a man, who was at the stove and was yet to acknowledge Max. There was a kind of Henry the Fifth abruptness to the line of his haircut which cleared the top of his ear by a good inch or so. He was wearing a black T-shirt, wide-legged trousers and shoes with soles so thick they had an inescapably remedial quality.

'Yeah, but would you have ever actually got round to it?'

He looked at her sullenly.

'I'm doing six shifts a week.'

'I know you are,' she said kindly. 'You don't have time. It's fine.'

'I would have made time.'

'Cal,' she said. 'It's fine. Max was happy to do it.'

Max stood at the top of the steps leading down in the space, listening to all this with interest. The combative edge to the exchange, to his mind, was ordinarily the preserve of couples. Yet something about the energy between them made him question whether they were together.

'I thought we were trying to keep things contained,' continued Cal, not looking at her as he chopped some coriander.

'He's only showing me how to use the software. We shot some random footage and used that.'

Max turned his head through ninety degrees to look at her, pretending to be wounded. Zoe's reaction was to grimace in a not-you-too kind of way, but there was a hint of a smile, and he felt the thrill of a secret alliance recently formed.

'I could have done whatever editing we're going to need,' continued Cal. 'I've done plenty of it before.'

'Cal, you just said you're working six shifts a week. My god!'

Max walked down the three steps into the kitchen. It was obviously a kind of dick move, all of this. Unnecessarily public and embarrassing for all involved. But, still, he found himself begrudgingly admiring young Cal. He had spent his whole life avoiding confrontation, smoothing edges, looking for compromise, and there was something heroic about the man's obstinance.

'Can I do anything to help?' he asked.

'Yeah,' said Cal. 'Sure. You can wash up if you want.'

'*Cal*,' said Zoe.

The sink was full to overflowing, the top of the water slicked with grease, a pan handle protruding from it.

'No one else is doing it.'

'It's fine,' said Max cheerily. 'I'm happy to get stuck in.'

Max dug his hand into the water to pull out the plug, smiling to himself at the amount of effort he had recently found himself putting into weaponising the washing up. He emptied the sink and ran the water until it was hot, merrily squirted some washing-up liquid into the basin. They could call him names all they liked but until one of them was round at his, stacking the dishwasher, he surely now had the upper hand.

Ten minutes later, they sat down to eat. Max was next to Laurie, an expensive-looking American, who was doing a postgraduate degree and spoke in crisp, considered sentences.

Zoe was at the other end of the table, and as he listened to Laurie talking about a protest at the university on behalf of outsourced workers, Max found himself glancing over at her, trying to get a bead on her relationship with Cal, who was sitting to her right and talking to her intensely in a low voice so that he couldn't hear what was being said.

'It was a peaceful sit-in and they could tell it was a peaceful sit-in and still they called in a load of extra security,' continued Laurie. 'It was a spectacular overreaction and the most egregious waste of money.'

'Outsourced of course,' said Max dryly. 'The security, I mean.'

Laurie smiled.

'I bet my bottom dollar, the money they're spending on them is at least equal to the money they're saving by outsourcing the cleaners in the first place.'

She had her fork in her hand.

'The vice chancellor needs to go. He's a joke. His pay is indefensible. *And* he's holding out from divesting in fossil fuels even as all of the other universities are doing it.'

Max murmured his disapproval as he pinched some coriander from a bowl and sprinkled it onto his curry.

'Have you read that magazine piece? "The Uninhabitable Earth"?' she asked.

'Um, no ...' he said. 'I keep meaning to.'

'It's fucking terrifying.'

'Yeah, that's what I had assumed.'

'The other day I heard this phrase, "tipping cascades", and I can't get it out of my head. You read some of the dates and they're 2050 or whatever and I'm like I'll be fifty-three when the Gulf Stream collapses. Good to know. At least I don't have to worry about paying into a pension.'

Max smiled at the joke but found himself incapable of thinking about this future even though it would arrive when his kids were in their thirties. Every time he tried to contemplate the looming apocalypse it produced a kind of whiteout in his mind. He looked up and down the table at them. None of them were laughing. Perhaps you had to have been steeped in this since childhood to really be able to take on the enormity of it.

Laurie went to say something but was distracted by her phone buzzing.

'Oh god, it's my mom. This is so rude but I have to take this. I'm sorry.'

She shuffled along the bench and then out of the kitchen, leaving Max alone, at his end of the table, with a woman he had recently discovered was called Alexandra. Alexandra was wearing an elaborate headband and a too-tight lace top, her eyes heavily kohled. She was one of those young women who is too much and knows she is too much and has decided to make a virtue of it but is not yet in full command of her material.

Once Laurie was out of earshot, Alexandra looked at Max and said something, which he didn't catch but which he understood – from the set of her body, the look on her face – was a challenge to him, certainly to his presence there, perhaps to his very existence.

He stopped and looked at her rather more directly than he'd intended as he tried to work out how to react.

A blush started to rise up her throat.

Max froze. What could he do? He genuinely hadn't heard what she'd said. He looked at her and she looked at him. Around them, the table had gone quiet. Instinctively, he understood that it would be a further humiliation for her to have to repeat, in front of everyone else, whatever it was she had said. And so he said nothing, but even as he did so, he felt the power tilt in his favour in a way that he hadn't courted and didn't want.

He took a bite of the curry.

'This is delicious,' he said merrily. 'Thank you to all involved in its creation.'

Cal had finished his bowl and was sitting back in his chair, his legs stretched out.

'Is it true that you hang out with them all?' he said.

Max smiled and then explained the particularities of their situation. Karolina's working hours. His limited freedoms.

'They have taken me on like you would a stray cat. I'm kind of like a regimental mascot.'

'What are they like?'

'The boomers? They're all hilariously self-satisfied ...' He shrugged. 'But I guess you've earned the right to it by that age. I like them. They're a good craic.'

'How long have they all lived here?' asked Zoe.

'Oh, thirty years some of them. Maybe even longer. They paid nothing for these houses. I mean, nothing at all.'

'And the two at the end. In the big house?'

'The Coxes. They're the Isabella and Ferdinand of the set. You should see their joint. It's incredible.'

'You've been to their place?' asked Cal.

'A couple of times. She's an artist. Quite a big deal in certain circles, I think. She's got a glorious garden studio out the back.'

'He's a fund manager,' said Cal.

'Is he? I know he has funded things. Gallery shows.'

Cal snorted.

'And the rest.'

'He did some film distribution back in the day. A couple of Fassbinder films. Some Bertoluccis.'

Max stood up, started to clear the table.

'He met them both,' he said, but no one was interested.

He stacked the bowls and took them over to the sink, waiting for someone to discourage him from washing up again. No one did. Resignedly, he once again started filling the sink. He had just finished the glasses when a new song came on the stereo. Max listened to the first few chords. It was Radiohead, obviously, but not one of their more famous songs.

'Wait a sec,' he said. 'This is from *Pablo Honey*, isn't it?'

Cal was a couple of feet to his left, scraping some uneaten food into the bin. He nodded.

'I knew people your age liked "Creep" but I didn't realise you listened to the whole album. The later stuff, obviously, but not this. I thought even the band had kind of repudiated this now.'

He paused respectfully while Thom Yorke sang the opening lines.

'I haven't listened to this for years. It's great, isn't it?'

He ran the tap again, rinsing detergent bubbles off a clutch of forks.

'You know, I queued up for the release of this record. Me and Rick Gibbs, waiting for half an hour outside Pelican Records for them to open. For some reason we must have really wanted to be the first two people in Hertfordshire to have a copy of this.'

The chorus kicked in and he sang along to the words.

'I can't remember us doing that for any other record. Not for *Nevermind*. Not for *Loveless*. But we queued up for *Pablo Honey*.'

Max was conscious that he was wittering but Cal was showily offering him nothing and he felt that stopping talking would represent more of a defeat than carrying on.

'Funny to think back to those days. It felt like there was a completely new genre of music every eighteen months. We were so complacent about it ...'

He placed a clean bowl on the drying rack.

'I remember hearing jungle for the first time. It was so heavy. It felt . . . I don't know . . . kind of post-human or something. It wasn't intuitive. You had to teach yourself how to dance to it.'

Zoe had come over from the dining table and was now standing next to him, a tea towel in her hand.

'Back then, I thought it would carry on for ever. That kind of newness. But it didn't. It just stopped.'

'Did it?' she said. 'What about grime?'

'Yeah, grime was new. Or at least new-ish. But that's been it. For years now. That rich seam that ran through the sixties, seventies, eighties and nineties, it just feels exhausted. The Strokes and the White Stripes were the big bands of the noughties, and they're about as original as the Bootleg Beatles.'

He passed her a serving bowl to dry.

'I feel kind of sad for all those kids coming of age and there not being anything that's genuinely new.'

Cal scoffed.

'The music you are into when you are fifteen always feels new, though, doesn't it?' he said. 'It's new to you. And do you really think that anyone that age – when it all feels like life and death – do you really think any of them care if the band that they love is impressive to forty-five-year-old Glastonbury dads?'

Max turned to look at Zoe, wide-eyed. She was laughing. At Cal, he thought. But also him. And probably men in general.

Part of him was burning at the takedown, but as much as anything he felt vivified by the exchange, heartened that Cal felt him an adversary worth getting riled over.

'I'm forty-two,' he mouthed to her in mock horror.

Cal caught this and looked away in disgust.

'You've had it so fucking easy,' he said. 'You had to come to terms with the end of originality. We're coming to terms with the end of the world.'

Monday 9 July

'Boris Johnson has resigned.'

Early evening. The kitchen table at number fourteen. Tabitha. Gordon. Bryony and Jonathan. All four of the Gayle family cats. Fiona, sitting immediately to Max's right, wearing what appeared be a croupier's visor.

Douglas, who was ten minutes behind his wife, having apparently decided at the last second that he was wearing the wrong pair of trousers, had just walked in with the news.

'It was on the radio just now.'

'Thank god.'

'Boris as foreign secretary. What an embarrassment for the country.'

The tablecloth was wipe-proof and ever so slightly tacky to the touch. On the table was a big bowl of what Max was told was seven-layer dip, Tabitha's signature dish, about which they all seemed enthused, despite cold refried beans being one of its core ingredients.

'Incredible to think he was ever allowed near one of the great offices of state,' said Gordon as he took a tortilla chip and scooped up a great lump of avocado dotted with jalapenos. 'What would Eden make of it? Bevin?'

The room smelled of dry cat food and potpourri and damp towels. Max found it all deeply reassuring.

'Robin Cook,' said Douglas with sonorous deliberation.

'*Robin Cook,*' said Tabitha. 'He was a good man.'

'Johnson can flounce off in a huff,' said Jonathan, who was sitting at the top of the table, wearing a linen shirt. 'But it'll be a soft Brexit. May will get her deal through. It's what the markets want. And the markets always get what they want.'

Tabitha favoured tiny wine glasses, out of piety, Max had decided, compelling her guests to make a decision every time they topped them up. They were cut glass, barely bigger than thimbles, and looked ridiculous in Jonathan's large hands.

Jonathan took a crisp from the bowl and looked down the table at Max and Bryony, who were seated next to each other. The look on his face was impenetrable. There was no significance to the seating arrangements, Max felt, but he appreciated that this was open to interpretation. He smiled to himself, wondering idly if Jonathan had found out about the tree.

'I think we should re-run the referendum,' he said. 'Only those under sixty should be allowed to vote. People with a meaningful stake in the future.'

Jonathan didn't react.

'Yes, very good,' said Fiona.

'*We* didn't vote for Brexit,' said Tabitha.

'I think Fiona might have done,' said Gordon. 'Make it easier for Corbyn to collectivise the farms.'

Fiona looked at Gordon imperiously but also indulgently, before she turned back to the table.

'Max thinks that we're all just a field of sunflowers,' she said, 'who can't help but turn towards the sun as one.'

Max paused, a tortilla chip in his hand.

'Fiona,' he said. 'I have never and will never compare you to something so sunny and cheerful.'

Fiona pretended to be outraged. Gordon laughed his dirty old laugh.

'But you're right, though,' continued Max. 'As far as I'm concerned, anyone over sixty is basically the same person.'

'Well, we're not,' said Tabitha. 'And we won't take the blame for something that we didn't do. It's like blaming you because more men voted to leave. It's ridiculous.'

Bryony reached over and scooped some dip onto her plate, then fixed Max with a look.

'Enough chat about people over sixty, I want to hear more about people *under* sixty. Particularly some who are new to the area . . .'

'Oh, yes,' said Tabitha. 'You went to the house, didn't you?'

Max leaned back in his chair. He waited for a second, milking the moment.

'The door . . .' he said, slowly and deliberately, 'is a tabletop!'

A great cheer went up round the table.

'Where do they all sleep?'

'I don't know. In the bedrooms?'

'All eight of them?'

'I think so.'

'What are they like?' asked Bryony.

'I only met some of them. They're fine, the ones I met. You know, I prefer some of them to others. They're maybe a bit overly dramatic about the challenges they're going to face, but who isn't at that age? I mean, how old were you lot for the Cuban Missile Crisis?'

''62, wasn't it?' said Jonathan. 'I was twelve.'

'I was sixteen,' said Douglas. 'I remember it, of course. And I understood the seriousness of it at the time but honestly I think I cared more about whether or not Manchester United were going to be relegated.'

Fiona made a gesture of resignation.

'It was always there in the background of our lives, the threat,' she said. 'Funny how something can be so terrifying and also so commonplace.'

The room was lit by a standing lamp with a wonky shade, casting interesting shadows on the ceiling. On one wall there was a huge pinboard thick with keepsakes: family photos, children's drawings, birthday cards, flyers for plays, discount vouchers, cycling proficiency certificates, a horse-riding rosette.

'What do they do?' asked Jonathan.

'I think they're a mix of students and just young people starting out, working whatever jobs they can. Pretty standard stuff.'

There had been talk of a game of cards but too many of them had turned up and everyone seemed content with the dip.

'Should we invite them to the street party?' asked Tabitha.

The Pemberton Place annual summer street party was scheduled for the end of the month. Max had been charged with hanging the bunting and making guacamole.

'Would they want to come?' asked Bryony, directing this at Max.

'I don't know,' he said. 'You'll have to ask them.'

'Let's see how things go,' said Tabitha.

'Did you ask them about their bins and whether or not it's entirely necessary for them to be arranged as they are?' asked Fiona.

'I didn't.'

'If they could find the time to neaten them, it would make their neighbours very happy.'

Douglas, who frequently went for minutes at a time betraying no sign that he had been listening to a single word of the conversation, looked up and said:

'They're probably too busy scaling hypergrowth tech companies.'

At which everyone collapsed into immediate hysterics, except Max, who found himself looking around at them, smiling slightly desperately in that way that you do when you aren't in on the joke. It was an old one, clearly, but one of which they had not tired. Even Jonathan had lost it.

Max looked at Douglas sitting in his chair, soft and faded and unmoving, like an old and much-loved cuddly toy with black shining eyes glinting in the light.

Through his tears, Gordon clocked the bemused look on Max's face.

'Last year, Imogen had a boyfriend. Tabitha's Imogen. Tabs asked him what he did. And he told her that he scaled hypergrowth tech companies.'

He was crying with laughter, barely able to get his words out.

'She thought he meant he literally scaled the buildings.'

His chest shuddered and he was gone again.

'For five minutes they had a very earnest conversation,' said

Bryony, picking up the story, 'and the whole time Tabitha talked to him like he was one of those people who climb up big tall buildings and jump off them with parachutes.'

Tabitha wiped her eyes.

'I had seen it on television,' she said. 'These people climbed up the Gherkin and videoed themselves jumping off. I thought he was one of them.'

'"Do you scale other things?" she asked him,' said Bryony, which sent them all off again into great convulsions of laughter.

The laughter came in waves and seemed to contain unspoken references to yet other pre-existing jokes, connections that existed in their collective understanding and didn't need to be articulated. Max listened to it and understood that it could only accrue over time, this sort of thing, layer upon layer of memories and in-jokes and associations.

Jonathan had a hanky out to blow his nose.

'Work call in five minutes,' he said as he got up. 'Bloody New York. I have to go. Thanks for the dip, Tabs.'

He walked down the table, looking at Max, who was still an outsider, he realised, and always would be, however many glasses of their wine he drank. As Jonathan passed Bryony, she raised a hand and they brushed fingers, a gesture at once so casual and so certain.

It occurred to Max that marriages are like woods dense with undergrowth that thickens over time. You can see the tops of the trees but the roots are obscured. As he watched Jonathan go, he tried to fathom if his thoughts reflected an external reality or if they were simply things in his head. He had been trusted to chop down a single splintered branch, but what significance could that possibly have in the great forest of their lives?

A cat jumped on the table and somebody shooed it off.

'I met Imogen recently,' said Max, once they had all calmed down. 'She accused me of being a confidence trickster.'

'I heard about that,' said Gordon. 'I wouldn't take offence. Imogen has always been a very direct young woman.'

'Does she also scale hypergrowth tech companies?' asked Max.

'No,' said Tabitha. 'She does engagement, which sounds like the kind of thing that Jane Austen would have taken very seriously but is actually to do with websites and getting people to go on them. Or stay on them once they're on them. It's more complicated than that and she has explained it to me so many times but the information will not stay in my head.'

Tabitha looked momentarily perturbed.

'I could do you twenty, maybe even thirty, of the sonnets with not a word out of place. But Imogen's job? I can't retain anything about it. Anyway, she seems to enjoy it. Even if she is rather despairing at the ones coming up after her. They leave the office at 5 p.m. every day, which is anathema to her. She is her mother's daughter when it comes to graft, I'm afraid.'

Max picked up the unused pack of cards and stood it on its end.

'Imogen and I got the worst of both worlds,' he said. 'Our bosses treated us like indentured serfs when we were young, but by the time we were old enough to be department heads, line managers had basically become wet nurses to a whole generation of cosseted little princes and princesses.'

Gordon laughed.

'He's right, Tabs. Good thing we've been put out to pasture. We wouldn't survive a second now.'

He turned to Max.

'She used to tie belts around the students' chests to improve their postures.'

He mimed a belt being pulled tight round his own chest.

'Everyone did it,' said Tabitha, irritably. 'They did it to me when I was kid. It didn't really hurt. Not really. It was uncomfortable . . . OK, it hurt a little bit. But it was bloody effective. Look at you, you old hunchback, it would have sorted you out.'

'Oh, Tabitha, darling, I can't believe you're only offering now,' said Gordon, his eyes alight with mischief.

'All public-school-educated men of a certain age long to be on the receiving end of that belt,' said Fiona to Max.

'We do,' shouted Gordon. 'The tighter the better.'

'I've done a bit of guest lecturing at film schools,' said Max. 'I think you'd get a custodial sentence if you did anything like that now.'

'Tabitha nearly did!'

'*Gordon*,' said Bryony, furiously.

Tabitha, who until this point had been gamely smiling along at the tales of the belt, looked away and then stood up abruptly.

'I was only joking,' said Gordon.

'It's not something to joke about,' said Bryony.

'She shouldn't have been there,' said Tabitha.

'Tabs, darling. You don't need to go over it again.'

'It is an elite institution for god's sake. We pushed people. Of course we pushed them. We weren't doing am-dram.'

She looked slightly cruelly at Max.

'It *matters*.'

'Come on, Tabs,' said Gordon. 'It was a bad joke. I'm sorry.'

'People are forever saying it's not life and death, but it *was* life or death for me. And not just me. If you're going to do it, then you do it properly. And that means committing. All in. That means sacrifice. And sacrifice is sometimes painful.'

She was standing up, spine straight, delivering a variation on a speech she had delivered, Max imagined, many times before. He could picture himself, sitting in her introductory class, listening to these words and being absolutely terrified.

'That, I'm afraid, is the way of the world,' she continued as she stormed out of the room. 'And I, for one, am not apologising for it.'

Ten minutes later, Bryony and Max were alone in the kitchen. Gordon had gone home, somewhat in disgrace, with Fiona and Douglas leaving not long after. Tabitha had calmed down and was now in the living room with a cup of peppermint tea, having readily accepted their offer to tidy up.

While he cleared the table, Bryony had quietly filled him in. Ten years ago there had been the threat of a court case from an alumnus of the drama school. Accusations of systematic bullying. Mental cruelty. A colleague had taken the fall. Tabitha was thought, by some, to have been rather lucky to have survived.

'Tabs's problem is that she's a believer,' Bryony whispered, as she covered the remaining dip with cling film. 'And believers will do anything for the cause.'

She paused at the fridge door.

'I was only a kid when the Lord Chamberlain's veto was overturned and, to be honest, I don't remember it at all. But she was eighteen, just down in London for the first time and she finds herself in the middle of this utterly thrilling world which is full of geniuses dragging the country into the modern era. By the time she was twenty-one she had been in a Wesker play and worked with Peter Brook.'

Bryony picked up a tea towel and started drying.

'Did she go too far sometimes? Probably. It was all just too important to her; she wasn't able to compromise.'

She passed him a salad bowl to put on a high shelf.

'You understand, though, don't you?'

Max said nothing. Did he understand? He wasn't sure. His whole working life had been an endless stream of compromises and concessions and he had, he increasingly felt, been eroded down to a rump.

'How's the script going?' said Bryony in response to his silence.

'I'm making progress.'

'Jonathan can't wait to read it.'

Max felt his whole body contract a little.

'Really?'

'He likes you. He doesn't like many people, but for some reason he really does seem to like you. Even if you agitate him.'

'Agitate?'

'I think he's a little jealous of you.'

'Is it my great wealth and professional standing?'

Bryony smiled.

'More likely your youth,' she said. 'Although is it your youth? I don't know. Perhaps it's your ease. He has worked extremely hard to get where he is.'

Max rinsed the soap suds from a serving dish and placed it on the rack.

'And I don't just mean the hours at his desk.'

She was stacking glasses in the top rack of the dishwasher.

'He had to learn all the steps. He looks at you and sees someone who instinctively knows how to dance.'

Max looked at her. She was looking at him intently, her lips slightly parted. The light in the kitchen was low but still her eyes flashed. Fine lines ran across her forehead. She was beautiful in the way Bach is beautiful, in a way that transcended time.

He stayed his breath. In the quiet of the house, they could hear Tabitha moving about in the living room. Bryony's eyes were full of mischief and totally inscrutable. He felt, suddenly and shamingly, that she was playing him.

'I don't think he's jealous,' he said. 'Frustrated at me, maybe.'

'Frustrated?'

'I get the feeling he wants me to be something and I'm not it. Like, I'm close but not quite. And that's more frustrating than not being anywhere near.'

Bryony laughed.

'Do all men have such ...' she searched for the word. '*Colonial* relationships?'

'I don't think we can really help it. You want what you want.'

Bryony smiled.

'What is it that *you* want, Max?'

He swallowed. There were obviously two ways to answer this. One was clouded and complex and would compel him to think difficult thoughts. The other was clear cut. Even if it necessitated him adopting a kind of directness that ordinarily escaped him.

'I know Jonathan has been involved in film distribution before but has he ever financed one?'

If Bryony looked disappointed it was for the merest of milliseconds.

'Art films, for sure. A long time ago, though. His work is different these days. Less culture, more spreadsheets, but he has all kinds of projects on the go. And you never know with him. He knows a lot of people with a lot of money.'

She smiled a knowing smile.

'And he's never been afraid to take risks.'

The bedroom light was off when he got home, but the curtains were open and he could see that Karolina was asleep, lying on her side, the curve of her hips shrouded by the duvet.

Max grabbed his pyjamas and tiptoed past the end of the bed, back into the hallway. Arthur and Alma's door was open, as it always was, the room dimly lit by a moon-shaped night light.

He stood in the doorway, watching them as they slept. Alma was neat in her bed, her reindeer tucked under her arm. Arthur's cover had been thrown to the floor and he was lying sweatily on his back, his arms up in surrender, having lost, as he eventually always did, the nightly battle to stay awake.

He went first to Alma's side of the room and perched on the edge of her bed. She was just five, but already racing to be six. Mostly because of A. A. Milne. *When I am six I'll be clever as clever*, she told them most days in her lovely, ever so slightly lispy voice, *and I think I'll stay six for ever and ever.*

But she couldn't, Max knew. Stay six. For all that part of him would have liked her to.

He watched her as she lay there in her serene, motionless sleep, surrounded by her coterie of stuffed toys. He frequently found himself feeling sullied at the material excess of their lives. The piles of Christmas presents. The lavish birthday parties. The uncontrollable largesse of his in-laws and friends.

Apart from those who had experienced serious privation, had most people, he wondered, in their own mind, been indulged as a child to exactly the right degree? Enough material comfort to open them up to the world but also, crucially, just the right amount of want to keep them hungry?

Alma stirred and turned her head, her lips fluttering as she slept.

Max made a soft shushing sound, like a wind passing through long grass. What did he want for her and her brother as they grew up? In the long term, he had no real idea. Adulthood would be theirs to navigate in a world that he suspected would look very different from the one he knew.

Ahead of then, the thing he wanted most, if he was honest with himself, was for them to have teenage lives that were exactly like his. An impossible return to the prelapsarian nineties. The spaciousness of those days. Landlines and band T-shirts. Record shops. Paperback books and *Twin Peaks*. Boredom. Freedom. *Privacy*. He felt a momentary flutter of panic. Everything was already so different and it was just getting started. How did you stop their lives being swallowed whole by technology?

Max waited until he was sure that Alma had settled before he got up. He knew that the things that he wanted for them were the things that parents had wanted for ever: the navigable familiar, codes and norms they could understand. But there was also, surely, something particularly unsettling about the years ahead of them, a sense of looming cliff edges, precipitous changes that would be of a different order from those that had come before.

He sat down on the edge of Arthur's bed. Since his dinner at Zoe's, he had found himself returning again and again to the idea of *tipping cascades*. He hadn't dared to go online and find out what the phrase actually meant, but he could fashion a good guess and the speculative visualisations that it engendered – of surging water pouring from high ground, buildings collapsing like dominoes – were so graphic and overwhelming that he had found himself wondering for the first time if it had been a good idea to have children.

Arthur stirred, the elasticated band of his night nappy just visible above the waistline of his pyjama trousers. Max picked up the duvet from the floor and covered his sleeping son. They were the first generation to have children knowing that things were almost certain to get worse. That hadn't been the case when Zoe was born. Back then, perhaps a handful of people had had a sense of the trouble to come, but they were the seers, not the norm.

Max tucked Arthur's stuffed dog under the duvet. For reasons that he couldn't quite put his finger on, he had always felt – irrationally, he knew, but also enduringly – that his kids would somehow be fine. That there would be a boat for them. It wasn't a particularly noble thought, but to dwell too much on the alternative would be to drive yourself mad.

He walked back along the hall, pausing outside his bedroom to change into his pyjamas. Leaving his clothes in a heap, he opened and closed the door as quietly as he could. It was the second night that week he had crept into bed with Karolina already asleep. The first spent with Zoe, the second with Bryony. On neither occasion had anything actually happened, but still he felt an upwelling of guilt.

Max lay on his back, his head on the pillow, staring up at the ceiling. What was it that *he* wanted? Was it sex? Not exactly. Or at least not concretely. What he really wanted was to know that for all that he might have absented himself from the arena, he could still compete. Which was unbecoming, he recognised that, but it was not a betrayal. Not really.

Karolina was facing away from him. Max turned onto his side so that he could hold her, and felt her relax into his embrace. Her hair was freshly washed and smelled of rosemary and mint. He shut his eyes. It was all going to be fine. He had a backstop. A line he wouldn't cross.

Saturday 14 July

'You've got no bloody backhand!'

It was Saturday afternoon. Karolina had taken the kids to a cottage in Suffolk with a recently divorced friend and her two young children. It had been decided late in the day that Max's presence might be inhibiting and/or triggering, and so he had stayed in London, having made little effort to disguise his glee at this outcome, and was playing tennis with Jonathan on the fenced court at the back of the square.

'If you could hit it harder, I wouldn't have time to run round on to my forehand.'

Jonathan growled as he set himself to serve again.

The serve was down in the middle, hit with moderate force. Max got into position and hit his return deep towards Jonathan's baseline. Jonathan took the ball on his backhand and sent a shot to the centre of Max's half of the court. Max watched the ball bounce and set his wrist. As it dropped he swept his racket underneath it, taking all the sting out of the ball, and returned it neatly, just over the net.

'What the hell.'

'It's a drop shot.'

'I know what it is.'

Jonathan stood on the baseline with his hands on his hips.

'It's a bloody coward's shot.'

Max had watched only a handful of televised tennis games

in his adult life but had read enough Foster Wallace to bluster convincingly.

'What I love about the Federer, Djokovic generation,' he said, as he walked over to retrieve one of the balls over by the fence, 'is the way that that they evolved the game from a couple of grunts smacking it back and forth from the baseline. They introduced a new level of artistry to the game, like they were choreographing in three dimensions, fully embracing the spatiality of the court.'

Max used his racket to push the ball against the side of his foot so that he could flick it up into the air.

'Is spatiality a word?' he said.

'I don't fucking know.'

'If it isn't, it should be.'

Max bounced the ball twice on the ground before he knocked it back to Jonathan for him to serve.

'Anyway,' he said, 'love-thirty.'

The first set was over pretty quickly. Max won it 6–2. Which, for Jonathan, represented at least a modicum of saved face, as he had been 5–0 down at one point, and he was in good spirits when they sat down on the bench.

'You won that set but the momentum is with me.'

'The momentum is with entropy,' said Max cheerily. 'Always is.'

Jonathan smiled as he unpeeled a banana.

'Bryony told me your line about bosses being wet nurses,' he said, between bites. 'Made me laugh. You'd be straight off to HR of course if you said anything like that in the office, but it's absolutely bloody true.'

Max took a swig from his bottle of water.

'Yeah, but ... I don't know. I feel for them. The anxiety is a thing. It's endemic. I don't remember it being like that when I was young.'

It was late afternoon, and the sun had started its descent. Above them flew a swallow, gliding on its boomerang wings.

'I understand it,' he continued. 'They've lived with a sense of dread since they were kids. Must be awful watching your future being set on fire by the people who are supposed to be looking after you.'

Jonathan snorted dismissively.

'Come on,' said Max irritably. 'They're genuinely freaked out. They read the reports. They see the projections. Five hundred million refugees. Resource wars. Mass extinctions. It's terrifying.'

Jonathan swigged from a bottle of water.

'Look, I'm not saying it's not a thing. Of course it's a thing. But the solutions are there. We have the technology to do it. And once the dial flips, it'll flip hard. It's happening already in the markets. The price of solar is crashing. Batteries too. Carbon-capture tech is going to take off in the next ten years. Hydrogen has great potential. It'll be rocky but in the end we'll sort it out.'

'Oh, I am so glad to hear that the whole thing's just a fuss over nothing.'

Jonathan scoffed.

'Look,' he said, 'there's a lot of talk about negative feedback loops, but what about the positive ones? Solar prices will mean abundant electricity which we'll use to desalinate seawater and irrigate the desert. Once it starts, it will accelerate.'

'You seem a lot more confident than, like, *all* of the world's scientists . . .'

'The whole process is already underway. You've got to understand, Max. There's this stuff.' Here, he waved his hand dismissively at waist height. 'The stuff that's in the *Guardian*. Bryony politics. And then there's this stuff.' He made a rainbow with his hand, up at head height. 'The stuff up here is all that really matters. And the Chinese have gone hard on renewables. The Americans now have to play catch-up. Because they're not going to let the Chinese own the space. And the Chinese are going to keep pushing it because they *need* it to happen. The fertile belt hangs on it. We're talking the fertile belt that grows the rice that feeds two billion Asians. If the temperature goes up too much, China will get too hot and the fertile lands will shift north to Russian Siberia. And there is no way they are going to let that happen.'

'Well, I mean ...'

Jonathan was on his feet.

'The momentum has shifted,' he said. 'Everything else will catch up. You can go on all the marches you like but won't make an iota of difference.'

He tossed Max a ball.

'Your serve.'

The second set didn't last long. Irritated by their conversation, Max had stepped it up, forcing Jonathan to run for every shot, piling pressure on his backhand and punishing his second serves. He won it 6–0 and even that somehow didn't quite capture the extent of the defeat.

At the end of the final point, which had seen Max hammer a passing shot past his attempt at a volley, Jonathan stood at the net, flushed in the face and looking, to Max's mind, slightly repentant.

'Well done,' he said, once he had gathered his breath.

'Good game.'

'Not really.'

He took off his baseball cap and ran his fingers through his hair, a rueful smile on his face.

'Time waits for no man.'

In silence, they collected the half-dozen balls, both of them clearly reflecting on the game and what its outcome said about them. As athletes. And also men. Max felt vindicated and triumphant and slightly ashamed.

Once the balls had been returned to their tubes and the rackets zipped back into the cases, Jonathan stood at the net, his sports bag slung over his shoulder.

'My daughter is forever sending us delivery boxes of half-made food,' he said. 'Meal kits. Like we're incapable of cooking for ourselves. Anyway, they're backing up and need to be eaten. There are two or three that I think are curries of some sort and they look like they might be OK.'

'Is this an invite?'

'Bryony is going to the theatre and there is a bottle of Chenin in the fridge, which I think you'll like.'

'Still hasn't actually taken the form of an invite.'

'Are you coming or not?'

Back at number fifteen, Max stood in his en-suite bathroom, the windowless room illuminated by a light above the mirror. It was a long, thin halogen bulb and its blue tinge was unforgiving to the bags under his eyes, which seemed to get heavier and darker every year.

He pulled off his shirt and stood topless, looking at his reflection. Was forty-two a good age for a man? Possibly, but only if you put in the effort. Because it surely marked the point when you could no longer coast along, eating and drinking whatever you wanted. He turned and noticed that his flanks were puckering slightly like the fat trim on a side of beef. With a pang of self-disgust he found himself accepting that for all his aesthetic abhorrence of the gym, he could no longer pretend that the odd game of tennis against a seventy-year-old was going to be enough.

He turned on the shower and contemplated the prospect of having to find a new football game. For the nine years that he had been in Berlin he played an eight-a-side match pretty much every Tuesday night. It was a friendly game but the standard had been good. There were maybe forty of them on the email list. The first sixteen to respond got to play. Moksha, the organiser, picked the sides, which were different every week. It had been a truism among his fellow players that it wasn't the distribution of the good players that decided the outcome of the games, it was who got the worst player. The outlier. The guy who was ponderous on the ball, slow to turn, quick to panic.

For the first few years he had played, Max had always been able to identify that player and target him, harassing him off the ball, creating chances. Over time, though, he had come to find this distasteful as a tactic and had started to give the obviously worst player a bit of space and time. Towards the end, nearly a decade older, he had started to wonder if that player was him.

He stood waiting for the water to run warm. If not football, then what? It would have to be running or cycling. The utilitarian sports. The things you did when all you really cared about was the brute fact of the effort, the calories burned. And he wasn't there yet.

Max looked at himself again in the mirror, the light in his eyes, his still-brown hair. Forty-two had the potential to be a great age for a man. Whatever the cost to his dignity and his knees, he would find himself a game.

Ten minutes later, he was sitting at the kitchen table at number twenty-one, a glass of the Chenin at his elbow. The radio was playing classical music, a concert live from Wigmore Hall. Jonathan was at the stove, holding various packets and tubs up to the light so he could read the instructions. Bryony, still waiting for her taxi to arrive, was flitting in and out.

'I didn't dare ask him the score but judging by the huffing and puffing when he got home I sense that you might have been the winner.'

'He was very gracious in defeat,' said Max.

Jonathan grunted as he poured a tin of coconut milk into a pan.

'I'm sure he was,' said Bryony

She passed her husband a pair of reading glasses.

'God,' he said, once he had them on, 'you've got to make your own fucking rice.'

He pushed his glasses up his forehead and walked over to the pantry. Bryony took advantage of his absence to steal something out of one of the pans.

'It's a short play,' she said to Max. 'Only an hour. No interval. It's at the Almeida. We're going to eat afterwards on Upper Street.'

'How is the script going?'

'I'm making progress.'

'You need to get him a draft.'

'I know. I will. Soon.'

Jonathan returned with a packet of rice in hand and saw the look on her face. For a second he seemed perplexed but then he looked down at the pan.

'Did you just eat some of the chicken out of there?'

Bryony smiled impishly, made a great show of licking her fingers.

A ripple of anger rolled across Jonathan's brow.

'There were only three pieces.'

'I'm sure Max will share his spinach thing with you.'

Jonathan stood at the stove, fuming, but determined not to rise to it. Bryony flicked him with a tea towel.

Max picked a pistachio from the bowl in front of him, aware in a way that he hadn't been before of how frequently he had noticed her do this. The little licences she took. The calculated steps over the line.

He worked his thumbnail into the gap and cracked open the pistachio shell. Suddenly, it all made sense. How did you stress-test the contract other than by pushing it? It was how you checked something was alive, stopped it getting sleepy and docile. You poked it.

Behind his back, Bryony was leaning up against the oven, smirking. To Max, it all seemed freighted with risk, this. But he could see, too, how it might be the very thing that gave their relationship its animating force.

A car horn sounded in the street outside. Bryony picked up her bag.

'Bye, darlings,' she said. 'I hope you enjoy your romantic dinner for two.'

Neither of them said it, but her departure was a relief. Even a kind of victory. Like a siege that had been endured.

Jonathan topped up Max's glass.

'Marriage,' he said.

And he left it at that.

For half an hour, they ate and talked Brexit. Max tried to

convince Jonathan that its root causes were the decline of union power and a kind of generalised European civilisational exhaustion, but he was unmovable: it was all Michael Gove's fault.

Once they were done, they retired to the den with glasses of cognac and a cheese board. Jonathan flicked on a couple of lamps, one standing, the other on his desk, giving the room the feel of the inner sanctum of a private members' club. Mid-century furniture in deep cherry wood. The high polish of chrome. An aura of cigars once smoked. It sent Max into a kind of delirium.

Jonathan went to the Dylan section of his record collection and pulled *Blood on the Tracks* from the shelf. The opening track was 'Tangled Up in Blue'.

Max cut himself a slice of Comté and looked over at the wall of posters. It could be him misremembering but were there more now than when he had last visited? He couldn't be sure. He stood up and walked over to them, close enough to read the small print. There were six in total, spanning the years from 1972 to 1982.

'We put on a lot more shows than this,' said Jonathan. 'You lose stuff over the years. These are all the posters I have left.'

Max paused in front of one dated May 1977, which he felt confident hadn't been there before. It was a simple design, but striking. *The Now* in massive letters and the names of six artists underneath.

'*The Now*,' he said. 'Good name.'

'Seb came up with that. He had a talent for that sort of thing, did Seb.'

Max leaned forward to read the artists' names.

'They could have been anyone,' said Jonathan as he topped up their glasses.

Max looked at the list of artists. It wasn't by any means his most natural terrain, but he recognised a few of the names, one of whom had a foundation of some sort.

'Really?' he said. 'I mean, didn't he recently have a retrospective at the Serpentine . . .'

'*That show*,' said Jonathan, pointing at the poster, 'is the reason that he had a retrospective at the Serpentine. I'm not saying he wasn't good. *Isn't* good. He has talent. But a whole load of them had talent. He is where he is because of us. We were the kingmakers.'

Max turned round to look at him. There was a particular tone to his voice, slightly provocative, that Max recognised was a challenge, and he thought, with a swell of pride, a form of respect.

'We were two kids from crap towns who weren't interested in the way things had been done before. We imposed ourselves on the world.'

Max understood that the conversation was, at least at one level, a kind of audition – albeit one that took the form of a joust – and you didn't distinguish yourself in a joust by being passive.

'What was it Lenin said about power, back then? It was just lying in the street and we picked it up.'

He was still standing and Jonathan was sitting, looking up at him, and the light was low and they both had glasses of cognac in their hands and Max had a feeling that this was the sort of thing that he had basically been born to do.

'I envy you,' he said. 'You had an open field back then. It was there waiting for you to tear through it.'

Jonathan bridled, his knuckles whitening on his glass.

'We were overcoming centuries of people like us being held down in our place. It wasn't an open field that we ran into, it was a ceiling that we had to smash through.'

Max sat down, not least because standing over Jonathan like that made him feel a bit like a ceiling that might also have to be smashed through.

'Yeah ...' he said non-committally. 'But it all happened in the right historical conditions. You had a proper welfare state and cheap oil and housing that was effectively free by today's standards.' He gestured airily at the turntable. 'The order *was* rapidly changing.'

'The order was rapidly changing because people like Bob Dylan were rapidly *changing* it. It didn't just *happen*. He wrote that record,' he said, pointing at the shelf. 'Nobody else did. Nobody else would have done. Nobody else *could* have done.'

'Sure but something else would have been the thing that became the definitive thing, if you know what I mean. The shifts were tectonic and unstoppable and Dylan was just an expression of that. I mean, like the idea of Dylan rather than the man himself.'

'There is no idea of Dylan without the man himself.'

A flash of irritation shot across Jonathan's face.

'You had shot a whole feature film by the time you were twenty-whatever. That was you doing it. It wasn't the expression of anything.'

'I did it with a lot of help from the Arts Council,' said Max with a deflated little smile.

'Come on. *You* wrote it. *You* shot it. And it's not like they would have financed the whole thing.'

Max shrugged. 'It was 2002. The crash was years away. There was just so much cheap money kicking about. It was a particular moment. Those kids, across the road, they couldn't do it now.'

Jonathan looked incredulous.

'Do they have the desire to make it happen? Do they have the balls for it?'

The cognac had crept up on Max. Suddenly it had him by the hand and he realised it had taken him to a place that was warm and relaxing but didn't seem to have a through route.

'Are the conditions there for that?' he said distractedly. 'I just don't see it.'

'The conditions are always there for that. That's the whole point of youth. You rip it up and start again. You create the conditions.'

Max sat in his seat, uncertain where to go. His plan for the evening had involved two stags magnificently locking horns before one of them offered to finance the other's film. But it had gone awry.

He held his glass in his hand. He had, to some extent, felt like he had been failed his whole adult life. And only now was he starting to realise that the failure might actually have been his.

'For so much of my life I feel like I have been water flowing downhill,' he said. 'Just following the path of least resistance.'

Max went to sip from his cognac but put it down again, woozy.

Did he have the power to create the conditions? Did he even believe that that was possible?

'I don't feel like I have ever really *done* anything.'

Jonathan was unimpressed.

'Passivity is malign,' he said, not looking at Max. He held himself head up, like an emperor carved on a coin. 'The thing about water flowing downhill is that it's not neutral. It makes the possibility of doing something else much harder in future.'

'It deepens the groove,' said Max, drunk and defeated in his chair.

'Exactly,' said Jonathan. 'It deepens the groove.'

Sunday 15 July

'You really don't have any milk-milk?'
'We have oat, almond or hemp.'
'Hemp?! I don't even want to know what colour hemp milk is.'
Max leaned against the wall. He was queasy still from the night before and was doing his best to repress the thought that he had disgraced himself.
'Just out of interest, what happened to soya?'
Zoe closed the fridge door, a carton of oat milk in her hand.
'Nobody drinks soya milk any more.'
The kitchen smelled of toast. On the counter were supermarket herbs growing in their shop-bought pots.
'I drank too much last night and I really need a proper cup of tea.'
'Have it black?'
'It feels like a ravens leaving the tower sort of thing, this. When people stop drinking tea with cow's milk, England will have ceased to exist at some essential level.'
'I'm having mine with oat. You can do whatever you want but you have to decide now.'
'I'll have a glass of water.'
Zoe shook her head as she filled him a glass.
'I can do forty-five minutes,' said Max. 'And then I have to leave.'
He waited for her to ask why, but she didn't, so he told her anyway.
'Karolina is away for the weekend with the kids and they don't get back until at least 5 p.m. so I am going for a lunch with a

friend. Like a proper adult lunch with no crayons or high chairs or screaming.'

He followed her out of the kitchen towards the living room.

'We were at university together and he is now pretty high up on the news desk at *The Times* and after a couple of drinks he's always a reliable source of unprintable gossip.'

The living room was a mess. A wriggled-out-of sleeping bag on the sofa. Mugs of half-drunk tea, now cold and still and filmy. Crumb-covered plates. A rolled-out yoga mat.

'*The Times* news desk? Handy contact to have.'

'Not really, actually. I don't think he has ever even met their film critic.'

'How's the script?'

Max felt his skin tighten. The question elicited a complex slew of emotions. Because it was going well, at least at one level. Had he passed through into the realm of pure forms to make it happen? No, he had not. Or at least if he had, it had been an underwhelming experience that he hadn't really noticed. Nonetheless, it was ninety-five per cent done. Would it make for a landmark piece of cinema that changed the form for ever? Almost certainly not. And yet it had a kind of intrinsic wholeness, hit the right beats. As these things went, it was *good*. Which made his misstep with Jonathan all the more galling. He had pulled it back a little towards the end of their conversation, but he worried that he had prejudiced Jonathan against the project before he had even had a chance to read the script.

Still, it was nice of her to ask.

'It's going OK,' he said. 'It's nearly done.'

He looked at her quizzically.

'What is it that you do?' he asked, as he moved a laptop charger so that he could sit down at the desk. 'I don't think you've ever told me.'

'You mean for money? I have three zero-hours contracts. Mostly reception stuff. My main gig is at a co-working space.'

She laughed hollowly as she opened her laptop.

'People ask me and I say I'm working at a co-working space and I can see them thinking, *Oh, how cool she's there because she's working on her start up or whatever.* And actually I'm making sure the place doesn't run out of loo roll and looking for people's lost phone chargers.'

Max pulled his laptop out of his bag.

'That's not the long-term plan, though, is it?'

Zoe swallowed. A blush of recollection pinked the tops of her cheeks. She seemed to mull whether or not to tell about him about the cause of her embarrassment, and then decided that she would.

'The year before last, I did an internship. As an editorial assistant. Big publishing house. Three months. It was unpaid, obviously, or at least basically unpaid. We got money for our lunch and the bus. That was it. But it was competitive. *Lots* of people wanted it. I had to ask them if it would be OK if I didn't get in until 10.30 a.m. so I could live with my mum and get the train that is just about affordable, the one that's too late for the commuters.'

She took a steadying breath.

'Two years later and I am still blushing about it. I mean, asking the question... But also how I felt about asking. They were so nice as well, they let me come in at half ten and never once asked me to work a longer day to make up for it. I did, of course. I stayed late every day. But they never asked me. Not once.'

She breathed out with an involuntary force that made her nostrils flare.

'No one ever said anything about it but, honestly, you could practically *eat* the munificence. The fucking *understanding.*'

She swallowed.

'Four of us did internships that year. There was one job. I worked so hard and I wanted it so much. And I was the person who got things. At school. At university. I got things. Essay prizes.'

Zoe shut her eyes and shook her head.

'It sounds so pathetic now, doesn't it? *Essay prizes.*'

She drummed her fingernails on the table.

'The girl that got it had a first from Durham.'

Max shook his head.

'I mean, I . . .'

'*Don't say it,*' she said shrilly. 'She wasn't somebody's niece. Or, I don't know, an aristocrat or whatever.'

Before Max could say anything Zoe raised a finger and said, 'And no, they didn't give it to her because she got there before I did in the morning. Max, they gave it to her because she was really good. At everything. She just seemed to know how to do *everything.*'

Zoe shut her eyes and massaged her temples with the tips of her index fingers.

'I would have given it to her.'

She took a sip from her cup of tea.

'Her name is Jessica.'

A slightly glazed look came over her face.

'There are so few decent jobs, Max. And. There. Are. So. Many. Jessicas.'

Max pulled a face and did a little dance with his shoulders like he was literally tiptoeing round the subject.

'I don't know how to say this without it sounding really creepy,' he said, 'so I'm just going to say it. I don't know you particularly well but it seems pretty obvious to me that . . .' He paused, held his breath and then just said it. 'You're a Jessica.'

The look she gave him at this seemed to contain, confusingly, both gratitude and contempt.

'I have applied for so many jobs. Two hundred and fifty applicants is totally routine. It's five hundred sometimes. Interview after interview . . . You asked me about the long-term plan,' she said. 'The long-term plan is all about working out what to do now that I have finally realised that I don't want to be a Jessica any more.'

She sat up straight, took a long breath in through her nose.

'That's what all this is about,' she said, gesturing at her laptop. 'Liberating the Jessicas.'

Max smiled. Her righteousness was rousing, the kind that

picked you up and pulled you along. He didn't have the faintest idea what she was talking about but he wanted to be involved.

'OK,' he said. 'Let's get on with it.'

He leaned down and pulled his phone from his jacket pocket.

'But, I'm sorry. I just can't look at myself any more. We need to shoot some new footage.'

He turned his phone to camera mode and trained it on her.

'It's your turn, I'm afraid.'

Zoe groaned.

'Doesn't need to be profound or anything.'

Max started the recording.

'Tell me about something. I don't know ... tell me about your childhood.'

Just for a moment, a pained expression appeared on Zoe's face, and for a couple of seconds she looked away, lost in thought.

'A couple of years ago,' she said, looking back at the camera, 'a friend of mine got married in Mallorca and I went. Before you ask, yes, I flew. I tried to work out another way of getting there but all the other options were going to take so long and cost so much and so I flew. I try not to, but I did then.'

She mimed sarcastically begging for forgiveness.

'Anyway, the sun shone and the wedding was lovely and I swam in the sea and ate tomatoes and did all those things. And then it was time to go and I was getting a bus back to the airport when I saw this family. They were walking up a verge by the side of a slip road, six of them in a line, all of them pulling suitcases. It was one of those weird roads around airports that just aren't designed for people to be walking on. Like, there aren't even pavements. There are loads of cars coming round the corner. And there's no shade and it's really hot. And it's obviously really dangerous to be there and I could see that the parents were fighting furiously, and the kids were looking scared but also kind of resigned to it. And watching that family was like this incredible Proustian rush. Because that was my childhood.'

She gave a meek little smile.

'We were that family. We were the ones who had run out of water and were sunburned and were walking along some insanely treacherous path where we shouldn't be because my dad had some scheme or he had run out of money ... I have this memory of being on an industrial estate in the dark. It was pouring with rain. I was probably seven. Hours, we were there. No coats. Huge puddles everywhere. Why were we there? I have no idea. But it was so us, that. An industrial estate in the dark. No idea what was going on.'

Someone nearby was trimming a hedge and the noise filled the quiet as she paused.

'We never had adequate shoes. It wasn't that they were cheap. They often weren't. They were just inappropriate. Ballet pumps in the snow. A classic Dad decision.'

She exhaled scathingly through her nose.

'His whole life is just a litany of bad decisions. Over and over and over. His brother bailed him out. His sister bailed him out. And then there was no one left to bail him out. And he went bankrupt. This was like a decade ago. When I was a teenager. For at least a year, he slept on my older brother's sofa. He now lives in a rented flat and has nothing.'

Zoe shook her head.

'I'm not pretending that I didn't grow up in a house full of books. Or that I don't speak the way that I speak. I'm not pretending that my life is anything other than what it is. My godfather is a goddam theatre director. I really genuinely appreciate all the advantages that have been bestowed upon me, I really do. But actually, at the core of it all, there is materially nothing.'

It was a lovely summer morning and the light was bright through the curtainless windows.

'No, actually, that's not true,' she said. 'There isn't nothing. There is forty-five thousand pounds of debt, which grows every year.'

Zoe's expression had changed. She was staring straight down the lens of Max's phone.

'I guess everyone at some point in their lives realises that they've been sold a pup. Like a major one. One that you can't take back.'

She smiled, pushed a stray piece of hair behind her ear.

'The thing that we've come to realise lately is that when that happens the only option that's really left to you is to burn down the shop it came from.'

A few hours later, full of red wine and Westminster gossip, Max cycled his bike wobblily up Pemberton Place. A supermarket delivery van was parked outside number three, its driver loading crates of shopping onto a trolley.

He was locking up his bike when he noticed something out of the ordinary in the front garden of number five. He crossed the road to take a closer look and discovered that while he had been at lunch someone had rigged up a kind of cricket scoreboard facing out towards the street. It was an old-school kind of scoreboard, one with numbers that had to be updated by hand.

Max leaned over the garden to take a closer look. The numbers were original, clearly. Lovely old black metal plates with white sans-serif numerals, each one patinated at the edges. They had holes in the top, which allowed them to be hung on hooks.

The board they were hanging on, however, was clearly custom-made. Someone, Cal possibly, had done a nice of job it, cutting a large piece of hardboard into shape and painting it black so that it looked like a pavilion scoreboard of the sort that you found on village greens the country over.

Only, instead of columns for runs scored and wickets taken, this one had two rows, the letters painted onto the board, the numbers hung on hooks so they could be updated as often as needed:

TOTAL RENT PAID £ **3 0 0 0**
VALUE APPRECIATED £ **1 7 5 0**

Friday 20 July

'I think it's quite good,' said Douglas. 'The cricket scoreboard.' He sniffed.

'But then I was at Headingley in '81'

'Oh god,' said Gordon. 'As if anyone needed to be told.'

Douglas looked at Max, sizing him up.

'The greatest test match of them all,' he said tentatively.

'I wasn't there, obviously,' said Max softly in a way that was intended to communicate that he understood the reference. 'I was only five. But I've seen the highlights.'

Douglas smiled.

'Botham had one of those going like the clappers.'

'Don't be ridiculous,' said Gordon. 'They'd gone electronic by then. Test grounds weren't using manual scoreboards in the 1980s.'

'Not at Headingley. I can remember it as clear as a bell. The scorers battling to keep up with him as he smashed Lillee and Alderman all over the park.'

'Nonsense! I tell you what, Douglas Macallan, not for the first time I am harbouring serious doubts as to whether or not you were actually there . . .'

Max zoned out as they continued the argument. They were in the Coxes' living room, drinking Prosecco. Fifteen or so guests. Roughly half of them new to Max. It was Tabitha's birthday and, through in the kitchen, the table had been laid for a proper sit-down dinner.

He looked over nervously at Karolina, who was talking to

Bryony and Tabitha, the three of them laughing. He felt a pang of anxiety at the prospect of two of his worlds colliding, how they might navigate a potentially awkward encounter between their competing versions of his persona.

Karolina was between the two of them, smiling merrily. The conversation, much to his relief, seemed to be about her boots.

'Either way, the kids are right,' said Douglas. 'The housing market is an absolute joke.'

'They're absolutely right,' said Fiona, joining the conversation. 'We should be building social housing at the rate we did in the sixties. It's the only solution.'

'Half the social housing from the sixties is no longer fit for purpose,' said Gordon.

Fiona ignored him.

'I had a very interesting conversation with them in the street,' she said. 'They were smart and funny and I felt quite vitalised by them. I happen to think it's very imaginative, what they've done.' She looked pointedly at her husband. 'But then *I* was at Greenham Common.'

'For two nights,' said Douglas to Max, with a wink.

'At least we know she was definitely there,' said Gordon gruffly.

'You were at Greenham?' said Max.

'Just for a couple of nights,' conceded Fiona. 'I was pregnant at the time, which made it difficult to stay longer but they were two unforgettable nights.'

She drew herself up to her full height.

'I was very active back then. Women's lib. Arms trade. It was an exciting time.'

'I went on a few arms trade protests at university,' said Max. 'Although, if I'm honest, it was mostly because of a girl. It was to do with East Timor, I think.'

'That was a big campaign,' said Fiona. 'There were protests all over the country. Marches everywhere.'

She leaned forward, a wicked smile on her face.

'We didn't always just march,' she said. 'I had a friend, Sylvia

Jackson, who I was very tight with back then. Sylvia had a commanding voice. Honestly, anything she said, you would just do it. She always sounded so official. We would get wind that there was an arms fair coming up. Maybe Glasgow. Maybe Farnborough. They moved about in those days. Sylvia would call up the arms manufacturers and she would pretend to be calling from the fair, saying that she was organising the cars and she needed to double check which hotel their delegation was staying at. They always told her. *Always*. It was her voice.'

A large plate was circulating. Triangles of smoked salmon on soft bread, crusts cut off. Fiona paused so they could all take one.

'Anyway, a week before the fair we'd apply for housekeeping jobs at the hotel using false identities. They didn't look at your CV, let alone check the references. They were so desperate for staff. We were always hired on the spot.'

Jonathan was working the room with a bottle of Prosecco, topping up glasses. It was the first time Max had seen him since the night of their tennis game and he felt errant and uncertain and keen to reestablish himself.

'Three days before the delegates were due to arrive we would smuggle fish into work,' said Fiona, passing Jonathan her glass. 'Always mackerel, because mackerel were cheap. And we hid them, two in each room. One somewhere obvious so they'd find it and stop looking and one in a curtain rail because no one ever thinks to look there. Seventy-two hours out of the fridge on a summer's day and, believe me, a mackerel stinks to high heaven.'

She took her topped-up glass back from Jonathan, smiling triumphantly.

'You can't imagine the chaos,' she said. 'The rooms were unbearable. The hotels had to close. We ran rings round them.'

Jonathan looked at Max. Max looked back at him. Neither of them said anything about the ongoing rude health of the global arms trade. But neither of them needed to. Jonathan smiled and moved on.

'So I welcome our new neighbours,' continued Fiona. 'I think they have brought youth and energy to the street. And they have my full solidarity.'

'Am I right in thinking that the board is showing how much rent they've paid since they moved in?' asked Tabitha from across the room.

'That's right,' said Fiona. 'It's a scandal.'

'They've been there for a month and they have already spent four thousand pounds in rent? I thought the whole thing was that they were getting it for a steal?'

'That is a steal,' said Gordon. 'They're paying half market rate. Ask Max and Karolina.'

Karolina nodded with a grimace on her face.

'Eight grand a month!'

Tabitha did the calculation in her head.

'That's nearly a hundred grand a year,' she said tentatively.

Max nodded again.

'To rent one of these old things?'

'It's ridiculous,' said Fiona. 'We bought the damn thing for less than that.'

'Interesting to know, though,' said Tabitha, who was trying very hard to react detachedly to the news.

'Is it?'

'I mean, it makes you think funny thoughts, doesn't it? I'm not saying we would ever do it, of course. But it's just amusing to know that we could rent them all out and move to Bali, or wherever. If we wanted. From what my daughter tells me, eight grand a month would go quite a long way in Bali.'

Before anyone had the chance to properly consider the prospect of the residents of Pemberton Place moving en masse to the south Java Sea, Bryony reappeared with news: dinner was served.

They were a large group and so an extra table had been summoned up from the basement and called into service. As had more chairs. Four from the garden and a couple from Tabitha's. Max, being the youngest male, had to make do with a 1980s office chair on roller wheels, which squeaked every time he moved.

Toasts were made. To Tabitha, obviously, on this, her seventy-first birthday. And then to their hosts. And finally to Karolina and their collective delight at finally meeting her properly.

Once the soup was served, the table quickly settled into three conversational groups. Jonathan, Gordon and Douglas were at one end. Fiona and two other couples were at the other, talking about the terrible state of the local Tube station. And then there was Karolina, flanked on either side by Bryony and Tabitha, with Max, doing his best, despite his chair, to lean over the table to join them.

Karolina, who had drunk three glasses of Prosecco, was greatly enjoying the clubbable attention of her two immediate neighbours.

'How are you finding it, our little street?'

'I love it. It's like Mary Poppins with all the cherry trees and the pretty houses. I'm always half-expecting Julie Andrews to fly in on an umbrella.'

'Not that you'd need her of course,' said Tabitha. 'Not with Max on hand. Such a present father.'

'Is he?' said Karolina, looking across the table at him quizzically.

Max shifted in his seat.

'So present and so engaged.'

'Such a beautifully laid table,' said Max in an act of transparent desperation. 'The soup is delicious.'

'I remember him sleeping pretty soundly through the 4 a.m. feeding sessions,' said Karolina, looking pointedly across the table at him.

Max had his head in his hands.

'Oh, look at him,' said Bryony. 'He knows he's our favourite.'

'All of you are,' said Tabitha. 'You all just fit right in, my dear. You and your two Mary Poppins children. My goodness, they are so lovely.'

'*So* lovely,' said Bryony. 'And spirited. And such good hair.'

On it went like this for a while, Bryony and Tabitha lavishing them with praise, Karolina taking it all in good grace, Max getting ever more flustered.

'You didn't introduce us to your parents,' said Bryony.

Max looked at her, quizzically.

'They were here on Wednesday,' she continued.

'I know,' said Max, who was trying to work out why she thought that introducing them to his parents was some kind of priority.

'We would have loved to have met them.'

Max rolled a shoulder.

'They have total tunnel vision when it comes to the kids,' he said. 'My nieces and nephews are all much older. Our two are the babes of the flock. They are adored to an almost absurd degree.'

He picked a breadcrumb from the tabletop. He hadn't deliberately kept his parents away from them. But he hadn't tried to engineer an encounter, either. If they had met, it would have doubtlessly been polite, warm even, but still the thought of it made him squirm a little.

'Did they like our little street?'

Max looked at Bryony. They had been impressed, of course. By the street. The cherry trees and period stained-glass. But the deeper meaning had surely been lost on them. What these houses in this context really meant. A particular kind of *bien pensant* good taste taken to its upper limit, but not further. If that was what Bryony was angling at and wanted confirmation of, she wasn't going to get it here.

'Yeah, they liked it fine,' he said. 'They were particularly taken with the Square. And how easy it is to get to the Heath.'

Bryony smiled a non-smile and Max felt a brief flash of triumph on behalf of his parents. Had they ever wanted it, this life? His mum surely hadn't. Or at least if she had, it was a desire she had kept buried deep within her. London, for her, as least as far as Max could tell, was both overwhelming and slightly contemptible, a place you endured – for a West End show or your grandchildren or whatever – then got out as quickly as you could.

His dad? He was more complicated. A bright working-class boy. Passed the eleven plus. Became a teacher. Because that's what they did, boys like him. The ones predisposed to being contained by glass ceilings, rather than smashing through them.

On the face of it, he had had a happy life. Teaching chemistry GCSE. Never rich, but never poor. A well-liked man, active in his community.

But, intelligible perhaps only to Max, was there a nagging dissatisfaction that ran through his sensible demeanour, a splinter of regret at the paths not taken?

Max felt a familiar niggle. His dad had been so thrilled when *Flamingoland* had come out. *So* proud. And that had felt like a major accomplishment for Max because he had understood, even then, how as a son you could have obligations. Opportunities that you couldn't let pass by. And he hadn't. He had taken the chance. For himself, of course, but also for his dad. The film had been a kind of repayment on the ledger. But although his dad would never dream of saying so, Max knew that it wasn't enough. *Flamingoland* was supposed to have been the start of something. Not its apex.

'Truth be told, I think they preferred Berlin,' he said, which was a total fabrication but felt good, nonetheless.

He rolled his chair away from the table and got up to help clear the soup bowls. When he returned, the conversation had moved on to the new residents of the street.

'There is something fundamentally wrong with the way they wear clothes,' Karolina was saying, a wicked smile on her face after all the Prosecco. 'I know it's awful to say it but it's the truth.'

'We couldn't possibly comment, could we, Tabs darling?'

Tabitha mimed zipping her lips shut.

'Isn't the whole point of being young that you dress in a way that irritates people who are older than you?' said Max as he sat down. 'I remember coming home with a Bad Religion T-shirt when I was a kid. It had *Fuck Armageddon This is Hell* written on the sleeves. My mum made me take it back.'

'I bet she did,' shouted Tabitha.

'Obviously, I caved, but I think the point stands.'

'No, yeah, fine,' said Karolina, sounding more Swedish than ever. 'I totally get that. But my issue isn't that they're too sexy or risqué or – I don't know – *outré* or whatever. They're just wrong.

The shapes are wrong. When they wear baggy stuff it's baggy in the wrong places. They wear things that are the wrong length but not in an interesting kind of arty way. Just wrong!'

'The shape of their trousers,' said Bryony. 'It's just painful to watch sometimes.'

Karolina pointed at her in a gesture of gleeful confirmation.

Max, faced with the unlikely and slightly dizzying coalition of Karolina and Bryony, found himself oddly compelled to defend Zoe, even though they weren't, he felt fairly sure, talking explicitly about her.

'I don't know, sounds to me like that's them doing it right, doesn't it? I mean, if you're confronted with a basically unshockable world then perhaps a kind of studied incompetence is the only space you can carve out for yourselves.'

'But that's the whole thing, I don't think it's studied.'

'I don't know. I think they're sharper than we give them credit for. Or at least I have sometimes given them credit.'

The table was heaving with dishes. Green salads. New potatoes tossed in butter and chopped herbs. Carrots roasted in honey and spices. A chicken stuffed with yellow lemons.

'I'm coming to realise now that the nineties were a funny decade to come of age. The long nineties is like, what, '89 to 2001? The Wall coming down to 9/11. I was thirteen when it started. Twenty-five when it finished. A pretty definitive time in anyone's life.'

Max realised the table had quietened and everyone was listening to him, Jonathan included.

'Looking back now, I realise it was kind of like this geopolitical interregnum. Yeah, there was the war in the Balkans. And the genocide in Rwanda. And of course a load of other stuff, but it did feel that things were moving in a particular direction.'

'Fukuyama's book,' said Douglas in one of his characteristic verb-free utterances.

'Exactly,' said Max. He was looking at Jonathan now. 'It was literally called *The End of History*. I was fifteen when that was published. I didn't read it – I mean, I was fifteen, of course I didn't read it – but it did capture something of the spirit of the age. This weird ten, twelve years when it looked the Whigs might have been right.'

Jonathan smiled. It wasn't a father's smile. Max already had a dad. And Jonathan already had children. But it was indulgent.

'You know, that we really were on a path of progress,' he continued. 'That we were moving towards something and over time we'd finesse it and improve it. I was lucky to grow up in that environment. I genuinely thought things were only going to get better.'

He picked up his napkin, pulled it from its ring.

'And they've never thought that,' he said. 'Not ever in their lives.'

Later, once the babysitter had been paid and put in a taxi, Karolina was in her floral print pyjamas, sitting up in bed.

'I'm not saying you were flirting with her but you were not not flirting with her.'

Max pulled an incredulous face.

'And isn't that kind of flirtier than flirting?'

Max folded his trousers and hung them on the back of a chair which no one ever sat on, but was invaluable as a kind of staging post for the wardrobe.

'She's *sixty-five*.'

'I know. She's sixty-five. Why are you flirting with her?'

'It's . . . I *wasn't*. She's *sixty-five*.'

Karolina cocked her head.

'That conversation over coffee about your film. That was too much. *Our auteur.* How many times did she say that?'

Max felt suddenly ridiculous. This thing that to this point had existed wholly in his head had been given form. And it was a farce.

'Yeah, that's all . . . I mean, she'd had a few drinks by that point and I don't know how seriously she means all that . . .'

Karolina was laughing to herself.

'And the way she touches you.'

Max blushed. And with it came a stab of resentment that the feelings he had had were ridiculous to her.

'They both touch me. It's like I'm a dog or something. Something that it's OK to pet.'

'The way she touches you is different to the way that Tabitha touches you.'

'I don't think so.'

Karolina laughed again.

'Watch out, Harold,' she said. 'Maude's coming for you.'

Monday 23 July

The scoreboard had made page eight of that day's *Evening Standard*. A single-column story illustrated with a small picture.

'You've made the papers,' he said, passing her a copy that he had picked up on the Tube on the way home.

Zoe glanced over at it, but uninterestedly, having clearly already seen it.

'They're making out that we're a bunch of spoiled brats who think the world owes them a north London townhouse.'

She was at the desk already, her laptop open. It was Monday night. 8 p.m. Time for her third and final editing lesson.

'Are we talking about the same piece?'

'That's the subtext.'

Max hovered, wondering if he was going to be offered a cup of tea. Then, deciding he wasn't, sat down beside her. In the corner of the room was a large box, recently delivered and unopened, its edges bound with tape.

'That's not how I read it...'

She looked across at him.

'Lazy journalism in a shit paper.'

It was a lovely July evening. Pink clouds. Through the window, Max could see two blackbirds sitting on the garden fence.

'It's a hundred-word colour piece in the *Standard*,' he said. 'I think you're probably expecting a bit...'

'No one my age expects *anything* of the corporate media,' she said, turning her attention back to her laptop.

He pulled his laptop from his rucksack, making a big show of staying quiet so he wouldn't say the wrong thing. Zoe clocked this and clenched her jaw.

'This house will go up in value by more than we will earn this year. All eight of us combined. Whether or not anything gets invested into it. It will out-earn us just sitting here, doing nothing. And yet we're the ones who work in order to service the debt on the asset.'

Max made a gesture with his hands that was intended to illustrate both concession to the point and solidarity.

'It is hard to imagine a system that could be less optimally designed,' he said.

It was warm still and they were both in jeans and white T-shirts, which made it look, Max noticed, like they were colleagues on the shop floor of some self-consciously utilitarian lifestyle brand. He opened up his laptop, pulled his reading glasses out from their case.

'Just out of interest, why are you learning to edit?'

'We're working on a film.'

'Is the film part of this?' he asked, pointing to the *Standard* and then out to the front garden.

'I guess you could say that it's another chapter of the same project.'

'Right,' he said. 'Does that make me a collaborator?'

She laughed.

'Do you want to be a collaborator?'

'I don't know. I don't know what the project is.'

Zoe looked at him, took stock.

'Consciousness raising,' she said. 'At least for now. But that's where everything starts, right?'

She tucked a stray hair behind her ear.

'Housing is the gateway drug. Everyone gets it. San Francisco. New York. Amsterdam. Dublin. Paris. The crisis is everywhere and it's always people my age who are getting it in the neck. You start with the most obvious pressing thing and get people on side. Then you can start talking about other structural inequalities. The way we're selling out the future and everyone who will inhabit it.'

Max watched her as she spoke. The tattoos and her hair, which he was starting to think might be self-cut, conveyed a haphazardness, but he could see now that she was more strategic than he had realised.

'Why Pemberton Place?'

'It's where we ended up. We registered with like a dozen estate agents, told them we wanted to be somewhere round here and that it didn't matter what the terms were as long as it was cheap.'

'So it was just chance that you ended up here?'

'Yeah, but it's worked out nicely, hasn't it? These houses are perfect. You want to capture the insane misallocation of resources then this is where you come. Some of them have one person living in them. One person! In these massive houses!'

Max had the little chamois from his glasses case and was cleaning the lenses. He smiled.

'None of them have to downsize because they're on these massive final-salary pension schemes,' continued Zoe. 'The very same pension schemes which own thirty per cent of all fossil fuel shares. They're screwing us from all sides.'

She double-clicked on her mousepad.

'Talk to Cal about it. Pensions are his new obsession. There are two trillion pounds in British pensions. *Two trillion*. Think what kind of world you could build if you put that money to good use rather than just maximising returns for a load of already wealthy old people.'

Max nodded in agreement. He didn't have a pension either.

'I bumped into Cal yesterday,' he said.

'You did?'

'I complimented him on his woodwork skills.'

'He will have liked that. Even if it did come from you.'

'We had a nice conversation, actually. We talked tools. We share a weakness for a well-designed wood saw.'

'That's nice.'

'I couldn't help but wonder if it was all easier because you weren't there. He was a bit less territorial.'

Zoe didn't take her gaze from her screen, but Max detected a hint of a smile.

'Laurie's thinking about moving to Folkestone,' she said.

Max looked at her and thought about challenging this abrupt change of subject but chose not to.

'Laurie's the American one, right?'

Zoe nodded.

'The genetically superior hair. The strong Ivy League vibe.'

'She went to Noter Daym,' said Zoe, with a heavy emphasis on the American pronunciation.

'*Noter Daym*,' said Max. He smiled at the sound of it. The Americanness of it, the way it took something old and from it minted something new.

'Is Noter Daym Ivy League?'

'No idea,' said Max breezily. He stopped. 'Did you just say she's moving to *Folkestone*?'

'She's thinking about it.'

'Really? I mean, shouldn't she be living in like Seattle or Santa Monica or somewhere? What is she going to do in Folkestone? Play the amusement arcades?'

'Folkestone's kind of cool.'

'Yeah. Fine. I'm sure there are, I don't know, two nice restaurants, or whatever. But it's still *Folkestone*.' Max cast about despairingly. 'I'm just like . . . I don't know. She's so *expensive* looking.'

'She really likes it there.'

Max shook his head.

'There is part of me that can never not be slightly suspicious of Americans that choose to live here and not there.'

'Really? She makes it sound like hell on earth.'

'Yeah, OK. Some of it's awful and the bits of it that are awful are really awfully awful. But it's a continent. Of course bits of it are awful. Bits of Europe are awful. The UK is *mostly* awful.'

'For three months of the year her aunt has to wear a mask when she goes outside because of the forest fires, which is the absolute definition of karmic retribution.'

Max finally got round to putting on his glasses.

'I'm not pretending it's perfect. It's obviously not. But, I don't know, it's the *main stage*.'

'She says half her mum's family have fully signed up. They go to the rallies. Wear the hats. Believe the craziest shit.'

Max flinched. He found it almost impossible to reconcile the actually existing reality with the country of *Slacker* and *Midnight Cowboy* and *Paris is Burning* that existed in his head.

'I went to the local comp,' he said. 'Late eighties. Early nineties. We played football but not with the same enthusiasm people do now. Back then, it felt so English and parochial. All the really hip kids played basketball.'

He mimed shooting at the hoop, flipping the ball out of his right hand, guiding it with his left.

'Michael Jordan was in his pomp. We couldn't watch the games because they weren't on TV, so we had to kind of dream them. Honestly, the Chicago Bulls were the coolest thing you could possibly imagine.'

He smiled at the innocence of the memory.

'We played American football in the playground, or at least our approximation of it. We reverse engineered the rules from a computer game.'

'This is in 1980s Hertfordshire?'

'People went to France. You could get there on a ferry. It had no mystery. Nobody went to America. It was so far away. It felt like the most exotic thing in the world.'

Zoe smiled.

'Maybe that's how Laurie feels about Folkestone?'

Max laughed.

'I can just imagine her growing up on the Upper West Side, dreaming of the unknown mysteries of the south Kent coast.'

Zoe walked across the room and picked up a portable speaker, synced it with her phone.

'She said she saw you coming out of their house the other night. Laurie did.'

Max smiled. You couldn't live on Pemberton Place and not know immediately which house she was talking about.

'We were there for dinner. A birthday celebration for one of their friends.'

Zoe was scrolling through her music library.

'She's beautiful, isn't she?' she said, without looking up.

They weren't talking about Laurie any more.

'She is. Hers is the kind of beauty that doesn't require qualification. She isn't beautiful for sixty-five, she's just beautiful.'

Max looked at the top of Zoe's bowed head, the dark roots at her hair parting.

'Anyone can be beautiful when they're young,' he said. 'When you get to her age it takes on a different quality. It feels like the expression of something deeper. Even though it's obviously not. But it gives her a quality that's kind of hypnotic, I guess.'

Zoe finally settled on a song.

'Are you hypnotised?' she asked as the first bars of it sounded through the room.

'I'm a married man, twenty years her junior.'

'That's not an answer.'

'You can recognise the hypnotic power of something without yourself being hypnotised.'

'I don't think that's an answer, either.'

'I'm not hypnotised,' said Max, feeling at least moderately sure that this was true.

'Shall we get to it?' she asked.

'Let's.'

For forty minutes, they edited. Max took her through the audio tools. Showing her how background noise could be cleaned up and voiceovers laid over images. When they were nearly done, Max went to show her the professional version of the software, only to find that his subscription had just lapsed and his card details needed updating.

'Two seconds,' he said, pulling his wallet from his back pocket.

'You don't need to . . .'

'No, it's fine. Honestly, I need to do this anyway. Give me two secs.'

He took his debit card from his wallet and placed both on the desk in front of him. While he was filling in the details on the screen, Zoe pulled his driving licence from its slot.

'Nice picture,' she said.

'I don't know what was going on with my hair that day.'

'Sixteenth of September,' she said, reading his date of birth. 'I knew it! You are the most Virgo Virgo I have ever met.'

'I don't think anyone ever says that in a good way, do they?'

Zoe made a you-said-it-not-me face.

'Apart from it all being unalloyed horseshit, that's the main reason I've never been interested in the Zodiac. Being a Virgo is just so *meh*.'

He double-checked the sixteen-digit number against his card.

'If I was one of the badass signs, I might have got into it. Is Scorpio a good one? Scorpio sounds good. Who would want to be a virgin when you could be a scorpion? Or a lion? I would be into it if I was a Leo.'

'You have a lot of Leo rising about you.'

As he entered his card's expiry date, Max thought about asking what she meant by this but decided against it.

'The zodiac I *am* into is the Chinese one,' he said. 'In their one, I am a Fire Dragon. We only come around once every sixty years. There won't be any more until 2036.'

He turned his card over to read the three-digit number on the back.

'You're probably a rat or a sheep.'

Zoe smiled.

'You think that it's the big difference between us. The age gap. But it's not. It's that you're a Virgo and I'm a Gemini.'

Max rocked his head back and forced out a laugh.

'I was born in 1976 and you were born in . . .'

'1993.'

'1993! A great year. I remember it well. *In Utero. Modern Life is Rubbish. Siamese Dream* . . .'

He paused, thought hard about it.

'... and *Pablo Honey*!'

Zoe laughed.

'I was seventeen. You, on the other hand, were seventeen in 2010. And there are many actual clear-cut differences between those experiences. The times were so different. Not just politics, but culture and technology. And that has a huge impact, on our expectations, on the *imaginary*. It's massive. Whether you were born in September or April or whatever makes no difference at all.'

'That is literally the most Virgo thing I have ever heard.'

Max laughed.

'So you're a Gemini,' he said. 'That's the twins, right? Is it any good, Gemini? I obviously know nothing about it.'

'It's not a question of good or bad,' she said. 'That's not how it works.' She smiled. 'But Virgos and Geminis do actually work really well together.'

They were looking at each other now and there was, hanging in the air, an ambiguity as to whether *work well together* in this context was intended collegially or romantically.

His laptop made a pinging noise. The professional software had updated. He showed her its vast number of add-ons and applications and talked through its capabilities until her eyes started to glaze and they returned to the simpler package and the piece of film they were working on.

'And then if you click that it will sync the sound back in,' said Max eventually.

Zoe clicked on an icon and two lines came together.

'That's it?'

Max nodded.

'And so endeth the lesson,' he said. 'You have passed editing 101. That's us done.'

Zoe turned to look at him.

'I don't think so.'

The light was crepuscular. Kate Bush was singing about running up a hill.

'No?' said Max.

'You're our point man, Cishet.'

'I am?'

'We need a go-between.'

Max laughed. He looked over his shoulder, through the front window at the houses opposite. Tabitha. Gordon. Down the road, the Coxes.

'I told you the past was a foreign country,' he said with a wry laugh.

Zoe was smiling.

'OK. I accept it. You do things differently there,' she said.

Max folded shut his laptop.

'We do and we don't. They're all right, you know. They're mostly on your side. A lot of them were doing this kind of stuff at your age? They get it.'

Zoe's tone was light but determined.

'No, they don't,' she said. 'They might think they do, but they really don't. And soon they *really* won't.'

Wednesday 25 July

'Typical bloody *Guardian* going massively overboard about the whole thing,' said Gordon. He was eating salted peanuts and reading the newspaper. 'This dickhead is making out that they are the second coming of the Situationists.'

They were in Douglas and Fiona's living room: the two hosts on a sofa, Bryony, Tabitha and Gordon in easy chairs. Max up on his feet and prowling.

All three sides of the room were lined with bookshelves. One wall was occupied wholly by many decades' worth of *National Geographics*, the sun-faded spines running the full gamut of yellows from daffodil-bright to old straw.

'A single cricket scoreboard doesn't make you Guy De-bloody-bord.'

Max looked over at him. The broken blood vessels on his cheeks were like feathery calligraphy, the words no longer legible but the message clear: he had said yes to everything, at every opportunity.

'Look at his byline picture. Doesn't look like he's started shaving. We actually remember 1968, you little worm.'

'Rein it in, Gordon,' said Fiona.

The newspaper was spread out on the coffee table. The article in question had been published that day. Gordon read a paragraph aloud.

Pemberton Place is an exemplar of the gentrification that has reshaped many of London's neighbourhoods. Downtrodden as recently as the nineties, Dunstan Park has become one of the capital's most desirable areas. Since 1990, the average price of a house on Pemberton Place has gone up roughly two thousand per cent.

'Can you have two thousand per cent?' asked Tabitha. 'Is that how per cent works?'

'Means they've gone up twentyfold,' said Gordon. 'Which is probably about right. Prices had bottomed in the early nineties. Then, they were going for less than what we paid for them.'

The image accompanying the text had been shot in the middle of the day, the sun high in the sky. Zoe, Cal and their flatmates were assembled in the front garden of number five, some standing, others sitting on the low wall, the cricket scoreboard visible behind them.

'I see Max's little friend is front and centre,' said Bryony.

Max heard this and maintained, he hoped, an impassivity. It was interesting and slightly disquieting to know that his movements were being monitored. And intriguing, too, to hear the tone of Bryony's voice, which was, he thought, a little piqued.

Tabitha looked down her nose at the paper.

'She won't age well.'

A great roar went up. Douglas laughed so hard some gin and tonic dribbled out his nose.

'*Tabitha*,' said Fiona.

'Well, imagine being our age and covered in all those tattoos,' continued Tabitha.

Gordon clapped his hands in delight.

'You come for us and we'll come for you,' he shouted.

'I don't think anyone is coming for anyone,' said Max. He had his back to them, while he read book titles, looked at the assorted trinkets and curios.

'The implication of this piece is that it's us lot who are the problem,' said Gordon. 'And that the residents of this one randomly selected street should be forced to wear sackcloth and ashes and turn their homes into refuges for all of the world's waifs and strays.'

Max laughed.

'No,' he said, 'that's really not the implication of the piece.'

'Max, can you please tell them that we're on their side,' said Fiona. 'Whatever that old grouch says.'

The paint on the walls was pale green, the out-of-reach corners filled with cobwebs so thick with dust that they had a heavy, velvety look, like curtains in an old theatre.

'Speak for yourself,' said Gordon. 'I've had more than enough of them, thanks. They can all piss off as far as I'm concerned.'

Above the television, there was a shelf of VHS tapes. Some were shop-bought. *Three Colours: Blue*. *The Piano Teacher*. Others had been bought blank for taping from the television. On these, the spine stickers had been overwritten with every re-recording creating a palimpsest of the family's evolving taste in film. Max paused, reading the names. *Grease 2. American Beauty. The Reader. The King's Speech.*

'They're going to be gone as soon as the owner gets planning permission,' he said.

'Well, let's hope the council pull their bloody finger out,' said Gordon.

Outside, it was raining. Max paused at the window. Across the road, he could see number five. The had strung some fairy lights in the window. Music was playing. The front garden was filled with bikes.

'Anyway,' said Tabitha, rattling a cloth bag. 'Are we going to play?'

The Scrabble game had been in the diary for a couple of weeks. Max sat down next to Tabitha, suddenly aware that it was wearing a bit thin, all this. It was one thing listening to records and drinking twenty-year-old whisky in Jonathan's den, but another altogether to be spending your Friday night playing board games with a load of people old enough to be your parents.

'No French words,' said Gordon. 'I'm looking at you, Douglas Macallan.'

The bag was passed around, each of them taking seven tiles, Max slightly sullenly. Without Jonathan, the group dynamic suffered. Gordon was too dominant. Bryony was subdued. Max lacked an intellectual foil. He looked down at his hand, which was vowel-heavy, irritated at himself and the direction his life seemed to have taken.

For half an hour, they played. At times, the game felt like a one-sided linguistic conspiracy, with Max the lone voice of reason.

'Are we letting him have *coorie*?' he said despairingly at Douglas's second effort.

'It's an old Scots word,' said Fiona. 'It's what you do on a dreich day.'

'Surely, *elne* isn't a word,' he said as Tabitha counted up her points.

'My grandmother used to measure cloth in *elnes*,' said Gordon.

As the board filled and there were fewer spaces available, the game slowed down. Particularly when it was Douglas's turn. He was, Max had noticed, given to moments of absolute lizard stillness, sometimes mid-conversation. Max couldn't tell if they were occasions of total blankness, a kind of total neurological shutdown, or if during them Douglas was off somewhere else, lost in the farthest reaches of some extravagantly jewelled cave full of memories and associations and deep feelings.

'Is it my go?' he said eventually.

'Oh, for goodness sake,' said Fiona.

'Have you been waiting for me?'

'Since last Thursday,' said Gordon.

'Sorry,' said Tabitha to Max. 'We're not quite as fast as we used to be.'

Max waved a hand at her.

'I have a five-year-old and a three-year-old,' he said. 'I have discovered powers of forbearance I had no idea I possessed.'

He looked over at Douglas, who was rearranging his tiles for the hundredth time.

'This is nothing compared to the experience of standing for a full hour next to a Peppa Pig ride in a shopping centre.'

He looked up at the ceiling and found himself transported back to the mechanised pig and its strategic siting, just outside the toilets.

'Time takes on an almost exquisite slowness. I don't think the Buddha himself ever achieved the kind of absolute presence and clear-sightedness you get after forty-five minutes standing next to one of those machines, steadfastly refusing to put a pound coin in the damn thing. It's the purest kind of feeling, knowing that you can do it, that you're going to hold the line however loud and long they scream.'

Tabitha laughed.

'To be a true artist you need knowledge of the full range of human experience,' she said, patting him on the thigh.

Finally, Douglas took his turn. He placed an *n* and an *e* on the board for the word *net*. With the double-word score, it earned him six points.

'When he lived in Cuba, Hemingway used to go to watch the executions,' said Max, turning the board through ninety degrees. 'Each of us must take himself to the limit in his own way.'

He looked at the board, thought about it for a bit and then played. Outside, in the street, a dog barked.

'You could have had *qi* on a triple-letter score. Thirty-one points,' said Gordon.

'I'm not into those little Scrabble words,' said Max.

'Those *little Scrabble words* are how you win the game.'

'Yeah, probably. But where is the glory in that?'

'Scrabble isn't about glory. It's about who has got the most points at the end.'

Gordon picked the final tile from his rack and played it for eight points. He then laboriously went round deducting the value of their remaining tiles from everyone else's score.

Max finished third with 112.

'I win,' said Gordon.

'And we acknowledge your greatness,' said Max in a fantastically disingenuous voice.

Gordon scowled. He was a man who didn't do defeat. Which made it doubly difficult for him to deal with Max, who had accepted defeat as a way of defeating defeat. As a way to *transcend* defeat. And in doing so had turned defeat into a kind of victory, a play that was proving to be particularly successful in front of his current audience.

Gordon was muttering to himself as he got up to go to the toilet. Fiona followed him out, off to the kitchen to make tea, taking Tabitha along with her to help. Douglas stayed in his seat but was either asleep or in some unhearing sleep-like state.

Max took the opportunity to lean forward and whisper conspiratorially, 'It's nearly done, the script.'

Bryony, who had been quiet and withdrawn, was suddenly animated. She grabbed his hand.

'Really?'

'A couple of scenes need tidying up but then it'll be good to go.'

'Have you talked to him about it yet? I get the impression he knows nothing about it.'

She was still holding his hand and his gaze.

'I've been keeping my powder dry.'

'That's good. He'll like that. He's not interested in process. He wants the finished thing. He has an instinct. A *nose*.'

'You've been so kind,' he said. 'You've energised me more than you could know.'

'I believe in you,' she said. 'Totally.'

Max felt a kind of massing sensation in his chest. He looked at Bryony. Bryony looked at him.

The door creaked open.

'I still can't believe that we've been splashed all over the *Guardian*,' said Tabitha as she walked back into the room with a tray of mugs and spoons, a little jug of milk.

'We've got to stop talking about it being *us*,' said Fiona, who was just behind her with a teapot and a box of chocolates. 'What they're doing. It's not about us. It just happens to be *here*.'

Max looked over at her.

'You reckon?'

'Yes,' said Fiona as she poured the first cup. 'It's nothing to do with us.'

'I think it kind of is,' he said. 'I don't want to be indelicate about it but your generation have done pretty well from the thing that's causing them all the pain.'

'It's utterly ludicrous to talk about our generation as if we're a monolithic block. There are plenty of pensioners in poverty.'

'Yeah, but they're not doing this in Middlesbrough, are they? I'm pretty sure they don't have any beef with the old ladies in their mobile homes in Skegness. But...' He smiled as he paused. '... In *this* context, it kind of *is* a generational thing, isn't it?'

'It's such a lazy way of looking at the world. A sixty-eight-year-old care worker has more in common with a twenty-three-year-old care worker than they do with the man who owns the care home.'

'I hadn't realised Pemberton Place was full of care workers,' said Max innocently.

Fiona ignored him.

'All generations have different challenges to face and we would be able to overcome them far better if we all worked together.'

Max examined the guide to the chocolates in the box.

'That'll probably be easier for you lot on your final-salary pensions. The rest of us are going to be too busy working until we die.'

'Oh, come on,' said Tabitha. 'We've paid in.'

'No, you haven't,' he said, picking out a caramel.

'We *absolutely* have.'

'Yeah, you paid in, but it's not *your* money. You were paying for your parents. You're relying on us paying for you.'

Gordon scoffed. He had returned from wherever he had been with a full glass of red wine, despite the rest of them having moved on to tea.

'And you're relying on them paying in for you,' he said, nodding in the direction of number five. 'So good bloody luck with that.'

'The thing I don't understand,' said Tabitha, 'is why they've done it *here*. I mean, this is hardly Millionaire's Row.'

'I think that's probably the point,' said Max. 'That this isn't just about the one per...'

'Millionaire's Row?' said Gordon. 'It was more like Skid Row when we moved in. The state of the houses. My god, the damp in the walls.'

He reached over and plucked a chocolate from the box.

'The idea that all this fell in our laps, it's ridiculous. We worked bloody hard on these houses! Do you think they looked like this when we bought them? This place was barely a house when Tabs moved in.'

Tabitha sat up straight in her chair, readying herself for her moment in the spotlight.

'For years, it wasn't even a building site,' she said. 'There wasn't any building going on! It was just a site. The children loved it of course.'

'They loved it!' said Fiona.

'To them, it was an empty stage.'

'It was,' said Bryony, 'it was an empty stage.'

'Do you remember the plays they used to put on? Endless plays.'

'They would make tickets and up and down the street they'd go, knocking on doors, inviting everyone along.'

'What were those grey things?' asked Bryony. 'The insulation things for the pipes?'

'Polyethylene lagging,' said Gordon. 'Tabs's builder had ordered a bloody load of it and then the idiot went bust. And so there was a great pile of it lying about the place for months while she tried to find a new contractor.'

He stood up with surprising nimbleness and adopted the pose of a fencer, his right arm in front of him clutching a make-believe sword, his left raised balletically behind him.

'Was great news for the kids, though. Polyethylene keeps its shape nicely through the air and you can hit someone as hard as you can with it and it doesn't hurt.'

He feinted and then parried and then lunged.

'The perfect stage sword.'

'*En garde*,' shouted Douglas.

The mood had shifted. The light in the room seemed rounder, warmer. It was as if they had been transported back, the five of them, to those glory days. Postures improved. Eyes brightened.

'It was swashbucklers only for the Pemberton Players in the summer of 1992,' said Tabitha.

'I remember Jonathan having to play Cardinal Richelieu in a couple of particularly violent productions,' said Bryony.

Max was the audience. They had all turned slightly towards him, elders round a campfire passing on the codes and rituals.

'How many times did they do *The Three Musketeers*?'

'I remember a terribly wet week when I think it was on every night.'

To talk about it was to consecrate it, give it symbolic meaning. These were their lives, their extraordinary and never-to-be-repeated lives.

'It alternated with *Robin Hood*,' said Gordon.

'Jonathan was the Sheriff of Nottingham a couple of times as well,' said Bryony. 'It was death by a thousand cuts.'

'They were amazing days,' said Fiona. 'The children were in and out of each other's houses. It was practically a commune.'

'Think about them now, those rough and ready houses.'

'Do you remember when we stripped your wallpaper, Tabs?' said Gordon. 'And all the old plaster came off with it.'

'I thought the ceiling was going to fall down.'

'Right back to the lath, we went. The dust. My god, it was black as coal.'

'And so fine. It went everywhere.'

'It was a treasure trove, the inside of that wall,' said Douglas. 'A cigarette tin from the 1860s. Do you remember it? A lovely little metal thing.'

'There were tools in there. A chisel.'

'Pages from a newspaper. So faded you could barely read them.'

'Why are you looking at us like that?' said Tabitha, staring fixedly at Max.

Max was sitting back in his chair, smiling.

'I'm indulging,' he said. 'That's my role, isn't it? I indulge. And they're nice stories. The cigarette tin and the chisel. And the plays sound lovely. I would pay good money to see old Cardinal Cox trying to defend the kingdom with just a piece of polyethylene.'

'But that's not it, though, is it? You've got that bloody grin again.'

Max did his I-can't-win-here shrug.

'*What?*'

'OK,' he said. 'I don't want to be a ... you know ... I don't want to be a knob about it, or anything, but really we all know that the wallpaper is neither here nor there, right?'

He gesticulated airily over his shoulder.

'That empty lot where the swings are. If that had planning permission it would be worth, what, at least a million quid?'

Tabitha went to protest, until she saw Gordon's concessionary gesture, and stopped.

'Since they put that sign up, number five has gone up in value by £2,700.'

'That's their calculation,' said Douglas.

'Yeah, and we could argue the toss over the exact amount, but you and I both know that they're broadly right.'

Max smiled a meek little half-smile.

'For all the effort you no doubt put in, we can agree, can't we, that there have been forces at play beyond your DIY skills?'

Five minutes later, he was home. Eventually, they had all embarrassedly conceded his point and then moved the conversation on, which had been his cue to leave.

He threw his keys into a pot by the front door and walked into the kitchen. Karolina was sitting at the table drinking a glass of wine and eating peanut butter out of the jar with a stick of celery.

'You're down already.'

'Five minutes ago,' she said. 'We finished a bit early.'

She was tired, clearly; there were heavy bags under her eyes. She picked up her glass and took a pensive sip.

'Dare I ask?' he said.

'It was ... Oh, you know.'

'Let me guess. The Valet was on the call?'

The Valet was her name for the American lead on the project she was working on. Every time she, or indeed any other woman, suggested anything, he said, *let's park that over here for a moment.*

'He is *such* a dick.'

Max pulled a glass from the shelf and sat down in the seat next to her.

'I'm sorry.'

He poured himself a small glass of red, less because he wanted it, more out of solidarity.

'The thing that makes him so impossible is that he does actually care about the crisis. He might be a wanker but he is actually making a difference.'

Karolina put her bare foot up on Max's lap so he could rub it.

'He knows how to talk to them, the executives. And they're actually listening. They listen to him. And why not? These guys, they have kids, grandchildren, some of them. They don't want the world to be totally screwed.'

Max took her foot in both hands and started massaging the ball of her toe with both thumbs.

'If I have to put up with a few men like the Valet for a couple of years then so be it. Because if we can keep going like we're going, in seven or eight years we'll have totally changed the culture of the bank. And that is a thought, right?'

'It is.'

She put a second foot on Max's lap and smiled at him.

'How was your day?'

'Even by the standards of the things that I do for money it was fantastically pointless.'

Karolina grimaced in sympathy.

'Apparently it's like this every summer. We're producing all the work that was signed off at the end of March. The department heads at all these companies realise they need to spend money if they're going to get the same allocation again the following year so they come up with all this shit right at the end of the tax year. Proper back-of-a-fag-packet stuff. But we actually have to make it because they've paid for it. Whatever it is. A behind-the-scenes of their production process or some crap like that. Like *anybody* cares. No one is going to watch it. I don't even know if the *client* is going to watch it.'

Max shut his eyes. He forgot sometimes how pathetic it all was until he said it out loud.

'The thing we're making is terrible. Even by our standards. Everyone involved is barely even going through the motions. I couldn't even bring myself to take the piss out of it.'

'But it's paying for you to write.'

'It's paying for me to write,' he said. 'That's the mantra. I just have to keep saying it over and over again.'

Friday 27 July

The sign had appeared overnight. Max was certain that back when he was young it was the sort of thing that would have been handmade, painted on cardboard or an old sheet, but it was further evidence, he supposed, of just how cheap it was now to print things digitally. He looked up at the twenty-foot canvas banner that had been suspended between two first-floor windows so that it hung neatly above the front door at number five.

BOOMER RE-EDUCATION CENTRE.
WALK-INS WELCOME.

A council of war had been hastily convened at Tabitha's kitchen table. It hadn't exactly been cleared, but various things had, at least, been pushed up to one end. Three candlesticks. A pile of children's books. Two mobile phones long past their operational usefulness.

At the business end were Bryony, Gordon, Tabitha and Fiona. The tea was fresh in the pot. The biscuits were Garibaldi.

'I was wrong,' shouted Gordon as Max walked into the room. 'They're not Situationists, they're Maoists. I hated the Maoists the first time round.'

The morning light was horizontal, bright through the windows. Douglas was playing golf. Jonathan was off doing whatever it was that Jonathan was always off doing. Max was supposed to have been proofreading his script, but obviously wasn't going to miss it. He sat in the only available chair.

'Can we get them evicted?' asked Bryony.

'What for?' asked Max as he poured himself a cup of tea. 'And is that, you know, a good look, given the circumstances?'

One of the playwright cats jumped onto the table and was shooed off.

'It's a stab in the back,' said Fiona. 'That's what it is. It's a stab in the back.'

Max looked across the table at her, her eyes flicking back and forth, her lips forming silent words. He had noticed that a lot of the time she appeared to be conducting an internal dialogue, the two equally outraged sides of herself egging each other on to ever greater heights of exasperation.

'Do they think they invented this stuff? *We* invented this stuff!'

She picked up her teacup but then put it down again, too incensed to drink.

'But *we* targeted the right people. Heads of industry. Politicians. People in power.'

Max was about to say something when Tabitha's phone made a honking noise that would, he felt, have been appropriate only had it been warning of a nearby natural disaster. She put her glasses on and looked down at its screen.

'Oh god,' she said.

'What?'

'Sandra and Robert's sale has fallen through.'

Fiona made a keening kind of sound.

'They had a sale agreed,' she said, turning to Max, 'and now it's fallen through.'

'And you're saying that's because of the sign.'

'The buyer has said they didn't like the attention. The estate agent had already told them, that they didn't like the attention.'

'*They didn't like the attention?*' said Max, disbelievingly. 'Who are they? Kazakhstani oligarchs?'

'What does it matter?' said Tabitha. 'This isn't a game, it's Robert and Sandra's life. They'll probably lose the place they were buying now.'

'Oh, that precious little cottage,' said Bryony. 'Sandra showed me pictures of it. Right on the edge of the Peak District.'

'Someone else will get it now, I'm sure,' said Fiona. 'A cottage like that. They'll put it back on the market and it'll be snapped up straight away.'

Some people, over time, are worn down by injustices. For others, they are vivifying. She was upright, fizzing, her head shaking at a high, almost imperceptible frequency.

'Do they understand what they're doing? These are people's lives. Real people's lives.'

'It sounds like a very convenient excuse to me,' said Max. 'I mean, it's a canvas sign. Not a multi-storey carpark. It's hardly changed the character of the area.'

'Whose side are you on?' asked Gordon.

'The angels',' said Max.

He took a sip of his tea, enjoying Gordon's spluttering outrage. Earlier that morning, he had seen a man taking photos of the sign. His over-the-shoulder bag of lenses and the practised way he fired off a volley of shots made it pretty obvious that he was a professional news photographer.

'It's probably worth mentioning now that there are likely to be more pieces in the papers.'

'And they'll be casting us as the bogeymen,' said Fiona. 'As if we are responsible for years and years of underinvestment. As if neoliberalism is our fault. I haven't just voted for Corbyn at every opportunity, I have *campaigned* for the man.'

The cat flap flapped and another of the playwrights sashayed into the room.

'Oh god, it's that bloody smirk again,' said Tabitha. 'What now?'

Max sat back in his chair. He had held back his best card but now clearly was the moment to play it.

'There are some photos of you on the internet. You're literally protesting against the council building a block of flats on the square.'

'That was twenty-five years ago,' said Gordon. 'Ancient history.'

'And it wasn't the council, it was a private developer!' said Tabitha.

'And the plans were *hideous*,' said Bryony.

'Wait a second,' said Fiona turning sharply to look at Max. 'Did you know about all this?'

Max put up his hands, protesting his innocence.

'She mentioned that they'd found the photos but I didn't know anything about the sign. They're so secretive, honestly. They stop talking when I come into the room. It's like I'm in the Stasi.'

Tabitha rapped the tabletop with her fingernails. For a second no one said anything. Max grinned an irrepressible grin.

'I saw the pictures,' he said. 'You all look so different. There's a lot of big hair. And statement eyeshadow. And Douglas's sports jacket is a thing to behold. What colour would you call that? Penicillin yellow?'

'Honestly,' said Fiona. 'What do any of them know about that? They were barely out of nappies.'

Max leaned forward and took another biscuit off the plate.

'You were literally contributing to the future housing crisis. I mean *actually* literally.'

'It's a park and it's a hugely important community asset. Are you suggesting we pave over every green space in London?'

'I don't think anyone is suggesting that.'

'But it's fine to pave over every square inch of our street?'

Max made a non-committal gesture.

'I am not saying anything. I am merely the messenger.'

'I just don't understand why we are being singled out,' said someone plaintively.

Until this point, Bryony had been largely quiet.

'Am I a boomer?' she asked.

The table turned to look at her. The expression on her face was sheepish but also hopeful that she might have a get-out clause.

'I only ask because I'm a bit younger than everyone else and I wasn't sure.'

Max pulled out his phone, did a quick search.

'The internet says boomers are the generation born between 1946 and 1964. The end of the war to the invention of the pill.'

'Oh,' said Bryony, disappointedly. 'I am. Not even close.'

'But my parents aren't,' said Max. 'Which is interesting. Both of them are just too old.'

He skim-read down the web page.

'Oh my god! Lennon and McCartney aren't either!'

'So?' said Fiona.

'I don't know. I kind of feel like your generation has got away with a lot of shit because, you know, people really like a lot of the music and I think this information is bad news for you guys.'

Tabitha tutted.

'Mick and Keith aren't either!'

'Keith Richards is only a few years older than me,' said Gordon.

Max looked around at them all, a huge grin on his face, like he had just caught them all out in some unspeakable act of hypocrisy.

'You have had years of people giving you a pass for the whole living high on the hog and then pulling up the ladder thing because of *Exile on Main St.* and *Revolver*, but . . .'

Gordon scoffed.

'OPEC pulled up the ladder. Not us. '73. It was like a light was switched off. Things that had been possible before it simply weren't possible any more.'

He sat back in his chair, unusually contemplative.

'But that was the economy,' he continued. 'Which waxes and wanes. Live as long as we have and you'll see things go up and you'll see things go down. The things that mattered were the things that changed and didn't go back. Freedom. Selfhood. We tore off a straitjacket.'

Tabitha murmured in support.

'No one had ever had the guts to do that before,' said Gordon.

'Hear, hear,' said Douglas.

'What *are* you?' asked Tabitha pointedly. 'What generation? You're not a millennial, are you?'

'Me?' said Max. 'I'm Gen X.'

'What does that mean?'

'1964 to 1980,' he said, reading the dates off his phone. 'We're the generation who aren't a generation. We're too cool for it. We fly under the radar.'

He smiled.

'We're the Smashing Pumpkins to your Steely Dan.'

'Honestly, that was just a sequence of unrelated words as far as I'm concerned,' said Tabitha.

'The X represents the unknown,' said Max. 'I'm part of its latter cohort. The kids born in the 1970s. We defy categorisation.'

Bryony had apparently long ago stopped listening. She had the look on her face of someone with an intense and unrelenting headache.

'What are we going to do about the street party?' she said.

'We are *having* the party,' said Fiona.

Max smiled. Hitherto, Fiona had been the street-party refusenik, the one for whom it was all too parochial and Jubilee-like. Too close to the thing she had fled the countryside to escape.

'What will it look like with that sign up?' said Bryony. 'Won't we look ridiculous? Imagine the photos. All of us eating slices of quiche in front of the damn thing.'

Fiona took the last Garibaldi with titanium resolve.

'The party goes ahead *as planned*,' she said.

Zoe opened the door with a theatrical flourish. Her face, on seeing Max, was a complicated mix of disappointment and delight.

'Shame,' she said. 'I thought you might be a boomer coming for a walk-in appointment.'

She opened the door wider, ushered him in.

'But it's always good to see you, Max. What news brings the go-between?'

'You have officially wound them up now. Even your defenders have turned on you.'

'Good,' she said. 'We have been waiting for that kind of clarity.'

There was a bike in the hallway, too many coats for the hooks available.

'Let's have a cup of tea and you can tell me all about them.'

Zoe led him towards the kitchen. As they passed the open door to the living room, Max could hear what sounded like two or three separate phone conversations going on at once. He glanced in as he passed. Six or seven people. An air of clubbable concentration. Max had never known the hubbub of a campaign headquarters, but this, he imagined, was what they must be like. He felt a pang that there was a team, who were doing things, and he wasn't one of them.

The kitchen was dishevelled. Takeaway cartons. A pizza box slicked with grease.

'Apologies for the mess, we've been kind of busy.'

She flicked on the kettle, pulled a couple of mugs from the shelf.

'A sale has fallen through on the street,' said Max. 'It is being blamed on the sign above your door.'

'Really? I mean, I'm sad obviously for the people involved,' she said, betraying no such emotion.

'I'm sure you are.'

'But the thing is, house prices *do* need to come down. A modest eighty per cent or so would get them roughly back in line with earnings.' She smiled. 'And I guess Pemberton Place is as good a place to start as any.'

Max heard this and felt a jolt surge through him that filled him with a kind of thrilling foreboding.

'What's going on with the film?'

'We're still gathering together the footage. We're not at the editing stage yet. But we will be soon.'

'What's it about?'

'It's a call for genereparations,' she said, pronouncing it *je-ne-reparations*.

'Genereparations,' he said. 'I like it.'

'We had considered referencing it on the sign but when you write it down it looks like gene reparations, which sounds kind of eugenicist or something, so we decided against it.'

'Will the eight of you be accepting payments on behalf of your generation?'

'Oh, this isn't about us. It's about everyone. Our plan is to nationalise the Bank of Mum and Dad.'

She was impish and imperious, her eyes alight, her mouth pursed in a twitchy little smile.

'Seriously,' said Max. 'What is it you hope to achieve from all this?'

'Like I said, the first stage is consciousness building.'

'And after that?'

'Change.'

'Everyone wants change.'

'Do they?' she said. 'Do *you*? You're like *oh yeah, everything's awful*, but you don't really think that. You fit too neatly into the prevailing order of things.'

Max smiled.

'The rest of us have to struggle against the tide,' she continued, 'while you glide on through your frictionless life.'

'My life has had its fair share of frictions,' he said.

'But has it really, though?'

'You know nothing about my life.'

Zoe bit her lip.

'I know a way I could find out about it.'

'You could ask me,' said Max.

She was walking towards the door.

'No,' she said. 'I mean the deeper stuff. The stuff that you yourself don't know.'

Thirty seconds later she was back with a pack of tarot cards in her hand.

'Oh god,' said Max. 'Please, no.'

'You are the Virgoest Virgo in history,' she said, clearing away some books from the dining table.

She sat down and indicated for Max to sit opposite her.

'Do I have time for this? I'm not sure I have time for this. I'm supposed to be writing.' He smiled. 'You know, that centuries-old, tried-and-tested way of achieving actual genuine self-knowledge.'

Zoe looked up sharply from the cards she was shuffling.

'Self-knowledge isn't an end in itself.'

'Self-knowledge is the hardest knowledge.'

'Maybe,' she said dismissively, 'but it's only meaningful if it's a prelude to action.'

'Actually,' he said, as he sat down opposite her. 'I think you'd...'

'We're going to do a simple three-card spread,' she said, interrupting him. 'And we're going to ask the cards, *Who is Max?*'

She shuffled the cards one last time, drew three from the top and laid them face down on the table.

'First card is your past,' she said.

She turned it over. The Fool.

'Yeah, very good,' said Max.

'You *saw* me shuffle them,' said Zoe, smiling. 'And anyway, the fool isn't just a fool. It means expansion and possibility and hope. It's a lovely card.'

She tucked a loose hair behind her ear.

'Can you remember that boy? Before all the sarcastic jokes?'

Max cringed. He had, he had come to realise as an adult, been a princely and kind of performative kid, spoiled by his older sisters. Until they had turned on him when he stopped being cute.

'I think I was a bit of a dick when I was a kid,' he said. 'I was a better teenager. Or at least I hope I was.'

Zoe turned the next card.

'Your present,' she said. It was the Wheel of Fortune.

'There's a winged cow reading a book. That's nice.'

'The Wheel of Fortune is the card of change.'

'And a sphinx with a sword,' continued Max. 'That *must* be meaningful.'

'It represents upheaval. And destiny.'

She looked at him pointedly.

'And a search for meaning.'

Max said nothing.

'And that's what you're looking for, isn't it?'

He smiled. It was pretty broad-brush, this. Wasn't everyone

looking for meaning? Hadn't everyone *always* been looking for meaning? The one constant of the human experience. And yet ... He looked at her, tilted his head. He was more credentialled, experienced and richer than her. He had the stability, the wife and the children. But when it came to meaning, she could more than hold her own.

'You've totally rigged this.'

'I didn't,' she said, but she was laughing.

She went to turn the final card.

'Your future,' she said.

It was the Lovers. The pink came instantly to her cheeks.

'Oh my god, I swear ... You *saw* me shuffling them.'

'The Lovers,' said Max. '*Interesting*. I mean, beyond the obvious, what does this represent?'

It was the first time he had seen her ruffled.

'Um, well it's associated with ...'

'What?'

'Nothing.'

'Come on, what? They're your cards. All this was your idea.'

Zoe had been looking away. She turned to face him.

'It's associated with Gemini,' she said.

'Aren't *you* Gemini?'

'Yes,' she said.

Max felt conscious that she was holding his eye a little longer than was necessary and that he was reciprocating without really thinking through the implications.

'You have a quality of not-innocence about you,' she said.

'Not-innocence?'

'Yes,' she said.

She cocked her head as if to look at him at a fresh angle.

'I wonder if you are quite as attractive as you think you are?'

Max laughed his laugh, which came from the back of his throat and was both a genuine reaction and a masking device.

'Just because a bunch of old women are charmed by you ... Does that actually add up to anything?'

Max smiled. He had never fenced, obviously, but he understood that a parry was sometimes more appropriate than a riposte.

'You walk between the raindrops, don't you?' she continued.

Max sat back in his chair, looking at her indulgently.

'Why are you smiling like that?'

Max paused, the tip of his tongue between his teeth.

'I don't know,' he said. 'You're ... I don't know.'

'What?'

'Some people get to say this sort of thing. Do you? I don't know.'

'Uh, excuse me? What does *that* mean?'

'*Come on.*'

Here, Zoe looked at Max and there was a moment, he was sure, of recognition between them. Just a flash. And she could, they both knew, have left it there where it would have been honourably settled. A score draw. But she didn't. She chose to press on.

'*What?*' she said.

Max looked at her. It was a challenge, this, at one level. But it was also surely an invitation. And quite possibly a trap. He considered leaving it, but didn't. Couldn't.

'You can make comments like these, if you don't look like you. But if you look like you, and you've had a life of benefitting from looking like you, then you don't get to. That's the rule. I mean, it's never expressed but that's the rule.'

Zoe said nothing.

'And it's not expressed, this rule, because to do so is to bring attention to it. And then things that were unspoken get articulated and once they've been articulated they can't be unsaid.'

'I suppose they can't,' said Zoe.

She was maintaining what looked to Max like a kind of roiling implacability. Outwardly impassive, inwardly astir.

'I'm going to go now,' said Max.

She stood, but not to see him out. There was energy about her, a sense of achievement. Like she had just won something but it wasn't obvious what.

'Bye, Cishet,' she said. 'Thanks for popping by. I'll see you at the party.'

Max paused at the kitchen door.

'You're going to the party?'

'We didn't get an invite, but it's supposed to be a whole street party and so we thought we'd host our own.'

'What, like alongside theirs?'

'Exactly.'

Saturday 28 July

With the council's permission, Pemberton Place had been closed to traffic. Residents on both sides had parked their cars elsewhere to make space for a large roll of artificial grass on which quoits and garden skittles could be played. At the Coxes' end of the street, three long trestle tables had been lined up in the middle of the road. Between the lamp posts hung summer bunting in pastel pink and yellow. Two large garden umbrellas offered shade. On the tables, each with its own white tablecloth, were quiches and salads. Stacks of sandwiches. Cakes under clingfilm. As well as wine in ice buckets, there were two jugs of Pimm's, and one of elderflower cordial.

Thirty yards away, at the other end of the street, there was a door – *the* door – laid flat on two tradesmen's stands. Some desultory bunting cut from A4 printer paper had been hung at one end. Laurie, the American with the intensely brushed hair, was standing next to it, reading something on her phone.

'Well, isn't this lovely?'

She looked up and smiled.

'We did what we could with the budget available.'

Max nodded at the single bowl of crisps in the middle of the table.

'Is that all there's going to be to eat?'

Laurie gestured at the open door.

'She's in there making some other stuff. You can go help her if you want.'

Max paused. The bunting was hung and the guacamole made. Back at his, Karolina was doing an online Pilates class and the kids were watching an animated movie that told them they were special and unique and that nothing was more important than their own self-expression.

'Sure,' he said. 'Why not?'

Inside, the house was abuzz. As ever, there were boxes everywhere you looked, although it was never clear if they belonged to someone moving in or someone moving out. He walked past the living room door. Cal was in there with a couple of other housemates. Music was on. Laptops were open. The conversation was wry, punctuated with laughter.

In the kitchen, Alexandra was sitting at the table, talking on the phone. Max walked past her with the cast of his body semi-open so he could acknowledge her greeting if she offered one and also make it easy for her to ignore him, which she duly did.

Zoe was at the kitchen counter, cutting a lemon in half.

'Cishet,' she said. 'Perfect timing. You look like a man who knows how to finely slice a fennel bulb.'

The look on her face didn't seem to deny the conversation they'd had the day before, but it didn't suggest she was too bothered by it, either.

'Give me a sharp knife,' he said, 'and you'll be able to see through the slices.'

'That's what I like to hear.'

She tossed him the fennel.

'It makes me kind of nostalgic, seeing you all together like this,' said Max as he pulled open a drawer to get out a knife. 'I used to run in a pack. Shoreditch at the turn of the millennium. We were everywhere you looked.'

He ran the fennel bulb under the tap.

'But they've all gone now, my old friends. Hardly any of them live in London any more.'

He laid a chopping board flat, and topped and tailed the fennel.

'The really sad thing is that I'm basically fine with it,' he said as he started slicing. 'Last night, Karolina was out for dinner. I was on the sofa, watching this documentary about the England cricket team. I had a glass of red wine. A big bowl of spaghetti puttanesca. It was the kind of evening that makes you ask yourself: do I want company? Like, do I actually *need* friends?'

Zoe, who had a deeply sceptical look on her face, let him get to the end of this before she said, 'Doesn't puttanesca have anchovies in it?'

'And capers,' said Max. 'The capers are crucial. Italians go crazy if you put any parmesan on a puttanesca, but most of them will let you get away with a *pangritata*, which is fried breadcrumbs, parsley and ...'

He clocked the look on her face and stopped.

'Ah,' he said, sheepishly. 'Yes. I do eat occasionally from the bottom of the marine food chain. Anchovies. Sprats. Sardines.'

'So you're *not* a vegetarian,' she said, squeezing the first half of the lemon.

'I think of myself as a vegetarian, who very occasionally eats small fish,' he said, using his fingers to measure out a fish that was, in truth, quite a lot shorter than an actual sardine.

Zoe took a very pronounced breath in and out through her nose, like she was trying to stop herself from saying something.

Then she said it anyway.

'That is just *so you*, the half-arsedness of it.'

She poured the lemon juice into a bowl.

'It's not the eating fish,' she said. 'If you want to eat fish, eat fish. Fine. But either fucking do it or don't do it ...'

Max noticed that Alexandra had finished her telephone conversation and was now eagerly listening to them. Zoe twisted the second half of the lemon down hard onto the squeezer.

'*Industrial farming is analogous to slavery*,' she said mockingly, 'so let's have a bit less of it. Not *none* of it. Just a bit less of it.'

Max winced. He had got much mileage from his run-in at the barbeque.

'Oh look, the kitchen elf's back.'

It was Cal, who had just walked in. Max turned to look at him, thankful for the conversational shift. Cal came over and looked sceptically into Max's bowl, before begrudgingly conceding with a nod that the fennel had indeed been sliced satisfactorily thin.

'Which table are you going to be at today?' he asked.

'I plan to flit between the two,' said Max as he sprinkled flakes of sea salt onto the salad.

'Of course you do.'

He looked at Zoe.

'Incapable of committing. *Quelle surprise.*'

She looked back at him.

Max watched them looking at each other. It wasn't clear if Cal was warning her about his – Max's – incapacity for commitment, or if he was using the conversation as cover to challenge Zoe for her own inability to commit. To the cause. Or to him. Or something else. It was all fascinatingly opaque and intriguing and he, Max, was satisfyingly in the middle of it all.

'Do you have any dill?' he asked innocently.

Five minutes later he was back at home, turning off the television to howls of protest. Karolina had finished her Pilates class and was icing a carrot cake.

'The young people have set up a rival party at the other end of the street.'

'Weren't they invited to the main party?'

'I don't know if they ever were,' said Max. He was trying to get Arthur into any footwear that wasn't slippers. 'There was talk that they would be but I can imagine that the invitation might have been withdrawn what with that sign and everything.'

Karolina went over to the window and looked out at the two parties.

'Oh wow,' she said. 'Two base camps. Do you think it's going to descend into violence?'

Max laughed.

'The Battle of Pemberton Place?'

'It'll start off as a food fight,' she said. 'Vol-au-vents flying from both sides, but then it'll get really nasty. Gordon will take it too far. A pork pie right in someone's face.'

She was smiling wickedly.

'And that'll be it. Before you know it, trenches will have been dug.'

'We're talking Passchendaele right outside our front door,' said Max.

Karolina was down on her knees, velcroing on Alma's shoes.

'You've got to fancy the boomers if it goes that far,' she said. 'They are the ones who will know that it is logistical supremacy that wins out in the end.'

She checked her lipstick in the mirror.

'And they have Fiona,' she said. 'And Fiona will fight until the last man.'

Max smiled.

'Right,' he said, picking up the cake. 'Let's do it.'

Outside, the mood was determinedly jolly. Lunch had not yet been served and the street's established residents were milling about, chatting in small groups, most of them choosing to stand, Max noticed, with their backs angled at the rival table down the road.

He looked over his shoulder. Zoe and her friends had already started eating, all eight of them squeezed around the door. The crockery was mismatched and a couple of them were sharing chairs but there was much laughter and Max felt again that he really should be throwing his lot in with the punks and not the pensioners.

He put the cake down on the table and walked over to where Fiona and Bryony were standing.

'It's embarrassing,' Bryony was saying.

'If it's embarrassing, it's not embarrassing because of anything *we've* done,' said Fiona.

'Why don't you go and introduce yourselves?' said Max.

'Why don't *they* come and introduce themselves to *us*?'

'Come on,' he said. 'This could be like the Christmas Day game of football on the Western Front. Just walk over there with a plate of cheese straws and an open heart.'

'I will do no such thing,' said Fiona, and off she went to help Tabitha arrange the sandwiches.

'Poor Fiona,' said Bryony. 'You mustn't wind her up so.'

'She loves the drama.'

Bryony laughed. 'She does.'

Above them, the bunting flapped in the gentle breeze, straining slightly on its string. Max took a mini savoury muffin from a passing plate.

'Talking of drama,' he said. 'I've printed off the script for him.'

Bryony put her hand on his forearm, pulled him in.

'What brilliant news.'

'Did you want to read it?'

She leaned back.

'I'm not a words person,' she said. 'Scripts. Sheet music. They mean nothing to me. I need to hear the aria, see the film. The script is for Jonathan.'

'OK.'

'Give it to him today.'

Just then, Arthur appeared with a quoit in his hand and started to lead Max urgently away.

'I will do,' he said.

For twenty minutes, they played quoits, him and Arthur, in the company of the couple who lived at number nine, whose names Max had been told but could never remember. While father and son played, the couple stood close enough for Max to feel compelled to attempt what turned out to be an astonishingly one-sided conversation.

Finally, Arthur tired of the game and agreed to stop playing in exchange for a piece of banana bread.

Tabitha sidled up next to him as they approached the table of desserts.

'I saw you talking to the Ratcliffes,' she said.

'Arthur was deep into the quoits and they were just standing there so I had no choice. Ten minutes in and I had literally run out of questions to ask them.'

Max topped up his glass.

'It was like playing ping pong with Alma. You lob it up as gently as you possibly can and still you get absolutely nothing back.'

Tabitha smiled.

'You don't seem to be enjoying yourself, darling.'

Max pulled a kind of grimacy smile.

'I find the pretending painful.'

Tabitha looked along the road at the rival party. They were sitting around their improvised table, eating and talking. The bowl that had once contained his fennel salad was already empty.

'We're not pretending they're not there, we're just ignoring them.'

'Oh, I didn't mean them,' said Max. 'They're fine. I meant this pretending.' He gestured at the table, the bunting, the quoits. 'The 1950s role play. It gives me the creeps.'

Tabitha shook her head.

'Honestly,' she said. 'You are awful. People have made a lot of effort.'

'It just feels so forced.'

'People have been doing street parties for as long as anyone can remember.'

'I know.'

'It's a lovely way to get everyone together.'

'They do things like this in Spain or wherever and it feels so natural. We do it here and it feels so performed.'

Tabitha tutted.

'I'm sure there was a time when you could dance around a maypole in a non-parodic way but those days are gone.'

'Honestly, you are such a grinch. Is there nothing you can't find fault with?'

'It's not my fault we live in degraded times. If we had institutions worth believing in, I'd believe in them. If our rituals were worth honouring, I'd honour them.'

'You are chief grinch of all the grinches.'

The napkins on the table were gingham print. The potato salad was topped with chives. Max helped himself to a slice of broccoli quiche.

'I'm all up for stealing Christmas,' he said.

Tabitha looked at him, incredulous.

'The idea of a midwinter feast is great. I'm totally on board with that. But the crassness of the thing we do . . .' He shook his head. 'It's *awful*. Twenty per cent Christian piety and eighty per cent steroidal consumerism. It is the worst of all worlds.'

'I *love* Christmas,' said Tabitha. 'Exactly as it is.'

'Every year, I sit there at the lunch table and all I can think about are the millions and millions of Christmas crackers that will end up in landfill. For what? A ten-second window of diversion before the turkey gets carved. People only buy the damn things because everybody else does. *Nobody* enjoys them. *Nobody* cares.'

'Oh for god's sake.'

'Millions of people around the world performing an idea of Christmas for the Big Other . . .'

'Go over there,' she said, pushing him towards the rival party.

'What?'

She was actually physically pushing him.

'Go on. I have had enough of you.'

Max laughed, allowing himself to be pushed by her.

'I'm going,' he said.

He walked down the street under the gentle sun. Zoe was halfway from her house to the table with a fresh jug of water.

'Have you just been forcibly ejected?'

Max had a glass of white wine in one hand and a crustless cucumber sandwich in the other.

'I wasn't being sufficiently reverent.'

Zoe laughed through her nose.

'Your epitaph,' she said in a borderline unkind voice.

Max looked at her. *Which would put me in the company of Voltaire,* he thought. *And Wilde. And Peter Cook. And . . .*

'I'm exhausted,' she said hurriedly, by way of apology. 'I did the graveyard shift last night. The space shuts at midnight and this guy stayed right to the end so we didn't get locked up until half past and it's two night buses home.'

Max winced in solidarity.

'For ninety-two quid,' she continued. 'I mean, how you are even . . .'

Max was about to say something when he became conscious that someone was standing next to him.

It was Karolina.

'Hello,' she said. 'You must be Zoe.'

Zoe extended a hand.

'Nice to meet you, Karolina.'

Max breathed as steadily as he could, in and out of his nose. There was no need to feel guilty, he told himself, because he hadn't done anything wrong. At least not at an actionable level.

'Max has really enjoyed teaching you to edit.'

'He's been very generous with his time.'

'I keep telling him he should teach.'

'He's good at it.'

For a few seconds there was a pause, as they sized each other up, decided which way to take the conversation. Max's body clenched and then released when Karolina said, 'These numbers are ridiculous.'

She was pointing at the score board. The rent paid figure was now £5,500. The value accrued £3,200.

'They are,' said Zoe.

'I feel a little bit complicit because of our place,' said Karolina. 'And the ridiculous rent that is getting paid on it.'

'It's not your fault.'

Karolina smiled a sad little smile.

'I don't know how you are all supposed to get by with things as they are in London.'

'We can't,' she said. 'And we're not even going to try. When they kick us out, we'll be gone. There's no place for us here. London's over.'

Max felt a pang of sadness. His conversation with Tabitha had reminded him that in the past he had often wondered what it would be like to live in a society that you did genuinely believe in, a place that you could celebrate uncomplicatedly.

He looked out, across the skyline. He had, he remembered, once believed in London. The city he had arrived in back in 1999 had been a glamorously dishevelled place where you could sleep on someone's sofa and survive on your wits and remake the world. A place where anyone could turn up and choose to be fabulous.

But that London no longer existed. It had been leveraged and blast-cleaned and barricaded so comprehensively that it had become something else entirely.

'I don't know where we're going to go,' she said. 'Europe perhaps, while there's still time.'

Max looked at Zoe and realised that they were connected by a kind of homelessness. And then just as quickly sensed that hers was so total that she would have no choice but to build something new, whereas his was only partial and so he would endure it until it was too late.

'Good luck,' said Karolina.

'Thanks.'

Just then, a child screamed. The pair of them pricked up like prairie dogs sensing threat. Instantly, they both knew it was Arthur. And almost as quickly realised that it wasn't serious. Rage rather than serious injury.

'Sorry,' said Karolina.

'Don't be silly. Thanks for coming over.'

It was too much to run, especially in front of everyone, so they walked fast, the two of them, up the middle of the road.

'You haven't told them we're renting out our place in Berlin, have you?' said Karolina out of the side of her mouth.

'Nobody has ever asked,' said Max. 'And it has never felt like something that I needed to volunteer.'

Arthur was underneath one of the parasols, holding Tabitha's hand, tears rolling down his cheeks.

'There was a kerfuffle over whose turn it was at quoits.'

Karolina gathered Arthur in her arms. He buried his face into the nape of her neck while Max looked instinctively for Alma, assuming that she had been the other half of the kerfuffle, but she was happily sitting on Fiona's lap, being read to and eating a biscuit.

'It's important that they learn to play by the rules,' said Gordon gruffly to no one in particular.

'Do you want to go home?' whispered Max into Arthur's ear. He was still nuzzled into the nape of Karolina's neck.

He looked up and shook his head.

'Quoits with Daddy.'

'OK,' said Max, lifting him out of Karolina's arms. 'Let's have a game. My turn to go first.'

'No!'

'All right then, you can go first.'

For five minutes they played, Arthur having two goes to Max's one. To celebrate his son landing a quoit on the middle pole, Max gave him a piece of brownie. And then another when he did it again.

He was wiping chocolate from Arthur's mouth when he looked up to see Dom and Maude walking up the street with three of their children. Maude was carrying a plate of flapjacks.

He looked urgently at Karolina.

'Did you invite them?'

Karolina looked down the street at them and then back at Max.

'I bumped into her on the street a couple of days ago. She was talking about getting the kids together this afternoon and I said we couldn't because we were coming here . . .' She screwed one eye shut. '. . . and then I might have kind of accidentally invited them just in that way that you do. I didn't think they'd actually come.'

Max watched them as they walked down the street. The thought of Dom and Maude seeing them in this context – the Cath Kidston bunting and coronation chicken, the soft-focus Englishness – was excruciating enough. But the idea of Dom and Maude being understood somehow as emissaries of theirs – by Bryony and Jonathan and Tabitha and Fiona, but also by Zoe and her lot – was even worse.

'Hi,' he said as warmly as he could, as they approached. 'So lovely of you to come.'

'Love a street party,' said Maude in a voice that suggested that she really didn't.

They kissed twice, once on each cheek.

Maude was wearing white leather sandals, a red dress with oversized buttons, and a musky masculine perfume.

'How are you?'

'You know,' she said, looking around. 'Getting by.'

If she felt any contrition about the slight unravelling at the end of their dinner, it wasn't evident to Max. He poured her a glass of wine, topped up his own.

'*Boomer re-education centre,*' she said, reading the sign. 'I had heard about this. How amusing that it's on your street.'

'The two sides have cut diplomatic ties. Hence the two parties.'

Maude looked over at Zoe and her friends. They had finished their food but were still sitting round the door, drinking their bottles of beer. A couple of roll-your-own cigarettes were being smoked.

'Hardly the storming of the Bastille, is it?'

'No,' he said. 'It's not.'

'When I was their age I remember things being more squat party than street party.' She looked up and down the street. 'I guess there's nowhere left to squat any more.'

She picked up a chocolate-covered strawberry and gave it to her middle child. Max could feel all eyes upon them. Maude and Dom and their kids were the only people at the party who didn't live on the street and it occurred to him that this might constitute a breach of protocol. He had no choice but to start making introductions.

Bryony and Tabitha were hovering expectantly.

'These are our friends, Dom and Maude,' he said. 'They live round the corner.' He paused, smiled. 'And these are my neighbours, Bryony and Tabitha.'

'*Neighbours*,' said Bryony, hitting him on the arm.

'Sorry,' said Max. '*Acquaintances*.'

Tabitha and Bryony howled their disapproval with such vigour that they didn't notice Maude's eyebrow creeping up. Max blushed inwardly, aware suddenly that all the joshing and gentle flirting, which he had thought was innocent and playful, was actually, obviously, not cool at all.

'Come with us,' they said, leading Maude by the arm. 'Are you hungry? There's roast chicken and cucumber sandwiches and trifle and all sorts.'

He watched them as they walked away. Maude could get a little messy at times, but it didn't undermine her essential sangfroid. She had that thing that made you want to win her respect, not once but over and over. And right now, at least, he wasn't.

Clouds had rolled in. The temperature had dropped. Max wandered over to the food table to refill his plate. As he sliced himself a piece of asparagus tart, he became aware that Dom was standing next to him.

'How's it going?'

'I'm all right,' said Max. 'You?'

Dom yawned.

'Sorry,' he said. 'I was up late. Got stuck in a late-night Bill Hicks wormhole.'

Max smiled, relieved to find himself in his natural territory.

'Happens to me all the time,' he said. 'The algorithm knows what I want better than I do. Bill Hicks, Lenny Bruce, Richard Pryor, Chris Morris...'

'I can lose whole weekends to Chris Morris,' said Dom.

'The early radio stuff...'

'It's wild,' said Dom. 'Have you listened to...'

For ten minutes they ate and talked comedy, trying to ignore Arthur's increasingly agitated requests to play another round. Eventually, though, his son's insistence won out and while Max rounded up the discarded quoits, Dom drifted off to refill his glass.

As he stood waiting for Arthur to take his turn, Max watched Maude as she talked first to Jonathan and Gordon, and then to Douglas and Fiona. She was garrulous and gesticulatory, soliciting what looked, from a distance, like uneasy laughs. Max felt a creeping sense of anxiety. Maude was indiscreet. And inflammatory. And there were places you just didn't go with people this much older than you. Or at least there were places *he* didn't go. And he had no faith that she wouldn't.

Down the street he could see Dom chatting with Zoe and her friends. He had cadged a rollie off one of them and was smoking it surreptitiously so his kids couldn't see.

Suddenly, it all felt irredeemably sordid. The squat parties. The club nights and the raves. It was embarrassing to him. The way that they had lived their lives, the things that they had done. They had always taken things too far.

For five minutes he played quoits, feeling sheepish and sullied and saying little, until Karolina appeared with Alma.

'Can you look after her for a bit? She's being clingy and I really need the loo.'

'Sure,' said Max. 'Can you take him with you? He's desperate.'

Arthur was hopping from one leg to the other.

'No, I'm not,' he said.

Karolina scooped him up and sang him a song in Swedish as she carried him back to the house.

Alma loved nothing more than the company of other little girls, ideally slightly younger than herself, whom she could pet and boss about as she pleased. Max introduced her to Maude and Dom's daughter, Rosa, imagining that it might buy him some time and space, but instead found himself dragooned into a skipping game, which involved him holding one end of a rope in a supplicant-like stoop.

Over the girls' heads, he looked for Maude. She had wandered down the street and was talking to Zoe's lot. From a distance it looked like a couple of them seemed to know who she was. Which made sense, he supposed. They were her audience. The always online.

A few minutes later, she was back. Max dropped the rope, stood up straight.

'It's more fun at their end,' she said. 'But the wine is better up here.'

She stood next to Max and the two of them looked down the street together at Zoe and her friends and everything they represented.

'I was good at being young,' said Maude. 'Second assistant to the creative director at *Wallpaper*. The pay was terrible but I always seemed to make it from one month to the next.'

Max was finally allowed to let go of the rope. Alma and Rosa ran off, hand-in-hand, to play quoits.

'Magazines,' she said. 'They feel almost quaint now. All those openings and parties and launches. Is it all still going on and I'm just not invited any more? Or is it not? Part of me thinks it's just over, that moment.' She shrugged. 'Anyway, it was fun while it lasted.'

She looked over at Gordon, who was showily opening a bottle of sparkling wine, inching the cork out so that it flew in a long parabola over their heads.

'I read this thing about the U-bend of life,' she said with a crooked, slightly exhausted smile. 'People are happy when they're young and carefree, and then again when they're old and carefree, but the bit in the middle is just this joyless drudge of mortgage repayments and head lice.'

She looked back at Max.

'I mean, when did you last go to the cinema? Not to see the fucking *Emoji Movie* or whatever . . .'

Her attention drifted in the way it does after a few drinks on an empty stomach.

'Is there anything worse than having to sit through their films?' she continued eventually. 'The whole point of putting them in front of a screen is that you can get shit done.'

She motioned over her shoulder towards the high street and its retro Picturehouse.

'But they always put the kids' films on screen four, which is a bloody black hole for phone signal and so there's nothing to do but watch the damn thing.'

Max smiled.

'Life begins at forty,' she said bitterly. 'Maybe if you had kids at twenty it does. "Life begins at sixty" doesn't have quite the same ring, does it?'

'We got the timing all wrong, didn't we?' said Max. 'Doubly cruel to find yourself knee-deep in nappies just at the moment that you realise that you're really not going to do all the things that you thought you were going to do.'

Around them the party was entering its late phase. The coffee had gone cold. A red-wine stain was blooming on one of the tablecloths.

Maude looked left and then right. Tabitha was handing out bowls of trifle. At the other end of the street, Zoe was plunging a cafetière as her friends broke chunks off a bar of chocolate.

'This is ridiculous,' said Maude. 'They don't know they've been born, this lot.'

Maude placed her wine glass on the table determinedly.

'What are you doing?'

'I'm going to be the adult in the room.'

He watched in horror as she extracted Bryony, who was nearest to them, from the conversation she was having and jokily but also forcibly frogmarched her down the street. Zoe was standing at the head of the table, watching with an amused look as they approached.

Max felt his stomach bungee down into his feet and then up into his mouth. He watched as they stood there, the three of them, Maude doing most of the talking, the other two standing opposite one another, their arms crossed.

Karolina came over holding a half-eaten bowl of raspberry fool.

'Doesn't look like your age-inappropriate mistresses are really hitting it off.'

The tone of her voice was the usual dry register she used for jokes but her eyes contained a warning. Max held her gaze, for one and then two and then three seconds, hoping that this was long enough for her to recognise that he was both acknowledging the joke and accepting the censure, and also reconfirming the inviolability of their coupling.

When he looked back, Maude had left them to it, and they were alone, Bryony and Zoe. His first instinct was to run and interrupt but for all manner of reasons this was obviously impossible and so he stood there, holding on to his earlier defence, which was that he had done nothing wrong.

Other than be friendly.

And maybe a little lonely.

From a distance, he watched the two of them. Zoe was talking, Bryony listening with her arms folded across her chest. The conversation seemed to be quite adversarial. Both of them prickly.

But then she laughed, Bryony did, at something that Zoe had said. That honest, infectious laugh. And Zoe was grinning. And Max knew, he just knew, that they were talking about him.

When the rain came, it came quickly and wholly unexpectedly. At first it was just a few drops but then it was a downpour. Max looked up at the sky, mouthing silent thanks, and then he picked up Arthur and ran him back to the house.

Once Karolina and the kids were safely ensconced at number fifteen, Max ran back to discover that all the bowls and plates and jugs and chairs had been ferried to wherever it was they needed to go. All that remained was the door. He picked up one end of it, and helped Zoe carry it into their living room.

There wasn't any kitchen roll so they used toilet paper to dry it, chucking the sodden fistfuls into a carrier bag.

'I saw you talking to Bryony.'

Zoe said nothing.

'I think you'll look back on it as mistake,' he said gamely. 'Best to keep the enemy depersonalised.'

Zoe wiped the water that had collected in a groove of the door.

'I was expecting you to do something today,' he said. 'I don't know, a stunt, or something.'

Finally, she looked up at him.

'She's lovely, your wife.'

'She is,' said Max. 'But she's Swedish. And it's easy to be lovely when you're Swedish. Swedes can say anything they want and all people hear is *lovely, lovely, lovely.*'

Zoe picked up the bag of wet toilet roll and the two of them walked into the hall. Max was about to open the front door when she stopped him with a question.

'What if I had to ask something of you?'

Max stood where he was, one hand on the latch.

'You know, I have already taught you to edit and I did the fennel and now I've just dried your door. I think if anyone is going to ask anyone to do anything for them, it should be me doing the asking.'

'Can we just have a conversation,' she said, tensing her fingers, 'without the endless performance?'

Max smiled.

'I wish it was an act,' he said. 'But that would imply there were other layers and I'm afraid . . .'

'Oh, for god's sake, stop. I need to be able to talk honestly with you.'

'OK. Sorry.'

Zoe breathed in and out through her nose.

'OK,' she said. 'Tell me something. Tell me something true.'

Max considered this for a second and then he took her hand and looked straight in her eyes.

Slowly, he turned her wrist, exposing her inner arm. Very solemnly he said, 'That smiley face is by a long way the least good thing about Nirvana.'

'Oh my god,' said Zoe, pulling her hand out of his, 'you can't do it, can you?'

Max put his hands up.

'Sorry,' he said.

'No,' she said, walking out of the room. 'It's good to know. Who you can rely upon and who you can't.'

Ten minutes later, he was standing on the doorstep at number twenty-one. Jonathan answered, as Max had hoped he would.

'I meant to give you this earlier. But then the rain ...'

He handed Jonathan a copy of the script. One hundred and ten pages. Double-spaced lines. Typeset in Courier, font size twelve. Bound top and bottom with two brass clips.

THE RECKONING by Max Anderson

Jonathan looked down at the script and then up at Max.

'These days, I do pensions mostly. Lots of commercial property holdings. Spreading the risk. Hedging. Balancing. I haven't been involved in anything like this for a very long time.'

'Right,' said Max, doing his best not to sound too crushed.

Jonathan held the script in his hands, took a breath.

'But, let me have a look,' he said. 'I am always open to new things.'

Monday 30 July

*A*nother lovely evening. The hazy orange sun low in the sky. The kids were asleep. Max had eaten. Quiche, couscous with roasted peppers and a potato salad, all of it left over from the street party. He was halfway to the Coxes to return a now-empty serving dish when he heard a voice from across the road.

It was Zoe. She was singing.

'*Oh, Cishet, the dice was loaded from the start.*'

'Yes, very good,' said Max.

'*My Cishet, when you exploded into my heart.*'

Max was shaking his head.

She danced around him, pretending to swoon.

'*My Cishet, my Cishet.*'

She ended up down on one knee, looking up at him.

'I didn't have you picked as a Dire Straits fan.'

'My dad was obsessed,' she said, standing up and dusting down her trousers. 'It was on all the time in the car growing up.'

She was smiling sloppily, looking like she might have been celebrating.

'You're in a better mood than the last time I saw you.'

Zoe looked at him.

'You are who you are,' she said. 'But I kind of know that you'll come through when we need you to.'

She smiled again, her eyes a little glazed.

'And I've finished the film.'

'Great news. I'm looking forward to watching it.'

Behind her, he could see Laurie carrying boxes out to a waiting car.

'Is Laurie moving to Folkestone?'

Zoe looked over her shoulder, took a beat or two to answer.

'No, she's moving in with her boyfriend, south London somewhere,' she said eventually. 'I'm supposed to be helping her pack.'

The dusky evening smelled of barbeque charcoal and citronella candles.

'What were you talking to Bryony about?' he asked. 'At the street party?'

Zoe was walking along the kerb like it was a tightrope.

'We have a shared interest,' she said, a knowing little half-smile on her face.

As she wobbled along the kerb she seemed to notice something about the tableau he had created, standing next to one of the street's cherry trees while the day drew to its close.

'You know, Cishet, I have never in my life had the right person stand near the tree when the sun sank.'

The way she delivered this made it obvious that it was a quote from something that Max didn't know. He paused for a second but it wasn't the moment to ask and anyway he had no interest in advertising his ignorance.

'You're young,' he said. 'And the sun sinks every evening. And there's pretty much always a tree to hand.'

She was looking at him in her unsettlingly direct way.

'Or maybe I did and I was just too blind to see it?'

Max said nothing. She could have been talking about Cal, of course. But there was also, surely, a reasonable chance that she wasn't. And he knew which one he wanted it to be. He felt a stab of guilt. A couple of nights earlier Karolina had come down the stairs elated after a meeting at which she had helped secure five hundred thousand pounds more funding than she had hoped for, and the two of them had celebrated with wine and then sex and then more wine in the bath. It was long after midnight when they had finally gone to bed.

He did his best to usher away the guilty thoughts. All of this idle chat was just that. A game of wits and nothing else, whatever the tarot cards said.

Zoe glanced back at her house. Max felt she knew she should have been helping her friend pack but was looking for an excuse to stay.

'When am I going to get to see it,' he said, 'your film?'

'Tomorrow.'

'That's it? No more details?'

'It's a public information film for boomers.'

Max smiled.

'I like that. It's a medium they'll understand. They grew up with them.' He looked at her. 'But *you* didn't.'

Zoe made an easy breezy gesture.

'They were a big thing in our family. My dad's uncle worked in the Central Office of Information. Some families are into like horse-riding or whatever. We watched public information films.'

'Charley says …' said Max in the funny little boy's voice of the original.

'*Exactly*,' said Zoe, delighted. 'I know them all pretty much verbatim.'

For a couple of minutes they shared memories of Charley the cat and his charmingly animated warnings about the dangers of playing with matches and going off with men professing to have puppies. Briefly, the age difference between them felt inconsequential.

'Have you seen *Apaches*?' she asked.

'Yes!'

'Where all the kids die on the farm.'

'That kid who drowns in the slurry pit!'

'It's like *properly* traumatising.'

'The guy who directed it made *The Long Good Friday*.'

'Is that a movie?'

'Bob Hoskins is in it. He's a kind of cockney Don Corleone. It's amazing.'

Max was leaning against the tree, hugging the serving dish to his chest.

'It was a proper incubator, the Central Office of Information. Like a state-funded finishing school. Peter Greenaway worked there. Lindsay Anderson made films for them.'

He felt the sadness he always felt about the heroic era. How it was ebbing away from them and would soon be gone.

'Did you ever see the tombstone one?' he said. 'About AIDS.'

'I don't think so.'

'It was directed by Nick Roeg.'

Zoe looked at him.

'He's one of the all-time great English directors. *Performance. Don't Look Now. The Man Who Fell to Earth.*'

A supermarket delivery van pulled up opposite them and the driver started piling bags into a trolley.

'The tombstone ad came out when I was eleven. Don't die of ignorance. That was the strap line. I was petrified by it. I thought everyone was going to die. And I mean *everyone*. But they didn't. It was a catastrophe, obviously. Jarman. Mapplethorpe. That whole tragic generation. But the thing I thought was going to happen ... it didn't happen.'

Zoe looked at him, perplexed.

'I'm just trying to make the point that things don't always work out the way we think they're going to.'

'Yeah, OK,' she said, irritated now. 'Thanks for the fortune-cookie wisdom.'

Max took this with a smile.

'OK, imagine us two having a conversation in like 1963 or whenever about whether the world would make it to 2018 without a nuclear exchange. We would have said the chances of that happening were basically zero.'

Zoe pulled a slightly pained expression.

'We can't know ...'

'A hundred per cent, we would have done,' said Max. 'The equivalent of us, then. Me and you. People who like to think of themselves as looking at the world clear-sightedly. We would have bet the bank that there would have been an exchange. It would have been the *only* reasonable assumption in 1963.'

'I don't buy the comparison. Nuclear war would have been the result of a deliberate human decision. The threat we're facing is already in play and needs to be stopped. It's *drift* that leads to the apocalypse.'

'My point is that we don't know what's going to happen. I mean, Trump hasn't been so bad, right? We thought he was going to be the end of the world and he hasn't really done anything. He'll be gone in a couple of years and that'll be that. He'll disappear. Brexit is happening and the roof hasn't fallen in. We adapt. And we come up with stuff.'

'Oh my god, the fucking *complacency*.'

'All I'm saying is that we don't know what's going to happen.'

'Yeah, you're right,' she said as sarcastically as he had ever heard her speak. 'Will we see an actual species-level extinction or will it just be an unliveable hellscape? And *isn't* it going to be fun finding out.'

'My goodness, I don't think it's been this clean in forty years,' said Bryony, taking possession of the dish. 'I think it was a wedding present, this. Look at it, it looks brand new.'

She was wearing a denim shirt, a gold watch on a leather strap. Max could hear music playing in the kitchen.

'We were just about to have dessert. We got lumbered with enough of Angela's pavlova to feed the Mongol Hordes. Come in and help us?'

Max looked down at his phone. Nothing from Karolina, which meant that the kids were sleeping soundly.

'You'd be doing us a favour. It needs eating.'

'Sure,' he said.

Jonathan was in the kitchen, putting a couple of plates into the dishwasher.

'Max was returning our dish. He's going to help us try to make a dent in this great behemoth.'

On the table was the pavlova. The cream on top had started to stiffen and yellow, the banana and kiwi slices past their best. Not for the first time Max was bemused by their seemingly ideological aversion to putting things in the fridge.

'A big piece for Max,' said Bryony.

Max took a seat at the head of the table.

'I saw you talking to Zoe,' he said. 'At the street party.'

Bryony smiled.

'She's a spirited little thing, isn't she? I liked her, actually.'

Bryony gave him a look that communicated a kind of knowing.

'She talks about you a lot.'

'I have been teaching her how to edit,' said Max, uncomfortably.

'How selfless of you.'

Max did his best not to react to this.

'So you've forgiven her for the sign, have you?'

'Oh god,' said Jonathan, 'that bloody sign. I can barely imagine giving less of a shit about anything in the world.'

He speared a piece of meringue with his fork.

'I'm sympathetic to them,' said Bryony. 'I like a bit of agitation. Things should be poked and prodded. Disturb the comfortable and all that. We can take it.'

'They don't envy the house,' said Jonathan. 'They envy what the house represents.'

Jonathan looked at Bryony, admiringly.

'Twelve solo shows in four different countries. Two paintings in the Tate collection. That's what the house represents.'

Max smiled ambiguously at this. It was interesting to hear him talk reverently about Bryony's art, even if some of what he said was clearly aggrandising horseshit.

'Why did you stop putting on shows?' he said to Jonathan.

Jonathan thought about this for a second.

'I couldn't connect with the work any more,' he said.

'It happens,' said Bryony. 'You get older. The artists are younger. You start to connect with the work less.'

Jonathan sat side on to the table, his legs crossed. He had the profile of an eagle.

'Or the work just got worse,' he said.

Bryony dismissed this with what Max recognised to be a kind of supremely disingenuous largesse.

'There is plenty of wonderful work being made today.'

She turned to Max.

'He's never really been a visual person. Not like us.'

Jonathan slowly turned his head to look at her with an aquiline disdain.

'*What?*' said Bryony. 'It's true. You were always interested in art as a phenomenon. It was never about the work for you. Not *really*, darling.'

Jonathan rang a finger along the line of his jaw.

'As you get older,' he said, 'you naturally get more interested in the deep movements of the human world. The bond market is more interesting and way more significant than any film I've seen in the last twenty years.'

Bryony sat up straight at this, scandalised and delighted.

'Honestly, that is the most philistine thing I've ever heard.'

She was looking at Max with a kind of gleeful outrage.

'I'm sorry, Max, but we can't let him get away with that.'

Max breathed out through his mouth, a kind of long, steady sigh. Like all coalitions, marriages are made up of camps. It was inevitable that he would be forced to choose.

'As *artists*,' she said. 'We can't let him get away with it.'

Jonathan was looking at him. Penetratingly. Max knew a no-win situation when he saw one. He exhaled.

'The bond market speaks truth to power more effectively than any filmmaker,' he said to Jonathan with a concessionary shrug. He waited a beat, held his gaze. You didn't get someone to believe in you by disavowing the thing you were doing. 'But if we're being forced to choose between the ecstatic truth and the accountant's truth, I know which side I'm on.'

Jonathan snorted through his nose. Max could see that he had confirmed the thing that Jonathan had always thought.

He waited for a second or two and then he pushed his chair away from the table. 'Nature calls,' he said.

Bryony was elated.

'The ecstatic truth!' she said, once he was out the door. 'I *love* it!'

'It's Werner Herzog,' said Max, feeling rather small in his chair.

'And the *accountant's* truth,' she said. 'That's just perfect!'

Max had his elbows on the table, his head in his hands.

'Have I just really pissed him off?'

Bryony waved him away. 'Oh god, no. He'll have forgotten all about it before he gets back from the loo.'

She rested her chin in the palm of her hand.

'You do like to shake things up, don't you?'

'I thought so,' said Max. 'But ... I don't know.'

Bryony was leaning towards him, her eyes full of mischief and delight.

'What is it that you want?'

She had asked him this before, but the tenor of it was different now.

'What do I want?'

'What do you *want*?' she said again.

Max prevaricated. What did he want? He didn't know. His heart was scrambled, like a disordered Rubik's cube that would require much twisting and turning to be righted again, and he wasn't sure he was the man for the task.

In the hall, they heard footsteps.

'I can't talk to you now,' she whispered. 'Come round when he's not here. We need some privacy.'

Max looked down at the table. He barely remembered eating the pavlova but his plate was empty.

'I should go,' he said.

Jonathan drew out his chair to sit down again. 'Always a pleasure,' he said dryly.

Max walked down their hall, past the collection of Japanese silk prints and the belle époque desk lamp. In among the clamour of his thoughts, he could concentrate on one thing and one thing only.

His script had gone unmentioned.

Tuesday 31 July

The first thing to say about the film was that it was quite good. Max was sitting at his kitchen table, watching it on YouTube for a second time. It was shot in the style of a public information film, ostensibly targeted at those now collecting their pensions, but its true audience was transparently those of a similar age to its creators.

The first half of the film was built around the call for genereparations. They had shot footage on Pemberton Place, the houses looking empty and underutilised, and cut it with images of long lines of young people queuing up to view apartments and clips of young families in overcrowded social housing. Over the top of this a narrator outlined their plan for a bedroom tax on private property: every night a room was empty the owner paid a levy. Alongside this, they were calling for the introduction of a wealth tax – 'the nationalisation of the Bank of Mum and Dad', as they had it – that would be put to use building zero-carbon social housing.

Max paused the video. The speed of the cuts and the larky graphics made it obvious that it had been made by a generation who had grown up with social media. And he could see why they had broadened it out, tried to make it more universal, but the second half, which called for pension reform and the creation of a youth sovereign wealth fund dedicated to rapid decarbonisation and climate mitigation, would probably have been better as a separate, stand-alone project.

Still, there was no denying it, the film had tempo and shape and a propulsive forward momentum.

She answered on the first ring.

'What did you think?'

'It's good,' he said.

She squealed.

'It is, isn't it?'

'Although, I'm not sure that the other residents of Pemberton Place are likely to agree.'

'You don't think?'

'You've used footage of their actual houses.'

'It's nothing personal. They were just the nearest ones to hand.'

'I don't think they're going to see it that way.'

'They're all very open-minded, progressive people. I'm sure they won't mind.'

Max was up on his feet, wandering around the house while he talked to her.

'They've already summoned me to a meeting. I'm just about to head over there now.'

'Great,' she said. 'Ask them if they'll sign our petition calling for a bedroom tax. A hundred thousand signatures and they'll debate the motion in the Houses of Parliament.'

'Oh right.'

'Tell them it'll be kind of like an inverse Airbnb: every night the room's empty you have to chuck in a few quid.'

'Yeah, I can see that being popular,' said Max.

'It's never going to be a problem for us, of course. We've got eight in our place. Actually, seven now that Laurie's gone.'

Max was sitting on the bottom steps of the stairs lacing his trainers, his phone wedged between shoulder and chin.

'Does she own six bikes?'

'What do you mean?'

'There were like eight bikes in the front garden and now there are two?'

'People must just be out,' said Zoe breezily. 'That is what bikes are for, after all. Cycling to places.'

He was in the hall, looking for his shoes.

'Will Bryony be at your little meeting?' she asked.

'I'm not sure. I think she might be out doing something else. Why?'

'No reason, just curious.'

Max thought about probing this and decided against it.

'Anyway, I'll let you know whether or not you can expect a brick through your front window anytime soon.'

He was about to hang up, when she said, 'Max.'

'Yes.'

'Why don't you give them the impression that that's us done? That the film is the last act.'

Max contemplated this for a second or two. This wasn't her scared off by the prospect of a brick through the window, he knew that. It wasn't even really her window.

'Is it, though?' he said. 'Is it really you done?'

Somehow, he could *hear* her smiling down the phone.

'Let's just say for sake of argument that it is.'

'Max, we've been waiting for you.'

Tabitha's living room. Douglas and Tabitha on a sofa. Gordon perched on the edge of his chair. Fiona up by the mantelpiece, pacing.

'You've seen it, of course.'

He nodded.

'They use actual footage of our houses. Some of the shots you can see through our windows. That can't be legal!'

The drinks were on a tray on the coffee table. A cafetière, already plunged. Milk in a jug. Max poured himself a coffee and sat down next to Douglas. He had some experience of this from music-video location shoots.

'You can't film inside someone's house without their permission,' he said, 'but I think that anything shot from a public place is generally considered fair game.'

'Oh fine,' said Fiona. 'So it's open season for peeping Toms.'

'You point a tele-lens into a bedroom and you're going to get in all kinds of trouble. But they haven't done anything like that and none of you are actually in any of the footage.'

'But that's exactly the problem. They've shot it to make it look like we're barely there.'

'It's *so* irresponsible. It's practically encouraging burglars.'

'They're trying to make it look like we don't use these houses, when, by god, we use these houses.'

A cat was stretching ostentatiously along the top of a sofa back.

'Juxtaposing the footage with slum housing. How dare they?'

'It's not fair.'

'I think that's precisely their point,' said Max. 'It's *not* fair.'

Tabitha had been quiet up to this point.

'Did you help them make it?'

'No,' said Max.

He havered.

'I mean, not directly.'

'*Max.*'

'She asked me to teach her how to do a few things. How to edit. Overdub the sound. And, you know, the end result *is* pretty good. At least formally.'

'Oh god, Max.'

'I didn't know what the film was about. I promise you.'

'What else have they got planned?'

Max looked up. He wasn't going to do Zoe's bidding. But nor was he going to sell her out.

'I don't know,' he said.

'Because I don't know if we can take much more of this.'

Max laughed. '*This?*' he said. 'This is the rebellion of the head girls. You go on social media and you'll see the kinds of things the boys at the back of the class are talking about. This is *nothing*.'

'It isn't nothing, Max, it is a rebuke. It is a falsehood. I am *not* the enemy.'

Fiona expanded to fill the space, all unexpended lifeforce. She was wretched and divided and incapable of taking a backward step.

'If they weren't so blinkered about this inter-generational nonsense they would see that I am on their side.'

'So you're OK about the film?'

'*No!*'

'Very well then I contradict myself,' said Max, smiling.

'Yes,' she said, pointing at him instinctively, propelled, he felt, by the multitudes that she no doubt contained.

And then, 'No!' she said again, just as forcefully.

Gordon was up on his feet. He put a hand on Fiona's shoulder, but he was talking to Max.

'They don't get to compare the world they imagine they'll one day make to the one that we actually made.'

He had a kind of serenity about him.

'In the future people will look back at our generation and all they'll think about will be the honours board. The length and the depth and the breadth of it. The geniuses in every field. No one will give a shit about who was in which house.'

Douglas had been sitting on the sofa, staring out the window.

'I never imagined that we would one day be viewed as the problem,' he said. 'To be young in the sixties was to imagine that you would be young for ever. Or at least always on the side of youth.'

He smiled absently.

'But I guess that's the way it always goes. The cycle of creative destruction.'

Fiona and Douglas were first to go, off for a pre-arranged lunch date. Gordon followed soon after when he realised he wasn't going to be invited to stay for food. Before he too left, Max was carrying the tea tray back into the kitchen, Tabitha following behind him.

'I am not going to die anytime soon,' she said, 'or at least I don't plan to.'

'Good,' said Max, putting the tea tray down on the counter. 'A sensible approach.'

'But it is coming for me,' she said, sitting down at the kitchen table, 'in a way that it's not for you.'

He conceded this point with a nod.

'And that means the reckoning is coming. Not publicly, not demonstratively. But in my heart.'

'I'm not sure that's quite how it works . . .'

'I abandoned my parents.'

They had touched on her parents before. Her angry father and her domineering, disappointed mother.

'You play the hand you're dealt, Tabitha. My parents are nice. They drink hot chocolate in garden centre cafes. My dad volunteers at the local library. I didn't have to repudiate them to become me.'

'Neither did I.'

'Yeah, but maybe you kind of . . . *did*,' he said, trying to be as delicate as possible. 'I mean, I didn't know them, obviously. But the way you've talked about them . . .'

'I could have found common ground. I was better educated than them but I wasn't generous with it.'

'But you were also, what, seventeen or whatever, when you left. And who makes good choices when they're seventeen?'

'There were plenty of opportunities to reach out that I didn't take.'

Max was trying to leave but felt honour bound to stay. He sat down in the chair opposite her.

'I can have them all at once,' she said. 'All four of them. Their partners and their children. Christmas. Easter. Half terms.'

One of the playwrights leapt up onto her lap.

'The children are all cousins of course, but they're as close as siblings. There are seven of them. They can't fit all at once in any of my kids' houses, but we can all fit in here.'

She stroked the cat behind its ear.

'I lie in bed when they're here and I listen to the sounds as they float up through the house. The laughter and the hooting. The squabbling. The tantrums.'

Tabitha's eyes were filmed with tears.

'The three-year-old has the tread of a diplodocus. The house shakes when he runs. I lie in bed and I listen to it, the plenitude. The unbelievable plenitude. The thing that I hold tighter than anything else is the thing that I deserve the least.'

Max started to make a conciliatory noise, but she waved him away.

'I never did it for my mother. We could have stayed with her. We could have squeezed in, made it work. I could have slept on the floor. But we never did it. *I* never did it.'

She took off her glasses and wiped her eyes.

'I don't deserve it, Max. But I have it and I'll never let it go. So you can tell your friends down the road that they'll take me out of this house when I'm dead. And not a day before.'

Wednesday 1 August

'I don't know what it is that you're planning but I have this sense you're about to do something that is a lot more serious than a vaguely amusing sign and I don't want you to do something that you're going to regret.'

He was on the doorstep of number five. Zoe had answered the door but wasn't, it seemed, inviting him in. Over her shoulder, he could see through to the kitchen where the atmosphere appeared to be low-lit and intimate. Music was playing. Shadows were moving on the wall. Incredibly, the hallway behind her seemed even more crowded with belongings.

'If you get a criminal record, you'll never be able to visit America.'

'I'm never going to America. It's a six-hour flight. There and back is almost two tonnes of carbon.'

'By the time you're my age there will probably be a hydrogen plane. Or a wind-powered Zeppelin or whatever. But you still won't be allowed in if you have a criminal record, even if you row there yourself.'

'I'm never going to America. It's fine. I've accepted it.'

'But might you come to regret it? I know this is going to sound deeply patronising but I am forty-two, which at twenty-one I thought was as good as dead, and I am telling you now, I am so glad that that little prick didn't make any massive decisions on my behalf.'

Max did his best, here, not to look at her forearms and their ragtag tattoos.

'I know you're not twenty-one. And I'm not saying *you're* a prick of course.'

Zoe's expression was elaborately unimpressed.

'Any sentence that starts, *I know this is going to sound deeply patronising* ...'

'The Grand Canyon,' said Max, interrupting her. 'It's genuinely amazing. One of the few things that actually lives up to its promise.'

Zoe made a face.

'The Taj Mahal is a lot smaller than you think it's going to be,' he continued.

'I hope one day to go to India on the train,' she said. 'And I'm sure I'll be able to cope with the disappointment.'

She was leaning into the frame of the door, her arms crossed.

'I mean, why are you so bothered about what we do, anyway?'

'Oh come on. I'm fond of you.'

She softened.

'You're fond of us?'

'No, I'm fond of *you*. I actively dislike a couple of the others.'

'That's nice. The me bit, anyway.'

'Well, it's true,' said Max.

She looked at him. He looked at her. Did this shared look contain reservoirs of longing? It was difficult to tell.

'Whatever it is that you do, is it going to make any material difference to anyone?'

'Yes, actually.'

'So you *are* planning something. I knew it!'

Zoe shrugged.

'Look, I am completely on board with the righteousness of your cause but there surely can't be anything more self-defeating than a pyrrhic moral victory.'

'You're totally right,' she said. 'We're done with gestures.'

Max looked despairingly at the heavens.

'The point I'm trying to make is that something can come at great personal cost and still be a gesture.'

Zoe looked at him and smiled.

'But some gestures,' she said, 'are completely free and come at no personal cost at all.'

She raised her middle finger and then shut the door in his face.

'Are you sneaking out of that young woman's house late in the evening?'

Max turned round. Bryony. Dressed up and going out for the night, her arm in Jonathan's.

'It's 7.15 p.m. and I didn't go beyond the doorstep ...'

Max faltered. It had been a joke and he had reacted hastily and now it looked like he was genuinely trying to cover his tracks.

He smiled a subdued little smile.

'She doesn't have many friends on the street.'

'An understatement,' said Jonathan.

'You two were notable in your absence yesterday. You missed the full Fiona debrief.'

'Some of us still work.'

'And they didn't feature our house,' said Bryony. 'So ...'

Max looked at them. Off to the theatre or to dinner or whatever it was. Jonathan in a well-cut jacket. Bryony in a dress. A reminder that there was a whole world that wasn't beholden to bathtimes and bedtimes and accidents in the night.

'We're having the Archibalds round for dinner tomorrow night,' said Bryony. 'You should come.'

Jonathan was incredulous. 'Should he?! *Why* should he?'

'I want him to be there. I think Gwenda will like him. And we need some youth. Some zest. Max and Jasper will spark off each other.'

'I've already bought lamb cutlets for four.'

'It's fine. Max doesn't eat lamb.'

'Honestly,' said Max. 'I really ...'

'I'll do Max a piece of fish. You eat fish, don't you, Max?'

'Well, I only ... I mean ... Occasionally,' he said. 'But really ...'

'I'm going to be in Islington in the morning. I'll get a piece of sea bass from that good fishmonger's.'

'Honestly, Bryony, I . . .'

'No more ifs and buts. You are *coming*.'

Max looked at Jonathan, who was defiantly looking elsewhere.

'OK,' he said meekly. 'See you tomorrow.'

Thursday 2 August

The door rang. It was Zoe, which was unsettling as she had never come to theirs before and inviting her into the house felt like a different order of transgression, particularly with Karolina upstairs, ten minutes into a two-hour Zoom meeting.

'Come in,' he said with enough uncertainty, he hoped, for her to pick up on his unease and decline.

But she didn't and so he had no choice but to make the best of it.

'We're playing Happy Families,' he said.

Arthur and Alma were on the living room floor, the cards strewn around them.

'What happened to the game we were playing?'

'Arthur did an Arthur,' said Alma.

'Start again,' said Arthur.

'OK, fine. Let's do that. Let's start again.'

Max turned to Zoe, who was standing in the doorway.

'This is Zoe,' he said. 'Zoe, this is Alma and Arthur.'

'You can play, too,' said Alma. 'You can be Mummy!'

Max didn't look at Zoe.

'Well, we've got a mummy upstairs, haven't we? Zoe can just be Zoe.'

'I like your newt,' said Zoe, pointing at Alma's cuddly toy as she sat down next to her.

'It's an axolotl,' said Alma reprovingly.

Zoe looked bewildered.

'Their generation's amphibian of choice,' said Max. 'Shall I deal you in?'

'Sure,' said Zoe.

The game went much as anticipated. Arthur cheated. Alma cried. Zoe – who had not been briefed that in Anderson family card games all adult participants were supposed to sabotage their own chances and offer up sacrificial lambs – won at a canter.

'Again,' said Arthur.

Max looked over at Zoe, who was shuffling the cards and didn't seem to be going anywhere.

'Why don't you two watch something?'

'But it's Thursday,' said Alma, appalled. 'No screen time during the week.'

'Ordinarily,' said Max. 'But today is an exception. One episode of *Bluey*. Don't tell Mum.'

Once the TV was on, Max and Zoe walked through to the kitchen.

'Drink?' he said. 'Cup of tea? Glass of wine? I think *Bluey* episodes are about seven minutes long. I reckon we could probably knock one back in that time.'

Zoe was learning against the kitchen counter. Her sunglasses were hanging on the neck of her shirt.

'I need you,' she said.

Max was clearing away the kids' afternoon snack and used this fact as an excuse to keep his back to her. He had allowed, even *encouraged*, things to get to this point without ever really imagining they would. There was no way he was going to do anything about it, but still he felt a great stirring of desire.

'Zoe, I um . . . It's well, I'm flattered obviously . . .'

He turned around.

'And you are . . . But I . . .'

The look she was giving him betrayed nothing.

'*We* need you, Max.'

The humiliation hit him like a punch to the face.

'Right,' he said. 'Of course.'

'We're moving on from the housing stuff.'

'Good,' he said, the words tumbling out of him. 'I mean, I actually think you have some talent as a filmmaker.'

'It's time to focus on pensions,' she said.

'Ah,' said Max.

She walked across the kitchen to stand next to him while he washed a couple of potatoes in the sink.

'An opportunity has presented itself and you have to react when things present themselves unexpectedly.'

She was looking at him with discomforting intent.

'Right,' said Max.

'Later this year the government are planning on selling a load of student debt. Two billion of it. There's been consultations on it and all that. It's happening.

'Who would want to *buy* student debt?'

'Loads of people. You buy the debt then you get to collect the interest on the loans. It's a big money spinner. All those humanities graduates waiting tables, watching their liabilities grow year on year.'

'Right.'

'The postgraduate slate is particularly lucrative.'

'OK,' said Max. 'What does all this have to do with me?'

'There's a rumour that the bulk of the debt is being bought by the Coopers and Black Pension Fund. We need proof.'

Max's blood stilled for a second. He recognised the name. He had seen it on headed paper in Jonathan's office.

'Oh god,' he said.

'Cal knows a guy. Apparently he doesn't like being called a hacker, but I don't know how else I am supposed to describe him. Anyway, he is here, in London – and he leaves tomorrow. We need to get him the laptop so he can work on it tonight.'

Max could hear the *Bluey* credits rolling in the next room.

'You can have another one,' he shouted through to the living room. 'One more, but that's it.'

Zoe was standing uncomfortably close.

'We need his laptop.'

'Oh god,' said Max again.

'You're in and out of their house all the time,' she said.

Max felt leaden-footed, horribly out of his depth.

'You want me to steal his laptop?'

'We're really just borrowing it,' said Zoe. 'And only for a few hours. We'll do what we need to do and then give it back. We just need to confirm that they're buying it.'

'Why does it matter if they're buying it?'

'Oh my god,' said Zoe. 'It'll be just the most perfect illustration of the generational transfer of wealth you could possibly imagine. It would make headlines all around the world.'

'You think?'

'Definitely. And once it does, there's no way they'll be able to do it. They wouldn't *dare*.'

'I mean, it's not illegal or anything so I think they probably *would* dare, but even if they didn't, wouldn't someone else just buy the debt?'

'Sure, they might,' said Zoe, irritably. 'I mean, they will. Of course they will. But that's not the point. We're doing it to raise awareness. About the system. How it's loaded against us. This captures it so perfectly people won't be able to ignore it. It will fundamentally change the conversation.'

She looked at him disarmingly, her eyes soft and encouraging.

'*You* can fundamentally change the conversation.'

Max considered challenging her but decided against it. There was no perfect action. No cheat code for justice. They were doing what they could, when they could. And all that was beside the point, anyway. He understood the request for what it was. She was offering him meaning.

'Can't the hacker guy just hack into his email?'

'The fund uses a special kind of encryption. We need his laptop.'

'Couldn't I just take a look and then tell you if I saw something?'

'Do you know his password?'

Max didn't bother to reply.

'You just need to come up with an excuse to go round there. It shouldn't be difficult.'

He had his eyes shut, was pinching the top of his nose.

'No, I don't.'

He opened his eyes.

'I don't need an excuse,' he said. 'I'm already going there tonight. For dinner.'

An hour later, Karolina was down in the kitchen ahead of her evening meeting. Max was warming baked beans in a pan.

'I baked you a potato,' he said.

Karolina smiled.

'You're going out for a posh dinner, and I am eating like a five-year-old.'

'Sorry,' said Max.

'No,' she said. 'Thank you. A baked potato is actually just exactly what I fancy.'

She came up behind him and slid her arms around his waist.

'You OK? You seem a little . . .'

Max stirred the beans in the pan.

'I'm starting to wonder if listening to podcasts is actually the same as living a politically engaged life.'

Karolina laughed. She had let go of him and was over on the other side of the kitchen, filling the kettle with water.

'I've spent a long time kind of convincing myself that making films, or at least making the films I imagine I will one day make, is a contribution of sorts. You know, kind of moving the Overton window . . .'

'Your *whodunnin*?'

The incredulity in her voice was undisguised. Max blushed, his back to her. The film was about surveillance capitalism. At least glancingly. Or rather it *had* been about surveillance capitalism when he first conceived of it. Although he could imagine how someone coming to the script for the first time could read it, as it currently existed, and have no idea that this was the case. It was, of course, impossibly ridiculous to say any of this.

He took some cheddar out of the fridge and started grating it into a bowl, his cheeks still burning. You could roll your eyes all you liked about Bryony and her desire to break through to the realm of the divine and roam with the gods, but no one could ever say she was just a middle-ranking content creator.

'I need to do something,' he said. 'I need to contribute.'

'You're always *saying* that. At some point you're going to have to actually *do* something.'

She was standing there in front of him, this brilliant, beautiful woman.

How would you have fared in combat? Jonathan had asked him. Disastrously, was the obvious and only answer. But how much did that matter? It was whether or not you stood up that counted.

The kids' potatoes were sitting on the countertop. Max cut them open and added a knob of butter to each. He had always consoled himself with the thought that if it had been necessary he would have stood up, to whatever it was that might have required it. That it hadn't happened was simply a product of the way that the dice had rolled for him. You played them as they laid.

He felt a great swell of shame. Even so, he had played them wrong, he felt. At almost every turn. Made bad calls. Risked nothing.

'You've done things,' he said. 'You *do* things.'

Karolina threw a teabag into the bin.

'The thing I am doing at the moment is so boring and technical I can't even . . . But it could unlock money that could do good things.'

She shrugged. She was wearing her glasses, a simple cashmere jumper.

'I have to go back up.'

She had her cup of tea. She paused as she passed him, kissed him on the cheek.

'You'll know when it comes,' she said. 'You're Max, you always know.'

*

'Are you going camping after this?' said Jonathan. His delivery walked the usual tightrope between friendly joshing and outright contempt. Max noted that he was falling increasingly on the wrong side.

'Um, no.'

'You're wearing a backpack.'

He stood frozen on the doorstep. It was madness to even have considered doing what he was doing. And now he had raised suspicions before he even crossed the threshold.

'I was just dropping something off,' he said, as casually as he could. 'It's empty.'

As soon as the words left his lips he realised how ridiculous they sounded. Jonathan looked at him, nonplussed.

'Because I have already dropped off the thing that was in it.'

Jonathan raised one eyebrow. He hadn't wanted Max there in the first place and they both knew it. And now this. Max remembered being seven years old and unwelcome at his older sisters' playdates.

'You can put it under the coats,' said Jonathan. 'Cupboard next to my office.'

The Archibalds – Jasper and Gwenda – were already in the kitchen. Jasper was sitting at the table, his chair at an angle so he could cross his legs. White-grey hair. A black jacket over a black shirt. Gwenda was at the counter, helping Bryony assemble the starter. Her hair was cut short and styled up. Statement earrings.

Bryony did the introductions. Much was made of Max's unusual situation, his evenings that would otherwise have been spent alone.

'His wife lets him out while she's working but only on the street so he can pop back if one of the children wakes.'

'They've taken me under their wing,' said Max determinedly.

He did his best to smile. It was going to be one of those experiences that he was just going to have to endure.

'Film nights,' said Bryony. 'Card games. Barbeques. It's like he's been living here for years.'

The starter was asparagus, cooked on a griddle and served with finely chopped boiled eggs. Max sat at the head of the table, a seat that, with him sitting in it, felt more peripheral than it did patriarchal.

In the main, he let the others do the talking, following the conversation as it roved about. A holiday on Hydra in the 1980s. Meeting Robert Smithson. Their sadness that Gore Vidal hadn't been around to see Trump. It was a little performed, as these things went. But still maddeningly aspirational, Max felt, despite being kind of hateful at the same time.

The lamb cutlets came served on a Tuscan bean stew. Bryony hadn't made it to the fishmonger in the end, so Max had the stew with a roasted piece of feta.

'How's the troublesome painting?' asked Gwenda, once they were done.

'God, it's been a struggle.'

'Can I see it?'

Bryony put on a coy face.

'I'm not sure. I haven't shown anyone. Not even Jonathan.'

Max wasn't sure if this was true. He was fairly confident that *he* had seen it.

'Come on.'

'All right then, but just you.'

Max watched them go through the doors and out into the black of the garden. A couple of seconds later, he saw the light come on in the studio. Jonathan and Jasper were talking but he had zoned out of the conversation. The large studio window was a golden rectangle in the dark. He couldn't see into the space, but he could imagine them both in there, Bryony and Gwenda, talking confidentially in a place which he had come to think of, stupidly, as somehow his.

'We're just playing by the rules as they are,' Jonathan was saying. Max had lost the thread of the conversation but had a vague sense they were talking about money.

He looked at the two of them, sitting in their seats. Jasper was gesticulating a kind of reluctant submission.

'What else can you do?'

'Look,' said Jonathan, conscious that Max was now listening, 'the offside rule as it currently stands is ridiculous. Did you see that goal at the end of the season? Rashford's goal?'

Max knew immediately the goal he was talking about. It had been controversial. In the boring way these things were. He nodded.

'Totally ridiculous. Should never have been a goal. Anyone can see that the current rules are ridiculous, but they are the rules. And the law is the law. When Rashford plays football, he plays to the rules as they are currently configured, not to the ones he wishes were in place.'

He raised himself up to his full height.

'You play the game as it is in front of you.'

Jasper was looking at Max in a way that was making him feel self-conscious and uncomfortable.

Jonathan rapped the table with his knuckles.

'Nature calls,' he said.

Jasper sat back in his chair, still looking at Max. He waited until Jonathan was safely out of the room.

'You get younger every time.'

Max cocked his head.

'Sorry?'

'Bryony's little – what are you? – *amusements*, I suppose.'

Max said nothing but his expression clearly betrayed him.

Jasper laughed.

'You think you're the first? I guess you all think you're the first. Why wouldn't you? That full-wattage attention. From a generational beauty, no less.'

Max shifted uneasily in his seat. There was a way of responding to this, he was sure. A killer comeback. But it was eluding him.

'I've known her for twenty-five years,' continued Jasper. 'I used to be hacked off that I had never got a turn. Her looking at me like that, hanging on my every word. Christ, I would have been game. You should have seen her when she was forty-five. None of the photos do her justice. She was like a fucking Catherine wheel, sparks flying everywhere.'

He smiled nastily.

'But I came to realise that I never got a turn because we were *real* friends of theirs. All the guys, the ones like you, they're expendable.'

He leaned forward, his arms crossed.

'Nothing is going to happen.'

Max heard this first as an instruction but then realised it was simply a statement of fact. The thing that everyone except him had always known.

'It never has, and it never will.'

Jasper had his elbows on the table, was looking right at him.

'My brother is a farmer. Every few years he plants cover crops on his fields. They're not *real* crops. Nobody eats them. You don't even harvest them. You let them grow for a bit and then you till them back into the earth. They enrich the soil. A kind of sacrificial offering to the wider ecosystem.'

Jasper smiled again, looked at Max's plate.

'Legumes are particularly good.'

The patio doors opened.

'Look at you two,' said Bryony, 'chatting away like old friends. How lovely.'

'What are you talking about?' asked Gwenda.

'Farming,' said Jasper, still looking at Max. 'Regenerative agriculture. A particular interest of Max's.'

'Is it?' asked Bryony. She laughed. 'What's he planning on growing? Verbena or mint? Or perhaps it doesn't matter?'

Max sat in his chair, shattered – obviously – on many levels, but galvanised at another. He picked up the bottle of wine and filled his glass.

Jonathan came back, humming to himself. The plates were cleared away. Pudding was served, an Eton mess. Max dutifully ate one bowl and then another, saying almost nothing.

Once they were done, he cleared the plates and cutlery so Bryony could serve the cheese. The dessert spoons were silver, a decorative relief at the bases. Max separated them from the rest of the things and was turning on the tap when Bryony stopped him.

'Just stick them in the dishwasher with everything else,' she said. 'Life's too short to be hand-washing spoons.'

He looked at her and she looked at him. There was a flicker of a smile. A moment of recognition, an exchange, but he no longer had any idea what any of it meant.

'Excuse me,' he said.

He walked into the hall. Opposite the downstairs toilet was a series of hooks for coats, his rucksack lying empty underneath them. He picked it up and walked to the door of Jonathan's den.

The door was open. The light was off, but the curtains were half-open and there was sufficient moonlight for Max to see the desk, the beautiful Danish desk with its suspended drawers. And on the desk, the laptop.

He stood in the doorway, staring. If he touched anything there would be fingerprints. But what would it matter? If anything went wrong, they would all know it was him anyway. *Jonathan* would know it was him. And he would give no quarter. Max knew that he would be arrested, get a criminal record.

He took a steadying breath. All he had to do was grab it and stick it in his bag and, whatever happened, from that point on, he would be able to look at himself in the mirror and know that he had had it in him.

Thirty seconds later he was flushing the toilet, washing his hands and walking back into the kitchen. On the sideboard, he noticed a pile of things. A quartered newspaper. Two unopened circulars. And at the bottom of it, screamingly unread, his script.

Max looked at its unbroken spine. Whether Jonathan financed it or not was immaterial. There was still a version of his future that involved script meetings in LA and shooting on location in New York. It had outrun him so far but it could still be caught.

He sat down with a thump, glassy-eyed.

'Are you all right?' asked Bryony.

Max picked up his glass, didn't look at her.

'I might have to go to America one day,' he said to no one in particular.

Friday 3 August

Max woke up, his head heavy in his pillow. The wine had been that dangerous reddy brown colour like a rusty poisoned river. The sort that always made you feel terrible the next day. And, still, how many times had he refilled his glass? He tried not to think about it. Tried not to think about anything. But at the periphery of comprehension, he sensed that the citadel of his selfhood was under threat, shame massing at its walls, about to pour in and overwhelm the defences.

Desperate for a glass of water, he got out of bed and made his way downstairs. It was a cloudy day and the early morning light was hazy through the windows.

Arthur and Alma were in the living room. They were wearing matching pyjamas sent from Sweden, blue and white hoops with a little yellow sun on the chest. Alma was sitting on the arm of the sofa.

'Good morning, my love,' he said, leaning down to kiss her on the top of her head. As he did so she reached up and tweaked his ear. Their established method by which a five-year-old might turn her father into a daddy robot.

He froze. Alma was looking up expectantly at him. At some point he would have to turn on his phone and confront Zoe's disappointment that he hadn't gone through with it. But that could be deferred for a little while yet.

He flattened his hands, locked his arms at the elbow.

'I am a daddy robot!' he said in a staccato robot voice.

The two children shrieked joyfully.

Max walked haltingly round the room, buzzing and beeping as he did so.

'Clean up our toys, daddy robot!'

He made a piston-like noise as he leaned forwards, bending at his hips like they were a hinge. It would be the end of them, of course. Him and Zoe. Whatever it had been.

He walked across the room, his knees locked, and deposited three stuffed dogs into the toy chest. But she had been wrong to imagine that it could have offered him any absolution, taking the laptop. No gesture could.

'Turn on the television, daddy robot!'

'Protocol override,' he said. 'Protocol override. I have been programmed so that I am not able to contravene Mummy's rules.'

Through in the kitchen, he could hear Karolina, boiling the kettle, making breakfast.

Arthur twisted his father's nose.

'Daddy robot horse.'

'Oh please, no,' said Max in his normal voice.

'Daddy robot horse!' shouted Alma.

Max looked plaintively at Arthur. He still hadn't had a glass of water.

'Daddy robot horse,' said Arthur resolutely.

He sighed and then got down on all fours and started neighing in what he imagined to be a vaguely mechanical way. Both children climbed on his back.

'Giddy up,' shouted Alma.

The large living room rug was deep-pile and soft under his hands. Max crawled robotically across it, Alma spurring him on with regular kicks. At one level not stealing the laptop had been a failure and he would always know that. But doing so would have been to take a pointless narcissistic risk. One that threatened his livelihood. Imperilled all this.

He allowed himself to collapse flat onto the floor, the children on top of him.

'Malfunction,' he said, slurring his robot voice. 'Low battery...'

He shuffled the kids off him so he could turn over and lie on his back. Quickly, they snuggled back into this embrace, Alma's head resting on his right shoulder, Arthur's on his left. Max looked down at the tops of their heads, their fine golden curls. Ridiculous of anyone to expect them to be enough. And just as ridiculous to imagine that they weren't.

Alma tweaked his ear.

'Normal daddy,' she said.

Max sat upright with a snap.

'What happened?' he said, looking left and then right as if in a panic. 'Why are we lying on the floor?'

Alma started giggling uncontrollably.

He pulled a face of mock outrage.

'Did you turn me into a daddy robot?!'

Arthur hollered triumphantly.

Max got up, shaking his fist at them both.

'I can't believe you did that to me,' he said. 'Turned me into a robot. Is that all I am to you, an unthinking mechanical slave?'

'And then we made you a robot horse!'

'Tell me you didn't ride me round the room like an animal?!'

The pair of them roared.

Alma reached up to twist his ear back to the robot setting but Max was up and out of the door before she could.

'Pancakes,' called Karolina from the kitchen.

From the hall he could hear the children running through for their breakfast. He was about to join them when he noticed that on the doormat there was an envelope, his name handwritten on it. Inside was a press release printed on headed paper. Coopers and Black Capital. Jonathan's firm. An announcement that they had just invested £30 million in a new long-term, ultra-progressive climate fund.

Max stood in the hallway, surrounded by shoes, trying to hold out against a deep sense that his universe was about to collapse in on itself.

Still in his pyjamas, he put on his thickest winter coat, opened the front door and walked across the road.

The front garden at number five was empty of bikes. Only the cricket scoreboard remained. It had been updated overnight to total rent paid: £6500 and value appreciated: £3600. Max walked up the drive, disassociated, like he was underwater, the sound of the sea booming in his ears.

He rang the doorbell. For ten, maybe twenty seconds, he stood at the door, waiting, knowing that no one was going to answer. Only when it had reached the point that he could wait no longer, did he take a few steps and peer in the front window. The door was there still, resting on its trestles. But that was it. Otherwise, the room was empty. They had gone.

He sat on the front garden wall and got out his phone. It rang and rang but he didn't relent. Eventually, she answered.

'Please tell me that this isn't what I think it is.'

'I don't know what you think it is.'

'The press release. That was you, obviously.'

Zoe laughed a triumphant laugh.

'You're a man who appreciates good design, right? We nailed the press release, didn't we? That paper stock doesn't come cheap, but boy does it feel good in the hand.'

Max felt like an explorer discovering a new island for the first time; he sensed he was at the immediately visible edge of something but did not yet have any real sense of its enormity.

'How?' was all he found he could say.

'The fund is genuinely radical. It invests in the most amazing things. Mass-scale rewilding. Coastal defences. Apparently it takes some pretty speculative financial jiggery pokery to conceive how it will ever turn a profit, but looked at over the ultra-long term it does kind of make financial sense.'

'No, *how?*'

'It was actually a lot simpler than you'd think. First we had to create a mandate. We just googled his colleagues and picked one at random. William Keegan, one of the advisors. We then created a false instruction in his name which we sent to Cox's email. Then all we had to do was ratify it as if we were Cox and send it on as a purchase order to the team who then move the money.'

She laughed at the simplicity of it

'The fund uses a special email authentication system, which is why we needed his laptop.'

'I don't understand. They just transferred the money because you emailed them?'

'You have to move fast to secure the best rate, Max! There's no time for lots of silly questions.'

Max was sitting on the front garden wall. It felt like there was an enormous weight on his chest that was stopping him breathing.

'But you told me it was all about you wanting to know whether or not they were buying the student debt.'

'Oh, yeah,' said Zoe. 'I mean, they are going to but we're not going to make a fuss about that now. Probably best to keep a low profile, if you know what I mean.'

'No, shit, Zoe. You stole thirty million pounds.'

'No, we didn't. We simply re-invested it. The policyholders of Coopers and Black Capital still own it.'

She laughed.

'Although it's a fifty-year non-transferable bond so some of the current crop will have to live to like a hundred and twenty to see much of a return on it.'

'When they catch you, you're going to go to prison for a very long time.'

'They're not going to catch us because no one is going to report it.'

'Thirty million pounds, Zoe. Of course they're going to report it!'

'Coopers and Black is famous for its rectitude and integrity. Their entire pitch is all about security. They literally use the word safekeeping in their strapline. There is no way they're letting this get out.'

'It's *thirty million pounds*, Zoe.'

'Thirty million is chicken feed to them. They can just say it's just one investment. Part of the wide range in their portfolio.'

'Oh my god.'

'People have already picked up on the press release online and they're buying it. An NGO in Australia have already called them pioneers of the pensions world. You think they're going to turn around and say, *Actually it wasn't us and if you don't mind we'd rather spend the money on profiteering from student debt?* They're never going to do that.'

Max shut his eyes. He was struck by a sudden piercing thought.

'Was it really punctured?'

'What?'

'Your tyre. Was it really punctured?'

'Oh, *Cishet*.'

'Was it . . . I mean . . . Just tell me.'

'Of course it was punctured.'

She laughed.

'Really, Max darling, this was never about you. I mean, you at the centre of it. It's almost sweet that you think that. But honestly, you're such a minor player in this.'

He could hear her yawning down the phone.

'Sorry, I haven't slept. We've been up all night.'

Max left this hanging there, his mind exploring its many interpretations.

'Now that I think about it, it is actually perfect you calling this early. Can you do me a favour? The laptop is in a plastic bag under the garden waste bin in their front garden. Can you message Bryony and tell her to come down and get it. I'm sure she'll be up.'

'*What?*'

'How do you think we got his computer?'

'*She* gave it to you?'

'Well you didn't, did you?'

Max sat on the wall, stunned.

'You're right to be infatuated with her. She's the real deal. You don't have to be long in her company to realise she's . . . *serious*.'

In the background, Max could hear a noise. Zoe said something to someone. It was muffled, indistinct.

'I've got to go,' she said.

'Where are you?'

'Far away. And soon even further.'

She paused.

'Do your best, Cishet.'

He held the phone tight in his hand, resisting the urge to scream.

'Because I don't think you really have yet, have you?'

The line went dead. Max sat on the wall. It was a thing he had always known but could now see with a new clarity. They had absented themselves from all the meaningful arenas of life. Aimed low. TV box sets and flat whites. Paint colours and dinner parties. *Glastonbury*. They had settled for Glastonbury.

Heavy footed, he dragged himself to his feet. The residents of number five had only left that morning, but already Pemberton Place felt diminished; without them it was just another street.

He walked over to the Coxes'. The laptop was in a plastic bag, under the garden waste bin, as she had said it would be. He pulled it out. It wasn't a MacBook, he noted, which made him feel momentarily superior and then like he was the biggest twat in the world.

He sent Bryony a WhatsApp and waited as one tick appeared and then another and then the two of them went blue. Thirty seconds later, she was opening the front door.

She was in a dressing gown, her feet bare. The look on her face contained a kind of ecstasy.

'Did it work?'

'Yes,' he said.

She reached out for the laptop wrapped in its plastic bag and he passed it to her.

'I don't get it, Bryony. *Why?*'

'It felt right,' she said.

Max looked at her. That was it? *It felt right.*

'But he'll know it was you and he'll . . .'

She shrugged.

'You think?' she said. She smiled. 'I suppose we'll have to wait and see.'

Max shook his head, but there was a kind of mad logic to it. The further you pushed the perimeter of something, the greater the territory it covered.

'Why did she ask me to get it if she knew you were going to?'

Bryony was standing on the doorstep in her dressing gown, hugging the laptop to her chest.

'It seemed particularly important to her that you were given the choice. I never got the impression that she actually wanted you to do it but she wanted you to know that you could have done.'

The intentional cruelty sat underneath Bryony's demeanour like a weed in a pond: not quite visible at the surface but you knew it was there.

'She is one to watch, that girl. She has the temperament to go all the way.'

Max felt a sudden urgent sense that Zoe's life would deepen and it would go on deepening, and the thing at the centre of it would harden until it shone brilliantly and lit up the world. The dice had been loaded against her, but she was taking on the house nonetheless. He faltered. He had no idea if her name was really Zoe.

Bryony smiled at him fondly. It was a goodbye smile. The thing between them had run its course. She put one hand on the door to close it.

'Everybody likes you, Max,' she said. 'And that's not nothing.'

Acknowledgements

Thanks to the wonderful team of people behind the scenes who put the whole thing together, particularly David Bamford, Gabrielle Chant, Alice Watkin, Amy Richardson, Lucy Martin, Asia Khatun and Charlotte Stroomer.

Thanks to Will King for reading an early draft and Amy Grey for all her brilliant insights and comments.

Thanks to my dad, who just isn't a boomer, and my mum, who just is.

Huge thanks to everyone at Wylie, particularly Nicholas Allen and the beyond wonderful Luke Ingram. Similarly huge thanks to Sarah Castleton, queen of editors and great friend.

Endless thanks to Tom Morton. You're the best first reader and the best pal.

And finally biggest thanks of all to my great loves: Naomi, Amelia and Gideon.

RAISING READERS
Books Build Bright Futures

Dear Reader,

We'd love your attention for one more page to tell you about the crisis in children's reading, and what we can all do.

Studies have shown that reading for fun is the **single biggest predictor of a child's future life chances** – more than family circumstance, parents' educational background or income. It improves academic results, mental health, wealth, communication skills, ambition and happiness.[1]

The number of children reading for fun is in rapid decline. Young people have a lot of competition for their time. In 2024, 1 in 10 children and young people in the UK aged 5 to 18 did not own a single book at home.[2]

Hachette works extensively with schools, libraries and literacy charities, but here are some ways we can all raise more readers:

- Reading to children for just 10 minutes a day makes a difference
- Don't give up if children aren't regular readers – there will be books for them!
- Visit bookshops and libraries to get recommendations
- Encourage them to listen to audiobooks
- Support school libraries
- Give books as gifts

There's a lot more information about how to encourage children to read on our website: **www.RaisingReaders.co.uk**

Thank you for reading.

hachette UK

---

[1] OECD, '21st-Century Readers: Developing Literacy Skills in a Digital World', 2021, https://www.oecd.org/en/publications/21st-century-readers_a83d84cb-en.html

[2] National Literacy Trust, 'Book Ownership in 2024', November 2024, https://literacytrust.org.uk/research-services/research-reports/book-ownership-in-2024